#How to F*ck

A CANTALOUPE

#How to F*ck

A CANTALOUPE

A NOVEL BY PETE YOUNG

Publisher: Scrambled Head Publishing

Cover photography by Jaime Evans Creative.

Cover design by Jaime Evans creative.

Finished Art by Christian Baculo

Editor: Edited by Wilde.

Edited by Wilde

The author of these works strongly advises against the actual performance of any sexual act on or with a cantaloupe, or any other seasonal fruit for that matter, and accepts no responsibility for injuries incurred or summer snacks ruined by the replication of events from this book.

For Polly,
Who believed in me before I was real.

Special Thanks

To Rebekkah, my editor, without whom this book would not be nearly as complete. Thank you for your guidance and support. I couldn't have done this without you.

'You fuck one person—one time—at a centre for disabled youths and suddenly you're unemployable. That's the start, I guess.'

The start, dear reader, is a curious thing, and is often a matter of perspective. For example, when Daniel Savage guessed that was the start, what he really meant was that was the point where his entire life was turned inside out; the catalyst for the cataclysmic chaos and catastrophe that followed. But as perspective dictates for Dan that the moment alluded to was the start, it may also be suitably argued that the start was in fact the moment some twenty-four years ago when he was spewed forth from his mother's innards in a painful—or confusing (dependent on whether you were to ask Mrs. Savage or Baby Savage)—torrent of blood, shit and placenta. However, that would be the beginning of a much longer and much less interesting story, which

I doubt very much could be contained to the pages of this book. And so the start, as Dan so aptly guessed, is where this story will begin.

But not right away.

First, let us take a closer look at the man in question. Dan wasn't a bad person. At least, he didn't think he was a bad person. He did a lot of bad things, but surely no more than the average suburban semi-arsehole. He didn't consider himself a bad person, because he considered himself to be an apple. Sure, he had a couple of bruises, but if you could get past them you would see that there was still a lot of goodness beneath. He was, dear reader, by no means bad to the core.

I'm sorry. I can't do this. Let's cut the shit. Let's do away with the *dear reader* bit. I'm bored of this tone and I'm bored of this perspective. I've been writing for a whole two minutes and if I have to carry on writing in this style for a minute longer, I'm afraid I might eat my own head out of frustration. Let's do away with the whole omniscient, impartial narrator altogether. You be you and I'll be me. Let's lift the veil.

I've never written a book before.

My name is Dan Savage, and this is my story.

Chapter One

As you read before, I don't consider myself to be a bad person. I'm not sure why I used the apple analogy, but it seems fitting. However, I can tell you now, since I've dropped the guise of the humble narrator and made the call not to bother with painting myself in any other light than the one I'm under, this apple has more than just a couple of bruises. If I were in your fruit bowl, you would certainly pick me last and, having done so, you would discover that I was just unbruised enough to be edible, but if dropped one more time I'd be better off as compost.

I do a lot of shitty things. I can't help myself. I'm selfish, self-absorbed and self-interested. That's just who I am. The trick is, I balance out all of the shitty parts of who I am with charitable acts.

Cue *The Karma Exchange*.

It sounds stupid, but I swear by it. The Karma Exchange is why I know I'm not bad person. I'm pretty sure I'm not a bad person. Well, maybe I am a bad person, but I'm a karmically balanced bad person.

The way it works is like a credit card for karma. Not an actual, physical credit card, but one that operates solely within the confines of my own conscience. Basically, if I do something bad, I have to balance it out with something good to keep things on an even keel. If a *negative* action is committed, there will be a debit from the karmic account, which will only be credited back once a *positive* action of equal or greater value has occurred. The longer it takes to repay the debt, the more interest it accrues, and in turn, the bigger the positive action has to be.

The main reason I live by the rules of the Karma Exchange is to keep myself in check. I will be the first to admit that I can be a bit of an arsehole, but keeping the karmic scales balanced allows me to live my life without tipping over into the territory of *complete arsehole*. I perform just enough charitable actions to make up for all of the shitty things I do.

For example, if I were to steal an old lady's park at the supermarket, when she clearly had her indicator ticking away at it, I might pop a few dollars into the charity box as I exited through the supermarket's self-serve checkout. Now, if I were to use the aforementioned self-serve checkout for my own nefarious gain and scan a T-bone steak through as navel oranges, therein only paying $3.90 for the kilogram of meat, I might help out the homeless guy who sometimes hangs out at the front of the supermarket. If I were, hypothetically speaking of course, to secretly go through my best mate's mums delicates drawer without their knowledge, have a hypothetical sniff, and hypothetically pocket a particularly racy pair of underpants for a hypothetical, cheeky, self-romancing session later on, I might buy my mate a few beers at the pub, and maybe do some odd jobs for his mum.

As I exited the self-serve checkout at Woolies, I popped a couple of dollars into the little tin that was chained up next to the scanner. *The Royal Association of Seeing Eye Dogs.* Leaving the supermarket proper, I walked toward the car park, rummaging in the pockets of my shorts for car keys. I reached the kerb and stopped, forcing myself to turn back.

Sitting on a soiled mat beside the trolley bay was a dishevelled bloke with a cardboard sign and a near-empty glass jar of coins. He scratched at red skin beneath a well-worn eye patch. I went over to him.

'Could you spare some change for a meal, friend?' He looked up at me with his one good eye and rubbed a dirty hand across his scabby, grizzled beard.

'Sorry, I can't mate,' I replied. I couldn't. I'd just given my last few dollars to the *Royal Association of Seeing Eye Dogs.* 'Hang on,' I told him, digging through my pockets.

The search returned a bountiful yield of three Ghost Drop lollies and a button. It didn't quite balance the scales for the steak so I dug some more, finally pulling out a crumpled packet of cigarettes. I offered one to the pirate-double. *Winfield Blue.* He was stoked. Right as the grubby hobo was gearing up to give me a hug, my phone rang. The personalised ringtone was unmistakably the one I'd assigned to long-time-best-mate, Jake: *Pussy* by *Rammstein.* Saved by the signature drum solo, I dodged the homeless man's embrace and answered the phone.

'Hey buddy. How's tricks? I was just about to call you.'

'Oh yeah, what for?' came Jake's voice through the phone

'Just thought you might wanna go for a few beers? My shout.' Never one to pass up free beer, he agreed.

'Meet you at *The Irish* in halfa?'

'Done.'

The Irish was a poor attempt at an Irish pub. Tacked on to the back end of a shopping centre, the only thing remotely Irish about it was the name, *Flanagan's Irish Pub*; although, I don't think it was ever owned by anyone named Flanagan. As long as I'd known, it had been owned by an old Vietnamese bloke named Phuc. It was a bit of a dive. The floors were sticky, the bar was stickier, and the back half smelled like a toilet, namely due to the bathrooms being located at the back of the pub. Private booths lined the walls in the back part; the front half was crammed with tables and chairs that got pulled aside on Thursday nights when it was busier, making way for a small, sweaty dancefloor of Uni students and night owls. I liked the back part. You could always get a booth, even when happy hour was on, because people couldn't put up with the smell.

I walked in and took a seat at one of the end booths, old faithful, where someone had scratched *Sally is a Scrag* into the tabletop. I ordered two pints and rolled a cigarette while I waited for Jake to rock up. That was the other thing I liked about the Irish: the laws banning smoking inside pubs and restaurants had come into effect ages ago, but the Vietnamese family running the place didn't care. If it was quiet they would bring you an ash tray and let you smoke inside. Phuc told me once that he did this so that the back half of the place wouldn't smell so bad. I wasn't convinced it was working.

As I lit my cigarette Jake arrived, sliding into the booth opposite me. He picked up the pint I'd gotten for him and clinked it against my own glass. 'Cheers!'

Jake was a tall, semi-athletically built guy. He had a big, friendly mouth and brown hair that hung down in loose curls and always reminded me of a mop.

'Hey man. Were you at my joint today?' Jake asked.

Fuck. My hand moved reflexively to my jacket pocket, resting on Jake's mum's knickers. 'Nah man. Wasn't there today,' I said, hoping that would satisfy the inquisition.

'Well I know you were there, mate.'

Fuck. I fingered Mrs. Saunders' delicates nervously.

13

'Because someone left the back door open, ate my leftover pizza and played my guitar.'

I relaxed. 'Ah shit. You got me.'

'So now you owe me half a pizza, ya dickwit,' he grinned, one eyebrow raised.

'I'll get you a parma and you can shut up,' I said, laughing it off as I made certain Jake's mother's underpants were deep in my pocket.

'Oh, and next time you want to pretend you weren't at my place, ya strange cunt, don't get cheese on my guitar.'

Jake was one of those guys who dropped the c-bomb all the time. He never really used it in an aggressive way, he just weaved it through his conversations. I personally never used the word much at all. It always sounded forced coming out of my mouth, never really rolling of the tongue like it did for Jake. I only ever used it when I got really pissed off, and one time when I was trying to be sexy. She laughed at me.

'So why were you there?'

'Huh?' I feigned distraction, finishing my beer.

'At my joint.'

'Oh right... What about it?'

'What were you doing at my joint?'

'Oh! Just eating pizza and playing guitar,' I said, looking at something stuck to the ceiling.

'But *why* were you there to begin with?'

'I was looking for you, but you weren't home, so I left.' It wasn't untrue.

'After eating my pizza.'

'Yeah.'

'And playing my guitar.'

'Yeah.'

'And going through my mum's undies.'

Oops. There it was. I imitated offense, 'Jake! Honestly, I'm shocked that you would even think that. I have far more respect for Mrs. Saunders than to go rifling through her personals'.

'You left a pizza crust on top of her dresser!'

I squirmed in check. I didn't remember leaving the crust on her dresser. 'Maybe it was you?' I offered.

'I eat my crusts, you sick fuck. And you left the drawer open.' *Checkmate.*

An uncomfortable silence ensued. I went to speak, but someone else got in first. A third voice, not mine or Jake's.

'You fucking germ!' it said. I turned toward the voice at the edge of the booth. It was addressing me. I recognised the face that the voice belonged to. It was attached to a head that joined on to a neck which sprouted out of a set of shoulders, sporting two arms with soft, skinny hands, one of which was throwing a glass of water in my face. As I blinked through the liquid onslaught, I noticed that the hand without the glass was holding a large water jug, which was making short work of replenishing the vessel. I blinked twice. I recognised the face. I recognised the whole body. To be honest, I'd recognised the voice right away, and had only turned to it for visual confirmation of its physical source, because I prayed that it didn't belong to the body I knew it did. A body, face and voice I had gotten to know quite well over the last couple of years.

Christina Emery.

'Chris,' I tried to say, but was met with a supplementary aqueous affront. As soon as the glass was empty, she went right back to filling it up from the jug. I wiped the water from my eyes as she stood at the end of the booth and absolutely blasted me.

'You are a germ, Dan Savage. You are a complete pig of a man and I can't believe I wasted the last two years of my life with you!' She geared up to throw another glass of water at me.

'Wait! I can explain!'

She waited. I couldn't explain. There was nothing I could say. The water crashed across my face like an angry sea. I looked up at her. Her face was red and her cheeks wet with tears.

'I'm sorry,' I said.

'Don't bother coming home for a while. I'm moving out.' She slammed the jug and glass down on the table before turning to leave.

'Jesus. What did you do?' Jake said to me.

'He fucked Natasha,' Chris shouted over her shoulder as she left the building.

#howtofuckacantaloupe

Oh yeah, I fucked Jake's sister.

Chapter Two

The house was empty. At least, it *felt* empty. My shit was still all through the house, but every last trace of Chris seemed to have left with her. There was no music playing, no pictures of us on the walls, no waft of experimental Moroccan cooking coming from our small, cluttered kitchen. That was her favourite, Moroccan. She'd just been to Morocco when we'd first gotten together, and ever since she'd been desperate to get back. We'd never gotten around to it.

The first day was the hardest. She'd really done an immaculate job of clearing out. There didn't seem to be a single possession of hers left in the house. There didn't seem to be, until I sat down on the couch at the end of the day, and in between the cushions that always swallowed up the remote, I found a blue-green hairpin with a brightly coloured bird moulded into the end of it. A gift I'd given her in the first year we'd been together. I turned it over in my hands as the sun went down outside, the last long shadows of the day stretching out to our front window. I put the T.V. on to distract myself and ordered a pizza.

A couple of days later I got a call from Jake.

'Hey man. Can I come live with you?'

It was very direct. Jake was never one for beating round the bush. We hadn't really spoken since The Irish, apart for a couple of texts. He'd told me he needed "time to process everything." I'd never seen him *process* anything, ever.

'What's wrong with your flat?' I asked him.

'I can't do it mate. Every time I look at my sister I think of your cock and her vagina, going in-out, in-out. I don't like to think about my sister's vagina at the best of times, especially not with your cock going in and out of it.' There was a pause. 'I always pictured her with no genitals. Like a Barbie doll, just a smooth patch of skin,' he said.

'How would she take a piss?' I was intrigued by how much thought Jake had put into it.

'I don't know. Like a bird maybe, all out the back hole.' I laughed; Jake didn't. 'All I know is, I can't be sitting there eating my bowl of Coco Pops, happy, and then all of a sudden Tash pops into the kitchen and I'm knocked over by the image of you lobbing one into her. I can't do it.'

'Lobbing one into her?' I could barely stifle a snort.

'Whatever. Can I move in or not?' he asked. He sounded desperate, and I felt bad for fucking his sister, so I told him yes.

Jake came over that afternoon with a single box and a backpack. When I asked him where the rest of his stuff was he declared that he was a minimalist and only owned the essential items. This was news to me; he'd always had heaps of useless crap around the house. I suspected it was more likely that he just couldn't be arsed packing it all up.

He unpacked the box in my lounge room. It contained one large glass bong and a Nintendo 64 with a couple of games. In the backpack was another t-shirt, a pair of shorts and an impressive assortment of ramen noodle packets.

'Just the essentials?' I laughed. 'Got Mario Kart?'

'Of course I do, ya silly cunt. It's the only game worth having—that and Goldeneye.'

'Set her up then. I'll sort out some beers.'

When I came back into the room, the Nintendo still wasn't set up, and there was the distinct smell of pot hanging in the air.

'Want a hit?' Jake asked, leaning the massive bong in my direction.

'I can't mate. I've got work in an hour.'

Work, for me, was doing the night shift at a petrol station a few times a week. The money wasn't great, but the work was easy if you didn't have to get up early the next morning. I never had to get up early the next morning.

'Come on mate, it's our first night living together. Let's celebrate.' He held the lighter out to me. 'Just call in sick.'

Consider my arm twisted.

#howtofuckacantaloupe

It was a simple, happy couple of weeks living with Jake. Life seemed to be falling back into place since the clusterfuck-breakup with Chris. I missed her most days, sure, but I was a big boy and I knew it was my own fault she had left. I had no one to blame but myself, and that was something I was slowly coming to accept.

I could still smell her in the bathroom some mornings. Jake said it was just the toilet-blue.

Chapter Three

'I AM NOT A PAEDOPHILE!' I screamed to the street.

'Good for you!' shouted back Roy the postie as he cycled by. It was about four weeks since Chris had left and I was standing in the driveway, staring at the big red letters that had been sprayed down the side of my van: P-E-D-O. As I took in the rough paintjob, I tried to figure out exactly how I'd come to be in this position.

In the last four weeks, things had really gone downhill. In just four weeks, I had lost my girlfriend, lost my job, and was about to be put on the sex offenders register. *Four weeks.* Clearly a lot can happen in just four weeks.

I guess we'd better jump back a bit to give this scene some context. After Chris had broken it off with me, I was feeling pretty terrible for having cheated on her with Jake's sister, and it was becoming more and more apparent that it was time to make a deposit into the Karma Exchange. I was long overdue; this time it would need to be a big one. Something decent. Some real Mother Theresa shit. I opened the front door and stepped out into the world looking for somewhere I could shovel goodness for a while. As it turned out, I didn't have to go very far at all.

My van had been boxed in at the end of the driveway by a big blue bus. My house sat directly opposite a home for disabled youths, and the bus seemed to be dropping off a few of them that morning. There was a young guy, who looked like a carer, in a red t-shirt helping a wheelchair-bound boy off the bus and wheeling him towards the building's main entrance. He was incredibly tanned, and his hair bounced in tight curls (the carer, not the wheelchair boy).

'Oi!' I called out to the tanned man; no response. 'Oi!' I tried again, a little louder this time. Still, all I got was the back of his head. I crossed the road and jogged after him, catching him as he pushed the wheelchair up a ramp at the main entrance.

The building was never designed to be used as a disability centre. It had originally been a school, a long time ago. I guess there had been fewer people in wheelchairs back then, because when the place had been bought, they had to change all of the stairs to ramps. So rather than wheeling straight from level ground into the main entrance, as you might expect at a disability house, you had to go straight up a fairly steep front-entry ramp.

'Oi!' I said, tapping the tanned man on the shoulder as he got to the top of the ramp. He spun around and smiled at me with

23

a set of perfect white teeth, pulling his headphones out of his ears.

'Sorry, I was listening to Enya. I guess I must have sailed away.' He laughed enthusiastically at his joke.

Oh God.

The carer stared expectantly at me, and now that I had the man's attention, I wasn't too sure what I wanted to say. I had never thought this about a man before, but he had the most beautiful blue eyes that seemed to stare straight into me. He was probably the most handsome man I had ever seen. I got a little nervous.

'How can I help?' asked the handsome man, smiling.

What I wanted to say was: 'I cheated on my girlfriend by fucking my best mate's sister, so I need to volunteer to balance out the Karmic Scales and not feel like as much of an arsehole as I really am.'

What I actually said was: 'I want to volunteer.'

As I told him this, I couldn't help but think about pumping away at Jake's sister, and Chris crying at The Irish. I tried to shake the thoughts out of my head. I needed to volunteer. He beamed at me.

'Well that's just swell! Mrs McCormack will be thrilled!' He clapped his hands together, then added, 'I'm Carlo by the way.'

I don't recall ever having heard anyone actually used the word *swell* before. Aside from in American films that were set in the fifties, of which I'd seen very few, I didn't think people actually used the word swell. Carlo said it with such gusto.

I'd spoken with him for less than a minute, but it hadn't taken me long to form a pretty strong opinion of him. He was one of those wankers who volunteered his time out of the goodness of his heart, rather than out of some skewed ideal that he had to balance a set of karmic scales. His karma account was probably bubbling over with credit. What a tosser. He'd be the kind of guy who wore a skivvy, and had a library card, and drank soy milk because he *preferred the taste*. He probably still went to church.

I say *still* went to church, because it seems to be a dying fad. I say he *still* went to church, in the same way I might say that someone *still* believes in Santa, or *still* believes in the Tooth Fairy, or the Easter Bunny or midgets. I'm an atheist, or maybe agnostic, I never really learnt the difference. Either way, I don't believe in God.

I used to believe in God; the Christian one. I used to go to church every weekend with my Mum. I would listen to the stories and sing the songs and feel good. After a while, the stories didn't make sense anymore and I found better songs to listen to, so I kind of just grew out of it. I suppose most people do. Some still maintain their beliefs in a higher power, but for the most part people seem to drop off with the whole church-going thing.

When I started high school I stopped going to church altogether and, strangely enough, Mum stopped going too. I suspect she'd only been going for my sake, as part of some self-imagined civic duty; an attempt to provide the world with a well-rounded, morally intact young man. Maybe she would have insisted I keep going if she knew I would be a registered sex offender before my twenty-fourth birthday. I think she just got over it though, going to church. Some people can convince themselves that the stories are true but giving up your Sunday mornings for life can be pretty testing. She still goes at Easter and Christmas, I suspect just to cover her arse in case there is a God up there. Anyway, I suspected Carlo probably *still* went to church.

He pointed me to a little waiting area inside the main entrance, and I took a seat as he wheeled the boy in the chair down the hallway. He returned a few minutes later, sans wheelchair-boy, but accompanied by a large woman with yellow eyes and a plaid pants-suit. She looked like an armchair with a hairy chin.

Carlo introduced us: 'Dan, this is Mrs McCormack. I've just been telling her about how you wanted to volunteer.'

Carlo had said she would be thrilled. If this was thrilled, I would have hated to see what displeased looked like. She looked as though she had just sniffed the milk to see if it had expired and found that it had. I imagined this was her permanent face.

'Why do you want to volunteer?' she huffed, seemingly annoyed by my very presence.

'I just love to give,' I lied, recalling the sound my balls made whilst slapping against Jake's sister's arse.

She snorted, 'Bullshit.' Carlo quivered with discomfort at the sound of the profanity. 'Nobody loves to give. Except maybe this cheese-dick,' she said, nudging Carlo hard in the ribs. He looked as though he may pass out.

'Honestly, I do. I just want to help these people live more comfortably.' The lies were flooding out of me now.

She eyed me suspiciously for a long time. 'We don't have any vacancies,' she said flatly, turning to walk away.

'Actually, there's my job,' Carlo piped up, having recovered from the shock of McCormack's profanities.

'Ugh?' the big woman grunted.

'I'm leaving at the end of the week. I'm travelling to the Philippines with my church group to work at an orphanage there. We're going to refurbish the prayer hall and build a games room!'

'Of course you are...' McCormack rolled her eyes, further exposing the jaundiced whites.

'I did tell you about this a couple of months ago, but I can understand you forgetting, Mrs. McCormack. You are so busy with all that you do here.' Despite his chipper tone, Carlo looked a little crestfallen that she'd forgotten. McCormack breathed heavily out of her nose.

'Right. Well, it looks like I've got little choice in the matter. We are going to need someone to fill Carlo's shifts, and I guess it may as well be you. You two will work together for the rest of the week and then you're on your own, so pay attention to what goes on around here.' She pivoted her bulk around on one swollen heel and trumpled down the hallway, grumbling under her breath.

Perhaps it was a little pre-emptive, but I quit my job at the petrol station that same afternoon. There was no way I was going to be able do nights at the servo, backed up by morning starts at McCormack's. I had no idea what I was going to do for money, but I had faith in the system, and decided to let the Karma Exchange figure that one out. I quit via text message. I was no good at confrontation. "Sorry for the late notice. Got a new job. Can't work tonight," was my resignation. "Who's this?" was the response I received. I didn't bother to respond. I just saved the number under *Do not answer* and turned my phone off.

Chapter Four

I spent the next day shadowing Carlo, doing everything he did, learning exactly what a typical day would consist of. It wasn't that hard, really.

I arrived at 7 a.m., by far the hardest part. I'm not naturally an early riser. Working nights at a petrol station meant that I never had to see the morning if I didn't feel like it. Most days I wouldn't get up before 11 a.m. But, I reasoned, the bigger the Negative Action, the more challenging the Positive Action needed to be to make up for it. It wasn't meant to be enjoyable. So, at 7 a.m. I arrived at The McCormack Home for Disabled Youths. I was greeted by Carlo on the front steps. He handed me a hot mug.

'Oh, I don't usually drink coffee,' I said, trying to be polite. I detested it, in all honesty; it was bitter and awful and made me need to have a shit. Occasionally I would choke one down with about twelve sugars if I'd had a big night, but that was about it.

'It's not coffee, Dan; it's cocoa,' he said reassuringly.

'Cocoa?' I wondered if he had modelled his entire life on old American movies—and not the good ones, either: the ones where they said 'swell' and drank warm cups of cocoa. I had never heard of anyone in Australia ever drinking cocoa. Having said all of that, the cocoa was good. It was very good. Carlo smiled brightly, flashing his impeccable teeth as I took my first sip. The drink warmed my body down to my toes and made me feel awake.

'I add cinnamon to make it more fun, don't tell anyone!' He put a finger to his lips.

Christ.

Whilst I drank the Cocoa, Carlo gave me a tour of the institute. The McCormack Home for Disabled Youths was divided into four main areas, or wings. There was The Playhouse, The Hall, The Lunch Room, and The Beds. The Playhouse was where Carlo began our tour. It was a large room that resembled an oversized daycare centre. This room was where the kids spent the bulk of their day. The kids, as Carlo called them, were the disabled youths that attended McCormack's'. Their ages ranged from thirteen to twenty-five, but Carlo referred to them all as 'the kids'.

The Playhouse was a recreational centre where the attendees of McCormack's could relax, play, and engage in free-learning. There were building blocks and wooden train sets for the younger or less advanced kids to play with. For those who needed some time out, there were several bean bags and brightly coloured cushions spaced out around the room. For the more advanced kids, there was a PlayStation and a row of computers in the corner. In the corner adjacent to the computers, behind some low tables, stood a tall cabinet of pigeon-holes, filled with arts and crafts materials in plastic tubs.

I helped Carlo push in some chairs and tidy up a few things that had been left out from yesterday, then we moved on. Next stop was The Hall. We walked down a few steps that led to a set of glass double doors and went outside. We crossed a small courtyard and headed for the large timber-clad building opposite us. It looked a little neglected.

The entire building was divided into two sections. As we walked through the double-doors from outside, we entered a small anteroom that housed a vending machine, a plastic rubbish bin, and a noticeboard that still had last year's badminton schedule pinned to it. Passing through the underwhelming anteroom, we headed for another set of double-doors on the opposite side. Through these doors was a much larger, but equally underwhelming, gymnasium of sorts.

'This is The Hall,' Carlo said, casting his arm in a grand arc as if we had just entered the Sistine Chapel.

The Hall consisted of two basketball rings at opposing ends, and a handful of benches strewn around the perimeter. At one end of the hall, to the right from where we had entered, there was a burgundy crushed-velvet curtain. Hanging partly agape at the front of a haphazard proscenium arch–style stage, it looked as though a giant Hugh Heffner had discarded an old smoking jacket and flung it against the back wall. The stage itself was raised a little over a meter from ground level and had a set of stairs at one side, and a ramp at the other side, leading up from the basketball court.

'This is where the real magic happens!' Carlo exclaimed as he sashayed up the stairs, whistling a showtune I was unfamiliar with. He flung his arms out and did a bit of a twirl when he got to the middle of the stage. Finishing his whistled tune on a high note, he tossed the curtains open with gay abandon and pranced through. I was beginning to suspect it wasn't just his abandon that was gay. He was as camp as an arseful of tent-pegs.

I followed him through the curtains to the stage behind. There were loads of poorly constructed bits of set and costume lying around in the wings.

'Every December the kids put on a Christmas Concert for the public. This year it's going to be—' He very theatrically mouthed something to me with no sound. I had no idea what he was doing. He did it again.

'Huh?' I said.

One more time, even more dramatically, he mouthed something to me. I thought his head might pop with the effort of it all. I could half make out what he was saying. *Mmm*-something-*th*. I got it on the fourth go.

'Oh, Macbeth!'

'SHH!' He hissed, looking at me as though I might've just kicked his grandmother. 'It's bad luck to mention *The Scottish Play* inside a theatre!'

'What, Macbeth?' I said, half fucking with him. He looked like he might just cry. He started running along the backstage wall and out onto the basketball court, following the perimeter. I couldn't stop myself from laughing.

'What are you doing?' I called, through the laughter.

'I'm running—around the theatre,' he called back between puffs as he loped around the building.

'Well, I can see that, but why?'

He had a serious pace about him. I think he could have been a professional athlete if he wanted to.

'To break the curse!' he panted, well into his second lap.

I watched him in wonder as he ran another lap-and-a-half, finally coming to a stop next to me. He bent over double in front of me, panting like a madman.

'If you say the name of—*The Scottish Play*, out loud inside of a theatre—it's bad luck. You have to run around the theatre—three times—to break the bad luck curse.' He straightened up, his breathing slowing gradually, and wiped a bead of perspiration from his forehead. It seemed stupid to me, but Carlo said it with supreme seriousness. I suddenly had a flashback to a high school drama class.

'Oh yeah, I remember that from… *Cosi?*' We had studied it in year nine. In the play *Cosi*, a guy puts on a performance with a bunch of mental patients. Someone mentions Macbeth and one of the mental patients runs around the theatre in a panic. I'm not sure why I remembered that. I'd only ever taken drama for a bludge.

'Ah! A fellow thespian! How wonderful!' Carlo proclaimed. As he said this, he extended his arm outwards, pinched the air in front of him and drew his hand back to his face with performant flair.

'Not really,' I said, 'I took drama in high school but wasn't very good at it. Why are you doing Mac—'

'Ah!' he interjected.

'Right, sorry. Why are you doing The Scottish Play?' I asked.

'Because it's one of the classics! One of William's finest works, if you ask me.'

'Yeah, but I mean, why are you putting it on as part of a Christmas concert? I'm not much of a theatre buff, but The Scottish Play doesn't exactly scream Christmas…'

'That's the real magic of the theatre, silly! We are using a bit of creative licence and making it a Christmas themed performance. *M* will be dressed as Santa Claus, and *Lady M* will be a Mrs Claus of sorts. It's going to be a hoot!'

Carlo looked down at his watch—he was one of the few under-fifties who actually wore a watch—and exclaimed, 'My goodness! Is that the time? We best hurry the tour along, or we'll miss breakfast.'

We left The Hall and crossed back across the courtyard the same way we had come that morning. We went back through the glass double doors, past the Playhouse, turning right when we got to reception. Carlo led us down a short hallway. When we got to its end, we went through a door marked *The Lunch Room*, which opened onto a large cafeteria area.

'This is the Lunch Room,' Carlo explained, unnecessarily.

He seemed a lot less camp now that we had left the theatre. His camp-ness appeared to drain from him the further we got away from the velvet curtain. Now he was back to his usual awkward, church-going self.

'We call it 'The Lunch Room', but it's actually used for breakfast, lunch and dinner. We would have called it 'The Breakfast, Lunch and Dinner room', but that wouldn't have fit on the door,' he said, chuckling at his own joke.

It was going to be a long three days.

We spent the next half hour setting the tables with plates and cutlery. Everything was plastic so the kids didn't hurt themselves. The plates and cutlery were all brightly coloured, and Carlo told me he tried to keep them in their colour groups, 'just for fun'. There was a ruckus outside a door adjacent to the one we had come in through. I looked at Carlo, startled by the sudden intrusion on the peaceful atmosphere in which we'd quietly been setting up.

'That'll be Jenny getting the kids ready,' Carlo explained matter-of-factly. He glanced at his watch. 'They'll have just gotten out of bed.'

It occurred to me that I hadn't had much experience with disabled kids before, and I was starting to feel a bit nervous about encountering them for the first time. I didn't have long to ponder this thought, though. A bell tolled three ascending notes over the P.A system. Before the chime had run its brief course, the doors burst open and a stream of disabled youngsters flooded through.

I don't know the proper terms for them, but there were wobbly ones, drippy ones, squat ones and stretchy ones. They filled the room up like a noisy river.

Then I saw her: Jenny.

The sight of her struck me like a slap to the face. A radiant smile lit up her features as she laughed along with the kids. I watched as she paused, stopping to help one of them into his chair, before carrying on across the lunch area. She adjusted one of two short, blonde tufts, that barely constituted pigtails, as she moved. Her lofty gait stirred some primal captivation within me as she lightly traversed the room. I traced her path, in a daze, finding myself unable to look away. Carlo's voice beside me was white noise under water. She was not beautiful in the commercial sense, which I was typically drawn to. There was something far more attractive in her uniquities: petite frame; pixie nose; slight, slanted eyes with long, natural eyelashes like Lola Bunny from *Space Jam*. I'm not sure why, and I've always felt a little guilty about it, but I always found Lola Bunny strangely attractive.

'Jenny,' she said, extending a hand. She seemed to glow.

'Savage. Dan Savage,' I replied, attributing my James Bond-style introduction to the cerebral constipation caused by the softness of her hand in mine. 'I'm new here.'

She smiled, and I died a little inside. 'Dan Savage? Like the writer?'

I was always getting this, and I hated it. *Dan Savage, like the writer.* I often wondered if people ever said to Dan Savage, the writer, 'Oh, Dan Savage, like the deadshit from Scoresby?' Typically, it instilled in me the urge to jump up and down and stamp my feet and scream at the top of my lungs, 'No! NOT like the writer—like me. Like the guy you are talking to, not some knob-head who wrote a bloody book. Me!' However, this time I didn't get any of those feelings. I had a flutter in my chest and my fingers felt pins-and-needly. I vaguely wondered if I might be having a stroke.

'Yeah, like the writer,' I mumbled, suddenly very interested in something stuck to the floor.

When I looked back up at her she said, 'Well, it's been very nice to meet you, Dan Savage. I'll see you round,' and gave me a playful bump on the arm before checking on a couple of the kids and then leaving the room, her feet barely touching the ground as she floated out of sight.

I don't know what happened to me. I'm generally pretty good with women. Not good *to* women, but good *with* them. I talk the talk, do my best to be charming and, on several occasions, have slept with women who should never have even considered going to bed with me. This woman, this *Jenny*, had short-circuited my brain, and she was all I could think of for the rest of the day.

The rest of the day consisted of Carlo and I playing minder to the disabled kids. We were essentially unskilled carers. Our job was to babysit—for want of a better word—and supervise, making sure they didn't hurt themselves or get into trouble. There were nurses on hand who were in charge of giving medication to the kids that required it, usually administered at breakfast, lunch, dinner, or all of the above. At breakfast, we ensured that everyone had a meal in front of them, and assisted those that needed help feeding.

Carlo got me to buddy-up with one of the kids, David, who was in an electric wheelchair. I never learned exactly what his condition was, but he had trouble with his lower limbs and could only say a few words. Two of those words were 'eggs' and 'woohoo!', which he chanted repeatedly as I spooned his breakfast into his mouth. David was nineteen years old but had the mind of a three- or four-year-old.

'Here comes the aeroplane,' I said, feeling a bit daft, unsure whether or not I was being condescending. I popped the spoonful into his mouth, to which he gleefully responded, 'Eggs! Woohoo! Eggs!' We weren't having eggs that morning. We were actually having porridge with bits of banana through it. Carlo later explained to me that David referred to a lot of things as eggs.

After breakfast, we went through and cleaned everyone up and took them all to The Playhouse, where the kids had a couple of hours of recreational time. Carlo and I supervised while they played games and participated in arts and crafts, creating poor representations of animals out of coloured pipe-cleaners. I wondered if the pipe-cleaners ever got upset about almost never being used for their intended purpose.

We stayed at The Playhouse until lunchtime. Lunch was much the same as breakfast, with David ever-excited about his eggs, this time triangled ham and cheese sandwiches with the crusts cut off. Following lunch, the kids had an afternoon nap. Carlo led me through the doors at the back of The Lunch Room to show me The Beds; the same doors Jenny had come through this morning. I felt a nervous anticipation kick off inside me. As we passed over the threshold of *The Beds* wing, I searched the hallway for Jenny. I thought I saw her at one stage, but it turned out to be one of the nurses. I asked after her with Carlo. He told me that Jenny's Nan was sick in hospital and she was probably off visiting with her. I felt a mixture of disappointment and relief. I was really looking forward to seeing her again today, but relieved that I wouldn't have to worry about making a dickhead out of myself by stammering through another awkward conversation. I made a deal with myself that tomorrow I would be back to my usual, relaxed self.

The Beds was just that. Rooms filled with beds, which branched off a short hallway. Each room had between four and six beds in it, except for those belonging to the permanent residents of The McCormack Home for Disabled Youths, who had their own rooms. The permanent residents made up around forty percent of the group in all, with the remaining sixty percent dropped off by parents or family members in the morning. They were collected in the evening, before bedtime, so their afternoon nap stations tended to get swapped around.

The day finished around five p.m., when the evening shift workers would relieve us. When Carlo told me this, I made a joke about the evening shift workers *relieving* us. He didn't laugh. I don't think he got it, actually.

As I was leaving Carlo took me aside. 'You did well today. If you find you like it, I'm sure we will have a spot here for you.'

'Thanks,' I replied. It was a good feeling, hearing someone say that about me.

'David can be a bit of a handful at times, but you two seemed to really get along. A lot of people struggle.'

'He's not so difficult,' I said, honestly.

'There aren't many full-time employees here,' he continued, 'it's mostly volunteers. But if you find you enjoy yourself and the work suits you, I'd be happy to put your name forward for a paid position when I leave.'

'Thanks,' I said again. 'That would be great.' I wondered if it was fair to accept payment for what was supposed to be karmic recompense, but reasoned that I would be able to do more good for longer if I could afford to live whilst serving the less-fortunate. Perhaps this was the scales tipping a little in my favour after quitting my job at the servo. I shook his hand and we arranged to meet at the same time the following day.

Walking out of McCormack's, a warm feeling was growing inside my chest. I felt proud of myself for the day's work that I'd just done; not only because I felt like I was giving back, but also for the fact that I'd managed to work a full day. It had been a long time since I'd worked more than a four- or five-hour shift. This would be the first proper job I'd had in ages. I'd just about resigned to the fact that maybe I wasn't designed to do a full day's work, that there was something in my genetic code that caused me to stare at the clock after the four-hour mark of honest work and dread each subsequent minute until it was time to knock off.

The last, and really only, proper job I'd had was laying pipes for water mains. I'd lasted maybe six weeks before my boss told me I was an egg. That was one of the last things he ever said to me before letting me go. He called me an egg.

I wasn't sure how to take it, really. I'd never been called an egg before. Was it an insult or a compliment? I like eggs, personally: they are very versatile, and I'd been called a lot worse than that.

I'd been working for Don for about six weeks casually and thought I was doing a pretty good job. I was a bit slow to start off with in the first week or so, whilst I got the hang of the way he liked everything to be done, but not long into the second week it was all starting to come pretty naturally to me.

At the six-week mark, I decided it was time for a bit of job security. Having been on casually for six weeks, and given that it was outdoor work, we had been rained-off quite a few times, which for me meant half days or even full days with no pay. The company was small, just me, big Donnie, and another bloke who was a couple of years younger than me, Dale. Dale had worked there for almost three years, and he was a full-timer. Whenever we had to call it quits because of inclement weather, he would go home with a full day's pay.

I remember having a conversation about it at the time, with Chris. I'd said to her, after a couple of days in a row of being off work due to a storm, 'Right, I'm calling Don tonight and I'm gonna

42

tell him: I'll say, "Look Don, I need to go full time or I'm going to have to start looking around for a new job"'. I was pretty confident he would sign me up straight away. I called him late that afternoon and spoke with him.

'Hi Don, I just wanted to call up and have a chat with you and see if there was any chance you might be able to put me on full time any time soon?' My earlier brashness seemed to have dissipated when Don answered on the first ring.

'Well if you've got something else, grab it.'

'Sorry?'

'If you've got other work lined up, take it.'

Someone had dropped an anchor in my guts.

'Uh, I think you might have misunderstood what I was saying, mate,' I said, trying to recover the situation that seemed to have already driven over the cliff screaming 'O'Doyle rules!' 'I wasn't pushing because I've got someone else waiting for me to get back to them, I was just after a bit more security. I really like working for you, and I wanted to see if you would put me on full time.' I waited, but he didn't reply. I think I could hear him eating something.

'Hello?'

Slowly he replied, 'Not likely.'

'Sorry?' I asked, confused.

'Not likely.' There was a pause. 'You asked me what the chances of me putting you on full time would be; that's the answer: not likely.'

'Oh.' Someone had punched me in the stomach.

'Yep.' He chewed something. 'Sorry mate, but I don't beat around the bush. You're just not where I thought you would be.'

Another crushing blow.

'Uh, okay. Well...' I wasn't too sure what to say at this point. 'Can you give me an example of what I'm not doing right?'

Then he rattled off some pipelaying terms. 'Well, your joints are good and you're a fast worker, you don't get leaks and you are good on the shovel.'

I waited for the *but.* It didn't come. It was as though he had answered a completely different question to the one I had asked, and now all I could hear was him chewing. I think it was an apple. Finally he continued, 'Look, come in tomorrow and we'll knock it all about.'

'Okay,' I said, a bit dazed, and then he hung up. I couldn't work out what he was on about, and I certainly didn't feel like going to work the following day.

Morning came, and I was still trying to make sense of what the big man had told me. I dragged myself out of bed and forced myself off to work. When I arrived, Don greeted me with a cheerful 'Morning mate!' as though nothing had ever happened.

He was a large man. Both long and girthy. If he were a penis, I would have been very happy to have him as my own. His big nose, red from too much sun and too many Melbourne Bitters, was the undercarriage to two squinty, dark eyes, and a thinning head of hair. He was by no means an attractive man, but frank and hardworking, built like a plough horse as though predestined for long days in the sun.

I said to him that I wanted to discuss what he had said on the phone the previous day.

'Later,' he said, 'we've got a test on.'

We were swabbing the water mains that day. That meant there would be consultants and inspectors from the water board there. I had to wait until the afternoon to speak with him privately. After a very uncomfortable day's work, I finally found a good time to 'knock it all about' with him.

'Don,' I began, 'I just wanted to go over our conversation from yesterday.'

'Oh yeah?' he said, as though he'd forgotten all about it, 'What's up?'

'Well, you were saying that I wasn't up to the standard you thought I should be. Is there anything in particular that I'm doing that's not up to scratch?'

'Nah mate, you're alright,' he said, scratching his chin thoughtfully. 'You're a good worker, and you're not difficult to get along with.'

I wondered who I had been having a conversation with yesterday, because it certainly wasn't him.

'Well what's the problem then?' I pushed, 'Is there anything in particular I could improve on, or... is that pretty much it for me?'

'Yeah, well that's pretty much it, mate.'

By this stage my head was spinning with contradictions and I felt as though I might fall over. Then came the kicker.

'Put it this way,' he said, 'I want to make a cake, and I need an egg, flour, and milk.' That sounded like a pretty fucking boring cake to me, but I let him go on. 'And right now, I've got two eggs,' he said with finality, gesturing at me, and then Dale. I resisted the urge to tell him that perhaps he was actually making an omelette.

'Okay...'

'Do you understand where I'm coming from?'

'Yeah,' I lied, and looked away.

By this stage, I just wanted to get away before he started baking or coming up with more obscure comparative examples for me to pretend to understand. We started packing up the gear and that was that. Half an hour later he shook my hand and sent me on my way. I didn't bother saying goodbye to the other egg.

I was still thinking about Don and his bizarre references as I walked in the door of my house. Jake was playing the Nintendo.

'How was the retard factory?' he said, barely looking up.

'Don't call them that,' I said as I walked past him. 'And it was good.'

'Good?' He raised an eyebrow.

'Yeah. I really enjoyed it,' I said, satisfied.

'You're not right, mate. It's not normal to get enjoyment out of wiping a spastic's chin.'

That was a bit much. 'You've got to let up with that sort of talk, man. It's not cool. You can't be calling them retards and spastics. They're just people.'

'Jesus. One day in and you're already flying the flag for the downie brigade,' Jake smirked.

'I'm serious,' I said firmly, 'cut it out.' I turned to leave the room.

'Alright, shit!' he called after me. 'I was just having a bit of a laugh. If you're in love with the, the—' he searched for the words '—"mentally challenged" then that's your prerogative. That's your new thing, go you. That's great.'

It was his version of an apology. It wasn't great, but I took it. I went into the kitchen and had a look in the fridge: there was a half can of coke and a tub of sour cream which had expired last month. Jake had refused to throw it out, reasoning that because it was *sour* cream, it was already off and wouldn't go off-er. Like how when milk goes off it has 'gone sour', sour cream was already there. I don't know, it was easier to leave it in the fridge than sit through the full explanation. What I was actually looking for was a beer, of which there were, disappointingly, none.

'Wanna go to The Irish?' I called out.

The answer was yes.

Chapter Five

As always, we were sitting at the back. I was telling Jake about my day and how I really felt like I could make a difference, working at McCormack's. He seemed to actually be taking it all in, nodding along as I talked, and not making any dumb jokes. Then he asked suddenly, 'Are there any hot ones?'

I was taken aback. 'Sorry?'

'The "special people", are there any hot ones?'

Sometimes you feel like you are actually having a normal conversation with Jake, and then he hits you with something like this.

'You're fucked,' I said. 'You're such an arsehole.'

'How?' he retorted.

Christ.

'They are disabled,' I levelled back at him.

'So, what? Just because they are disabled, they can't be hot? They have a disability, so that immediately means they're unattractive? And you call me an arsehole?'

I considered this. In some skewed way, he had a point. He stared at me intensely for a minute, then said 'Gotta shit', and left the booth. I had a big draught of my beer and puzzled over what Jake had said. You could always count on him to offer up a different perspective.

'Dan?' came a voice from over my right shoulder.

She slid into my booth, sat opposite me with her back against the side wall and one foot up on the seat in a very casual, lounging position. Jenny.

'This seat taken?' She had on a dark top and a pair of those black, faux-leather pants that girls in bands tended to wear. The wind was knocked out of me.

'Hi,' she ventured. Her eyes were searching my face, no doubt trying to work out if I was a bit slow.

'Hi,' I could only mimic. I didn't have an original function available to me.

'I thought I saw you from over there when I was getting a drink,' she pressed on. 'I needed one after the day I've had.' A shadow flickered across her features and she looked away. *Her grandmother.* I forced myself out of the stupor I was in.

'Your grandma. She's unwell? I'm sorry,' I managed.

'Don't be,' she replied with a wry smile. 'I can't stand her, to tell the truth. She's a bitter old cunt. Mum always said Grandpa died so he could have a break from her.'

It caught me off guard, *cunt,* such a sharp word coming out of such a soft face. The shock must have been plastered across me.

'Sorry, but she is. I can't handle her. Just because she's my Grandma, and just because she's on her deathbed, doesn't give her the right to force her outdated opinions on me. It's the twenty-first century for Christ's sake, if a woman wants to marry another woman, she should be allowed to, end of story.'

If I was stunned before, I was something else right now. I was experiencing a solid blend of shock and embarrassment, with a dash of relief. She was gay. I was shocked because I hadn't even considered it a possibility; even with her short, now clearly lesbian haircut staring me in the face. I was embarrassed for having developed such an immobilising affection for her, but relieved that I was now mobile again, not having to feel so timid in her presence. I was disappointed, but I could finally relax. All of this washed through me and suddenly I realised she was staring, waiting for a response.

'You're right. She does sound like a cunt,' I said, and clinked my glass against hers.

'Oh, thank fuck. You took so long to respond, I thought you must have been a homophobe.'

We laughed and ended up having a really good night. I told her about my recent break-up, and fucking Jake's sister, and she agreed that I was a dick. She told me that she was a guitarist in an eighties themed acoustic cover band. It sounded pretty interesting. She said that they were just starting out but seemed to be getting a good audience response.

Our evening was cut short by Jenny's phone vibrating on the table top. A name flashed across the screen in rhythm with the vibrations: Tara. 'Sorry, I've got to take this,' she said as she excused herself from the booth.

She stood against the wall with a finger in one ear to better hear the caller. Something in her face changed as she listened to the person on the other end of the line. She raised a hand to her cheek, her mouth tightening into a concerned frown.

'Just stay there, I'm coming 'round,' I heard as Jenny ended the phone call. 'I'm really sorry Dan, but I've gotta boot,' she said to me. 'Thanks for a good night.'

And with that, she necked the rest of her drink and disappeared into the crowd. I sipped the rest of my beer then ambled outside to call a cab; Jake never resurfaced so I figured he must have left while I was talking to Jenny. When I got home I found him lying on the couch, bong in hand, a fading wisp of smoke from his last hit escaping out the top.

I asked him where he'd disappeared to earlier. He explained that upon finishing his shit, he had walked out of the bathroom to find that he'd been replaced in the booth by an unidentified babe and, reading the play, he thought it best to carry on home and leave me to work my magic. I laughed and told him she was gay.

'Shame,' he said. 'What a waste.'

Chapter Six

Next day I arrived at McCormack's at 7 a.m. I expected to be greeted on the front steps by the ever-chirpy Carlo and his firm but welcoming jaw-line, but he was nowhere to be found. It annoyed me that I was disappointed at missing out on one of his warm cups of cocoa. I went inside to find him.

He wasn't there. Mrs McCormack, who I'd internally nicknamed The Trunchbull, for her striking resemblance to the Roald Dahl character, met me in the foyer instead. She told me that Carlo was packing his things and heading off on his mission that day, and I would be partnered up with Dennis, one of the part-time staff, instead.

Dennis was a squat man with an irritated scalp. He had a thin wisp of ginger hair adorning the summit of his lumpy, fat head. Beneath the ginger wisp sat a layer of flaky, weeping skin, which Dennis scratched at with vigour while he shook my hand.

He wore a faded gold wristwatch, baby blue suit-pants, a white shirt and blue tie; the height of fashion.

'Do you like dragons?' he asked, looking up at me with his beady, button eyes. I'd never really given the subject a lot of thought. I certainly didn't abjectly dislike dragons, but as I said, I had never really given the subject much thought.

'Yeah, I guess so,' I replied.

For the next forty minutes, I sincerely regretted my response. Dennis treated me to a full and very involved 'history' of the mythical beasts, all the way through the genealogy of the great sky lizards and how certain breeding patterns yielded more powerful or agile firebirds. He scratched feverishly at his inflamed scalp while he ran me through the sacred lineage of the most powerful dragons, all the way down to the scrawny scaled-finch dragon. It was too much to take in, and so I was relieved when we bumped into Jenny in the corridor on the way to the beds.

'...And that's why when they breathe fire, they don't burn their own throats,' Dennis concluded as we rounded the corner.

'Morning, Dennis,' Jenny said brightly. He barely looked at her, and instead picked off a crusted flake from behind his ear. 'Can I steal Dan for a bit?'

'Well actually, no. We are going to prepare the Lunchroom for breakfast this morning.' He folded his short arms across his chest and glared at Jenny, who remained unperturbed.

'I'll have him back in a jiff, I promise. It's just that one of the overnighters has shit the bed and I need someone to help me strip the sheets and clean it up.'

'Well, that sounds like a one-person job to me,' Dennis replied acidly. 'I'm sure you'll manage.' I got the feeling that Jenny must have told him at some point that she didn't like dragons.

'It's a big mess. It's soaked through to the mattress, it's gotten inside the pillow case; it's even on the walls. We will probably need to mop the floor. Actually, it would be a big help if you could give us a hand too, Dennis.'

'Mop?' Dennis had turned ashen-cheeked.

'Mmhmm.'

'With water?' He had seen a ghost.

'Yep. Might even need to scrub it.'

'Just take him!' Dennis declared, pushing me forward clumsily. 'I'll manage on my own for a while.'

'What was all that about?' I asked Jenny, as we headed toward the beds.

'Dragons don't like water,' she replied, smiling. 'Might wash his scales off.'

Relieved to be away from Dennis and his scabby-headed dragon ramblings, I smiled to myself as we walked down the hallway. My relief was short-lived when I remembered that I would soon be scrubbing someone else's shit off the floor. We stopped outside an unglamorous door in the hallway. Number seven.

'This one,' she said, reaching for the handle.

I braced myself for impact as she turned the knob, prepped for an all-out nasal and visual assault. As the door swung open—to my surprise and delight—the room was perfectly presentable. As far as I could tell, there wasn't a crumb of faecal matter anywhere to be seen.

'Where's the shit?' I asked, confused. 'There's no shit.'

'No shit!' she replied with a laugh.

'I don't get it,' I said dumbly.

'I wanted to apologise for running out on you last night. That was so rude of me.'

'Oh, nah, that's totally cool. I get it, you had some shit to sort out.'

She kissed me. I was dizzy. Her lips were soft and unexpected. My stomach sucked itself up into my chest and stayed there, putting me off balance.

'Sorry,' she murmured, pulling away slightly.

The smell of her hair hung in the air between us. It was earthy and invigorating, a blended aroma of elements I couldn't pin down. Something akin to sugar and soil, straw and honey. I steadied myself.

'What about Tara?' I asked.

'My sister?' There was a pause as I processed this new information. I'd automatically assumed that Tara was her girlfriend. Something shattered above me and an icy coldness washed through me. A freshness. Relief.

Excitement.

'I thought—' I stumbled. Smiled. 'Never mind.'

I put my hands on her waist and drew her into me. Her fingertips knotted into the hair at the back of my head and she kissed me, hard. I held her close to me and slid my hand up the back of her shirt, coming into contact with the warm, bare flesh of her back. I ran my fingertips along the smooth, defined curve of her spine, feeling the soft fuzz of the tiny baby hairs as they began to stand up along her back. I kissed the side of her neck as my hand came to rest on the clasp of her bra.

'Is this okay?' I asked. I didn't want to push things too far.

'Mmhmm,' was all she gave by way of reply, as she pulled my face back into the side of her neck. I took a concentrated breath in through my nose and squeezed my fingers together. Astoundingly, the clasp submitted on the first attempt.

She spun us around and pushed me against the wall, kissing my neck, down to my chest, lifting my t-shirt. It hooked awkwardly on my head and one arm as she slid herself downward. When I eventually escaped from it, I looked down and was met with Jenny's pale blue eyes staring up at me. She smiled brightly.

'Lock the door,' she instructed, and yanked my jeans down to the ankles in one swift movement. I felt my way along the wall with my right hand, not wanting to look away from her. My fingers trembled as they found the edge of the door frame and fumbled their way over to doorknob as she took me in her mouth.

'Uhn!' was the only sound that came from me as I curled my neck backwards and the ceiling melted into my eyes. I floated from my body and witnessed the scene from above. One moment blended into the next and we were facing each other. She threw me across the bed with surprising ferocity and we fell into each other in a flurry of mouths and hands and fingernails. She was wild. Wilder than I could have ever imagined. She sat straddling me, and bit into my chest.

'Fuck me in front of the mirror,' she said, tilting her head toward the adjoining bathroom. She had no problem being upfront with what she wanted. I was thankful of her size as I stood up with her, lifting her over to the tiny room. She laughed and put her mouth to mine again.

The room was small and contained a single basin, shower and toilet. I placed her down as gently as I could manage before the vanity. She turned to face herself and directed my hand up to the top of the nondescript white business shirt she wore on the job. Standing behind her I followed the direction, trailing down the line of buttons, separating them from their holes as I descended. I drew a sharp breath in to the top of my chest as, in the reflection of the mirror, her breasts became exposed.

I fumbled around downstairs for a short while as I navigated our near-incompatible heights. Sufficing with an awkward squat, I slid into her. Her small, perky breasts bobbed up and down as I pressed in and out of her slender frame.

Her hot breath fogged up the mirror until her reflection became just a blurred vision in front of me.

It was perfect.

It was exhilarating.

It was short-lived.

All of a sudden, I felt the fire rising inside of me. Passion's efforts were reaching the ultimate crescendo. I wasn't ready for it. Jenny moaned in front of me. It was all too much.

'I'm going to come,' I said to her reflection.

'Not yet,' she replied, eyes wide, biting her lower lip.

I held fire as best I could. Fighting the inevitable. Agonising. It took every bit of my mental resolve, but I managed to hold back a little longer. That battle scene from Braveheart flashed into my mind.

Hold.

She moaned louder.

Hold.

The William Wallace within struggled. Jenny's reflection stared straight into my eyes.

Hold.

A bead of sweat ran down my brow, stinging my eyes. I couldn't hold for much longer.

HOLD!

Then, all at once, without warning, our private world was shattered by the sound of voices in the corridor outside. Perched dangerously close to the precipice of climax, we froze. Jenny stared at me, wide-eyed.

'Please tell me you locked the door,' she said through gritted teeth.

I hadn't.

The throes of passion had overtaken my basic motor skills as I had reached out for the lock on the doorknob earlier. I'd faltered, then fallen into bliss. Her answer came a split second later as the door creaked open and two people began to enter the room.

Despite the inevitable peril that awaited just inside the room's entrance, I couldn't fight biology. The fire was still bubbling away just below the surface, threatening to take over. Before the intruders had fully crossed the threshold of the room, Jenny pushed herself backwards with an almighty shunt, sending me successively deep inside of her, then immediately back out, and careering into the bedroom.

The intruders looked up in shock. It was the wheelchair-bound David, being escorted along by Dennis, the dragon-lover.

'And as we all know, when dragons are born, they are hatched from large—' He froze mid-sentence as he unwillingly took in the scene before him. '—Eggs,' he concluded with a gulp.

The free men of Scotland would hold no more. My body tensed and a vein in my neck stood up. The solitary word 'No!' escaped my mouth as my life hit a new low, and I came onto the carpet in front of a disabled boy.

'Eggs! Woohoo!' he howled, clapping his hands.

I prayed to any of the gods to strike me down where I stood. They were absent. Silence ensued.

The silence was broken only by the slow, shocked scratching of Dennis's fingernails on his scalp. It seemed to be the only response he could muster as he stood in the doorway, flabby mouth agape, trying to make sense of what he had just witnessed.

I didn't know what to do. Standing there, frozen to the spot, penis slowly deflating, I honestly did not know what to do. The last thing I saw was the terrified face of Jenny in the reflection of the bathroom mirror.

And then I ran.

Seeing no other recourse, I ran away. I just about knocked David clean out of his wheelchair as I screamed past him. Hip-and-shouldering Dennis out of my way, I legged it nude down the corridor, leaving a trail of scalp-flakes in my wake. I ran home completely starkers, nearly getting taken out by a hatchback as I bolted across the road. Arriving on my doorstep, I yanked at the front door handle.

It was locked. It was never locked.

Jake must have locked it.

Why would Jake lock it?

An old woman walking a Scottish Terrier on the other side of the street copped an absolute eyeful as I bent over to dig up the spare key from the pot plant beside our front door. I drove the key into the lock and twisted it with such vigour I was surprised it didn't snap. I flung myself inside and slammed the door behind me. Falling back against it, I panted furiously, adrenaline thumping through my eyeballs.

Jake was just walking back from the kitchen, eating what looked like a peanut butter and marshmallow sandwich. He cocked his head slightly.

'I've fucked up,' I said. 'I think I'm in a lot of trouble.'

'Where are your pants?' Jake asked through a mouthful.

'They caught me having sex at McCormack's.'

There was a pause. Jake's eyes widened.

'No!' he said slowly, 'I knew there was some hot ones!'

'Not one of them—Jenny.'

'The lesbian?'

'The very much not-lesbian.'

I thought of the fearful face I'd seen in the mirrored reflection not more than ten minutes ago, standing behind the off-green vinyl shower curtain, willing me with her eyes to help. I hoped they hadn't found her.

'I don't know what to do, man. I think I'm in a lot of trouble.'

'Come on, it's not *that* bad,' he said, finishing the last of his sandwich, 'people get caught having sex all the time.'

'I came on the floor in front of a mentally challenged boy in a wheelchair!'

'Well, maybe it is *that* bad,' he said, offering no solace.

I slid down the door, my naked arse cheeks prickling on the worn-out hall carpet.

'Come on mate, chin up. I'm sure it'll all blow over soon.'

As he said this there was a heavy knock on the door. I froze. A second, louder knock followed.

'Dan Savage. We know you're in there,' came a deep, gravelly voice from the other side of the door.

'That's his house. I saw him go in there,' came a second, whinier voice. Dennis.

Fuck.

'Open the door, Dan. We need to speak with you.'

My breathing had been coming in quick, sharp gasps, but I managed to steady it now. I got to my feet, taking a long, steady breath deep into my chest.

Time to face the music.

Grasping the doorhandle in my palm, I prepared to meet my fate.

'Pants.' It was Jakes voice behind me. He handed me some blue and white striped pyjama pants. 'I think enough people have seen that todger today,' he said, without a trace of humour. I nodded and put them on.

As the door swung open, I was met with the hulking frame of a man-mountain in a policeman's uniform. His bald head shone in the sunlight, and his hard face remained authoritatively expressionless as he grabbed my wrists and held them behind my back with one meaty paw. I assumed he was going to handcuff me like in the movies, but he didn't. I guess I wasn't resisting at all, and his banana fingers were enough to keep my hands in check regardless.

As Officer Hulkhands turned me around, I took in the view from my front door. It was busy. Driven forward from my doorstep, I was met with the faces of what seemed to me like hundreds of people gathered on my front lawn. In reality there were probably only two dozen, but it felt like a lot more. Their expressions were a gamut of emotions, with the overwhelming note, disgust.

There was Dennis, at the front of the pack, accusatory finger pointed squarely at me. Mrs Ethyl, my neighbour of two years, looked on from her driveway, watering her plants in confusion. Other volunteers from McCormack's had gathered on my lawn, too, watching me with contempt.

Then my eyes locked with Mrs McCormack herself. The mighty Trunchbull shook her head slowly from side to side as I stepped forward through the swathe of persecutors, her eyes boring into my soul. She spat on the ground at my feet, as Hulkhands led me through the crowd toward the awaiting station wagon parked on the street. His partner held the back door open for me as we approached and I got in.

Chapter Seven

So, this was definitely a low-point in my life. Getting publicly arrested and labelled a sex offender, and not just your run-of-the-mill, flasher in the park sex offender either; I was the kind that gets off in front of disabled kids. That would have to be one of the worst kinds, surely.

At the police station they asked me a lot of questions. At the end of the questions, they read a statement from Dennis. 'We went in the room and it attacked us. The dragon flew at us with its talons outstretched, breathing fire from its snarled mouth. Obviously, I leapt before David to protect him from the great winged beast. I stared it down and commanded it to leave. Stunned, it turned in fear, and flew down the hallway back to its cave. We were lucky to survive.'

At the end of it all, the police couldn't quite make sense of what had actually happened. I'd watched enough *Law and Order* to know to keep my mouth shut, and with Dennis being the key witness, clearly not of sound mind, they only had the testimony of the carers who had seen me running nude through the building to go off. Jenny's name didn't come up.

From witness accounts, and what I had told them—which wasn't very much—they determined that:

I had been up to something unusual in the room by myself.

I had been nude.

Dennis had entered said room with David and, perhaps, startled me. Thus startled, I had run from the room, through the hallways, across the road and into my house. The end.

The officers didn't seem too concerned with the truth, but more so the chronology. They made it apparent that they didn't care what I was doing in the nude by myself, as long as it was by myself. If I had been doing... whatever, before David the disabled boy had entered the room, and then fled upon his arrival, that was more or less okay. If I was doing... whatever, whilst David was in the room, then that was a different story.

I signed their version of events and they told me that they would be in touch over the coming days. I was free to go.

I went.

The officers who had taken me to the station had neglected to inform me that it wasn't to be a return trip. I stood out the front of the police station in nothing but my pyjama pants, doing my best to avoid eye-contact with passers-by, and called Jake. He met me on the corner in his absolute shitbox of a car: a Cadbury-purple 1999 Honda HRV, with a big dint in the back, that was always pumping out clouds of blue smoke.

I got in. He handed me a t-shirt.

'Where to?' Jake asked as I pulled the shirt on.

'Home, mate. I've had enough of today already.' I could see in the car's blinking clock that it had only just gone midday. Jake looked over at me uncomfortably.

'You don't wanna go home yet. Those McCormack people are still hanging out on our front lawn. The flaky one hissed at me when I left.'

'Oh.'

'Irish?'

The Irish it was. We went for a few pints and I filled Jake in on the finer details of my morning. He hung off every word. After a couple of hours, we decided we would probably be safe to head home. As he pulled into our street, Jake slowed right down and proceeded with caution, just in case any of the mob from earlier were still lingering on the property. They weren't. We got out of the car and hurried into the house. Someone had done a shit on the welcome mat. I left it for the morning.

I smoked some pot with Jake and went to bed. I slept all the way through to the following morning. When I awoke the following day, for a fractured second the cataclysmic fuckball that had been yesterday happily eluded my memory. For that indistinct fragment of time whilst I lay in bed blinking back the night's sleep, staring at the ceiling, it must have danced along the edge of recollection, holding itself back before crossing over the delicate line that would cement it into reality.

That happy stasis couldn't be maintained forever. The line was crossed, the dance became a seizure, and my head was sucked back hard against the pillow, as though someone had just placed a large sack of sand on my face. Movement didn't appear to be an option as I lay there, images of the past twenty-four hours invading. They flooded back in quickly, and as they each took their indelible place in my mind, I groaned. Today was not going to be a good day.

Today was not going to be a good day, but I couldn't just spend it lying in bed. I forced myself upward into a sitting position. That was the first step. Each one after that came a little easier. I went to the kitchen and made some toast. I had to scrape a little bit of mould off the side of one of the slices, and we didn't have any condiments, so I had it dry. Not an excellent start to the day, but I guess that was to be expected. I took a dissatisfied bite, sighing internally.

THUD.

I jumped, and the toast flew out of my hand. It still hit the floor what would have been jam-side down. The thud was familiar but caught me off guard. It came around this time every morning. Chris used to read the paper. I really didn't care for it. I would read the comics and have a go at the nine-letter jumble, but that was about it. I was pretty good at the nine-letter jumble.

'Don't you want to be informed? Don't you think it's important to know what's happening in the world around you?' she would say. My answer was always, 'I don't know. I guess?'

Truth be told, I was comfortable with my little pocket of the world. I didn't feel the need to broaden my horizons or travel or keep up with latest on the political climate in Guam. Anything outside of my immediate area wasn't of concern to me. Even with the wonders of the internet and News.com, she insisted on getting the paper delivered each day. She must have forgotten to cancel her subscription because it kept coming after she left.

We were one of maybe two houses in the street that still received a newspaper delivery. The thud that caused me to drop my toast was just the paper hitting our screen door after it flew out of the delivery guys hand, over the roof of his Datsun. He was very accurate. I heard his engine popping as he burned off down the street.

Maybe it was time to see what was going on in the world. I opened the front door and there it was on the welcome mat, next to yesterday's shit, rolled up in a layer of plastic cling film. As I bent down to pick it up, I noticed out of the corner of my eye: red paint. I peered out of the front entryway a little further. Someone had sprayed up my van.

'I AM NOT A PAEDOPHILE!' I screamed to the street.

'Good for you!' shouted back Roy the postie, as he cycled by, having just deposited something in my letterbox.

The big red letters glared me down as I crossed the yard to the mailbox. My eyes were locked on the word 'PEDO', plastered down the side of my van. The red paint really stood out against the black. I went back inside to get some cleaning supplies from under the sink, tossing the mail on the bench as I went past. Just a few loose envelopes. We didn't have much in the way of car-wash gear. I figured a dish sponge and detergent would have to do.

I moved the van out into the street and sprayed it with the garden hose. I tipped liberal amounts of detergent onto the big red letters and began to scrub. The red paint was a lot more stubborn than I would have hoped. I had to start using the scouring side of the dish sponge. It wasn't doing wonders for the original paintwork, but the red was slowly coming off.

'Stephen Hawking died. Do you think they will bury him, or just plug him back into the charger?' It was Jake. He had the morning paper tucked under his arm. 'You're not supposed to be out here.'

'What?'

'Yeah, you're not supposed to be out here. I haven't measured it out yet, but I'm pretty sure that's right,' he said. He was squinting down at a piece of paper in his hand.

'Give me that!' I snatched it out of his hand and scanned over it. It was a letter from a law firm, Oscar and Oswald, acting on behalf of McCormack's. It was a jargon-filled three pages that I didn't fully absorb, but which essentially forbade me from going within twenty meters of the McCormack's Home for Disabled Youths, or else risk further criminal charges, as a direct result of the restraining order pending.

'What the fuck?' I said, exasperated.

A car two houses down started its engine quietly and its headlights came on. A black Chrysler sedan. It slowly pulled out from the curb and crept past us. The driver watched us through the glass as he passed. A narrow-faced man with a dark-brimmed hat and thin moustache He tipped his hat at me and carried on. As he went by, the sun caught the passenger door and bounced brightly off the gold lettering on the side: *O&O Legal Representation*. I took that as my cue to head back inside.

'What the fuck?' I said again, once inside the security of our lounge room. 'Twenty metres?' I re-read the letter now that I had time to properly absorb it. 'Twenty metres!'

I was flummoxed. Twenty metres, as it turns out, is the exact distance from McCormack's to the outside edge of the welcome mat at my front door. I know this, because after reading the letter for a third time and confirming that it certainly did say that I could not be within *twenty metres* of McCormack's, I made Jake go and buy a long tape measure from the hardware store. I stayed in our doorway whilst he wound out twenty metres of the tape.

'Seems a bit weird, doesn't it?' Jake said.

'What does?'

'The whole twenty metres thing.' He looked at me conspiratorially. 'I mean, you're a dangerous sex offender who preys upon disabled kids.' I pointed at him finger in protest. Jake put his hands up apologetically. He went on, 'I'm just saying, if they thought you were a dangerous sex offender, why wouldn't they make it a K? Why wouldn't they go, "Right, we don't want this creep within a whole kilometre of our place", and that would be that. They'd be sure you'd never set your lecherous eyes on one of their disabled youths again.'

I didn't love his delivery, but he had a point.

'I bet it was McCormack, that crotchety old bitch,' he said after a moment.

'What do you mean?'

'To spite you. Why bother making it a whole kilometre, when she can just as easily make it twenty metres and you're trapped.'

'Fuck.'

'Doesn't really serve her purpose though, does it?'

I wasn't sure what he meant.

'You can still be a sex offender at a distance. Standing on the threshold, having a pull on the welcome mat as the blue bus rolls in.'

'Well at least I couldn't *come* on anyone,' I said sarcastically.

'You'd be surprised,' he replied, deadly serious. 'You'd be surprised what can be achieved with a bit of determination and a powerful urethra. I've seen some impressive videos.'

I laughed. It was all I could do. That was one of the strangest things I'd ever heard, even coming from Jake. I laughed because it was funny. I laughed because there seemed to be nothing else to do.

'We've got no food,' Jake said, looking into our barren pantry. He was right.

'Don't look at me,' I said, 'I'm essentially on house arrest. You'll have to go to the shops yourself.' He grumbled, but eventually left for the shops.

I hadn't heard from Jenny since the *incident*. It had only been a day, I know, but I still thought she would have made some effort to contact me. Maybe she was shitty with me. She couldn't call me, anyway. She didn't have my number. I didn't have hers, either. We hadn't really gotten to the stage in our relationship that called for us to exchange phone numbers. It was odd; we sort of skipped that stage. It was as though we went from just being awkward work acquaintances straight to fucking in a disability bathroom—there was no '*What's your favourite colour?*' or

'*Where did you grow up?*' or '*How do you* really *feel about coriander?*'

>Uncomfortable silences in conversation.

>Torrid love-making sessions in the washroom.

That was the unnatural progression of our interactions, and I loved it. I was pretty sure I was in love.

It's funny, the effect of taking something away from a person. The forbidden fruit will always be the object of desire. I can remember a time that I didn't set foot outside of the house for an entire week. Sunday to Sunday. I only realised it had been an entire week because Monday is bin day, and we always put our bins out on a Sunday night for collection in the morning. When I'd gone to take the rubbish out to the bin, I'd found it still waiting for me on the curb from the week before. I remember feeling guilty, like I'd neglected the poor little yellow-lid. It was the sort of guilt I'd imagine you'd feel as a parent who'd left their kids in the car at the TAB, but in the 90s. Not as crushing as the guilt of leaving your kids in the car in 2018, but a pang of neglect nonetheless.

Anyway, the point I'm trying to make is that one time I spent an entire week inside the house without realising, but now that I had no way of leaving, all I wanted to do was be out of there. I was going out of my mind. I felt hot. I was getting itchy. I looked at the stupid fucking letter on the bench. I needed to get out. Who was going to know if I just quickly crossed the front lawn and went down the street? I needed some air, badly. *Fuck 'em*, I thought. I nearly tore the front door off its hinges in my eagerness to leave. I breathed in the freshness of outside as I stepped onto the welcome mat. My right foot slipped as it came down on the bristles.

Yesterday's shit.

The 'freshness of outside' was quickly tainted by the thick smell of human shit. I gagged as it reached my nostrils, stepping forward off the mat. An engine turned over across the street. I looked up, and the familiar emblazoning of gold lettering bounced sunlight into my eyes as the black car came to life.

'Oh, give me a fucking break, would you?" I stepped back onto the mat. "Cut me some fucking slack!' The beady-eyed law firm agent and I locked eyes through the tinted glass. I threw my hands in the air. 'Just piss off and leave me alone!'

Mrs Ethyl next door turned her nose up and made a disapproving noise as she watered her plants. The old bitch was always watering her fucking plants. She was always out in her garden, and it still looked shithouse.

'You can go fuck yourself too, Ethyl!' I yelled out to her, slamming the door.

I felt a bit bad telling my ninety-year-old neighbour to fuck herself, and made a mental note to make it up to her later on. Another debt to the Karma Exchange. Still, I was wild. I needed to get out. I paced around the living room like a caged tiger, the smell of the shit from my shoe hardly even registering as it peeled off into the carpet. I needed to get out.

The back fence.

My head snapped toward the back of the house as the thought hit me like a slap from a wet salmon. Our house backed onto the oval of the local primary school. Chris and I had been robbed three times because of it. Opportunistic thieves would pick houses that backed onto reserves or roads because of their easy access and getaway. I say we'd been robbed three times, but perhaps I should have said we'd been broken into three times, for the sake of accuracy. The enterprising burglar would break into our property, only to find it devoid of anything worth pilfing, so he (or she, let's not start assuming gender here) would be forced to suffice with the small amount of change in our coin bowl by the sink. Even when Chris was living here we never really had much to steal. We actually got robbed a fourth time whilst living together, but she never found out. Chris had come home and congratulated me on what a good job I'd done tidying up. I didn't have the heart to point out the broken flyscreen in the laundry window.

I felt pretty chuffed with myself as I swung my legs down to the other side of the fence, knowing I'd beaten them. They could try to cage me, but I'd outsmarted their prison. No one was keeping Savage in.

Chapter Eight

My feet touched down on the grass just as the bell rang. I supposed it was recess. As I crossed the oval, school children began to appear from the building on the opposite side; just a few at first, then more. They reminded me of ants as they crossed the grass, breaking off into their smaller groups of friends. I headed for the low fence at the street-facing side of the oval, adjacent to the school's buildings, which would be my exit from the grounds.

I don't know why, but I began to feel intimidated as I passed through the dappling of children. They stared at me like I was a leper. Passing through the growing mass of children felt more like passing through a very short, very widespread gang. I pictured it in my head: I was sure I could take three or four of them, but if they all decided to go me at once, I would be inundated and wouldn't stand a chance. It's like the old riddle Jake would often ask people: Would you rather fight one horse-sized duck, or fifty duck-sized horses?

Horse-sized duck. Every time. It seems daunting, but one-on-one, you might stand a chance. Sure, you could probably take ten, maybe twelve duck-sized horses, provided they came at you in a line; but even so, fatigue would eventually get to you somewhere in the mid-to-late teens. And if they swarmed around you, there could only ever be one outcome. The thought of being trampled to death by so many tiny hooves gave me chills.

My best strategy with the children, I mused, would be to pick one of them up by his feet and swing him round like a hammer-thrower, taking out as many of the others as I could with his top half. My inappropriate daydream was broken by a voice that had not. The very high-pitched question was posed to me by a thin, almost see-through ginger kid.

'Are you a teacher?'

I shook my head. This response was met by a lot of excitable whispering amongst the ginger kid's friends. They were an odd-looking bunch. They were the sort of group that I called 'the leftovers', a group of friends that forms not because they want to, but because they have to, as a means of survival. The social outcasts. They'd failed to meet the criteria for the usual circles and eventually banded together through their mutual interest in the avoidance of loneliness.

There was a drippy-nosed, freckle-faced one with sauce stains on his shirtfront; a fat one with jiggly little boy-tits; one with a hunched neck who breathed exclusively through his mouth; and of course, a staple for any group of left-overs, the pasty ginger-nut.

The whispering stopped.

Ginge looked up at me for a moment, then turned and ran toward the school buildings. His friends slowly turned and followed him at a less-enthusiastic jog, with boy-tits least-enthusiastically managing a sweaty lumber.

I wasn't doing anything wrong, I was simply passing through the school grounds, I reminded myself. I was pretty sure I wasn't doing anything wrong. I quickened my pace to a weird sort of skip-jog. Tiny fingers of primary school children pointed at me as I did my best to look inconspicuous, whilst standing out like dogs-balls in your Sunday lunch. The skip-jog metamorphosed into a canter, and for the last twenty meters, I dead-set legged it.

'Hey!' came the voice of a grown man wearing an 'approachable' and 'non-threatening' high-visibility vest boldly labelled 'Safety Monitor'. I paid him no heed as I hurdled the low, wire-mesh fence at the front of the school and disappeared down the street. My brain was stinging with déja' vu.

At least I was clothed this time.

I belted down the street and rounded a corner which opened up onto a strip of shops. There was a butcher, a fruit and veg shop, a trendy new café that served their coffees solely out of recycled glass jars, and a milkbar. I quickly ducked into the milkbar, and almost instantly felt safe. No one ever came into milkbars. I was pretty sure no one was chasing me anymore, but there was added solace gained from knowing I'd made entrance to the safe haven that was one of the most disused public buildings of the modern age.

The owner ambled out of the back room of the small, poky shop and made his way to the counter. He was an elderly Korean man who wore a white shirt tucked into khaki trousers. His head tilted forward slightly, while his eyes focused upwardly on me. He smiled kindly and I raised a hand in greeting. His teeth looked like a brick fence that had been hit by a car but hadn't fallen in yet.

I pretended to be interested in the lolly bags by the counter and kept my head down. I vaguely wondered why anyone would buy a bag made up solely of milk-bottles.

A TV screen flickered in the back room, and gunshots came from the speakers. It looked like some sort of Korean Western. There were Korean cowboys raiding a horse-drawn cart. I moved away from the milk bottles toward the door. There were a bunch of flyers hanging on the window. Someone had lost a pet bird. 'Indian Ringneck Parakeet: Answers to *Stephen.'*

Fuck me, I thought, as I stared at its stupid blue face. I had to laugh; *good luck getting that one back*. I imagined someone calling the owner: 'Yeah, I've spotted Stephen, he's just here in front of me…oh fuck, he's gone.' Another flyer advertised a ride-on lawn mower for sale. 'Runs alright, but needs a bit of love.'

The bell above the door jingled as someone else entered the tiny shop. The man behind the counter stood in shock, his eyes just about popping out of his head. Two customers in his store at once! He hissed something into the back room and a woman of similar age and appearance shuffled alongside him, by the register. Backup had arrived. Her eyes were huge in astonishment also. I decided she must be his wife.

'Can I put this up here?' asked the young girl who had just entered the shop. She would have been in her early twenties, and wore her dark hair in a long, black plait. The two behind the counter nodded vigorously and waved their hands for her to do as she pleased. I moved out of the way so she could stick her flyer up.

'Aww, someone's lost their bird. Sad,' she commented, as she stuck up a blue A4 piece of paper. *Blackwood Antithetical Cohabitation*, it read.

'Stephen,' I added, feigning sadness.

'Oh, Lucy,' she said, awkwardly balancing her pile of flyers as she extended a hand for me to shake. She'd obviously misread the situation, but I didn't have the heart to tell her that I was talking about the bird.

'That looks interesting,' I lied. I hadn't gotten past the title. *Fuck knows what 'Antithetical' means.*

'Yeah, it's a research thing for the psych students. It's for Uni. Here, I printed too many anyway.' She handed me one of the flyers and said it was nice to meet me, before giving a polite wave and nod to the store owners and exiting. They seemed more than a little disappointed that she hadn't made a purchase. It probably would have been their first sale in months.

'Esuse me, sir,' came some fragmented English from behind the till. 'Are you buying something?'

I felt bad for them, considering the Uni chick hadn't bought anything.

'I'll take the milk bottles,' I said, and handed him a couple of bucks. His wife had to help him pick his jaw up off the counter. I must have been the first person ever to have bought a bag of milk bottles. I wondered how long they must have been there. Years, probably. Maybe even a decade.

When I got outside I popped one of the milk bottles into my mouth. *Decades.* I nearly broke a tooth. It was as hard as an arseful of concrete and might have been older than me. I spat it out into the blue flyer and chucked the lot into a green metal bin that stood alone on the corner of the footpath out the front of the milkbar.

Time to head home. Jake would be back from the shops by now. My stomach grumbled as a reminder. Jake's idea of a wholesome meal was chicken tenders with potato gems and tomato sauce, so I didn't have much hope for nutrition, which was probably what my body was calling for right now, but anything would be a step up from rock-hard premillennial milk bottles.

A few blocks into my journey home my phone started buzzing in my pocket. I checked the screen: it was Mum. *Click.* I had low battery anyway. I'd call her later, I told myself. As I walked, my foot rolled over the top of a rock on the footpath, and it skittered out in front of me. It was about the size of a golf ball, a good kicking rock.

When I caught up to it, I kicked it ahead of me again. And again, when I came upon it once more. I kicked it and kicked it along the footpath as I walked. I thought about Jenny and kicked it ahead of myself. I thought about the dragon-man and kicked it a little harder. I thought about Mrs. McCormack and kicked it so hard it shot across the nature strip and onto the road. I followed it and continued kicking it along the road. I thought about Chris. I thought about every bad decision I'd made that had led me to the position in my life where I was indefinitely forbidden from setting foot on my own welcome mat. I kicked the rock again.

The quiet engine of a car stirred me from my rocky daydream as it crept up alongside me. A black Chrysler sedan. It matched my pace. I sped up and so did it, so I stopped. In perfect synchronicity with me, the car came to a halt. The man with the thin moustache stared at me through heavily tinted glass. I held his gaze. He didn't move.

'What?!' I exploded. 'What could you possibly want now? I haven't done anything!' I was getting angry, my voice climbing with every new word uttered. The man from O&O just sat there staring at me. A smile crawled across his lips.

'What do you want from me!?' I leant in close to the window so I could see his smug face better. My breath fogged up the glass. 'You gotta follow me round? Because I can't be trusted? Huh!' My voice grew louder. 'Because I'm such a fucking danger to society? Is that what you think, or are you guys just fucking with me? Am I that much of a monster, am I?' I was shouting now. 'That's right, I forgot! I AM a MONSTER! You'd better keep a good eye on me mate, because at any corner I turn, I might just start wanking off in front of a disabled kid!'

His head cocked to the front of the vehicle slightly. I followed the movement and my heart sank into my colon. At the end of the street ahead of us, maybe thirty metres away was a school, a man in a high visibility vest, and a police officer.

'That's the man! That's the one who was approaching the children!' exclaimed the guy in the high-vis.

As I watched them move toward me, I didn't even have the energy to run. I sat down on the side of the road where I was and waited for them to reach me. O&O pulled away and disappeared around the corner. I fell backwards into the grass of the nature-strip and stared up at the clouds passing by overhead. One of them looked like a cock and balls, so at least I had something to smile about for a moment. The clouds drifted on by above me; there was a wispy one, and one that looked a little like a dog, which then gave way to a more defined, shiny, baldhead-shaped cloud.

'Dan Savage,' said the cloud.

'The writer?' asked the smaller, whinier sounding cloud.

I blinked and the two faces above me came into focus; the bald one was extending a hand to help me up. It was the unmistakably meaty paw of everybody's favourite arresting officer, Hulkhands. I ignored it. His face looked decidedly more weathered than I recalled. The top of his head was still tight and shiny, but his face was more wrinkled than I remembered. He looked like a testicle with teeth.

'Dan, get up,' said the mouth of the testicle.

'Nope,' said my mouth. I felt substantially more relaxed than I should have.

'You're in the gutter,' said the policeman.

'We're all in the gutter, sir, but some of us are looking at the clouds,' I misquoth, laughing to myself.

'Were you in this schoolyard earlier today?' he asked, motioning in that direction.

'That's definitely him,' the man in the vest chirped.

I had déjà vu for the second time.

'Can't go out the front door,' I said.

'He was harassing the children,' squeaked the high-vis man.

'Were you harassing the children?' asked the officer.

'Nope.'

Overhead, an Indian Myna bird was swooping a magpie. I think it was trying to fuck it. Or kill it.

'Mr Savage, I think you need to start taking this more seriously. This is serious stuff. First the disability centre, now this?' came the stern voice of the bald-headed cock.

'A repeat offender! I knew it, it's a good thing I saw him before he had a chance to molest any of the children!' squealed hi-vis, bubbling over with excitement and nervous energy. His voice took on a more serious edge, 'You didn't have a chance to molest any of the children, did you?'

'No,' I replied. 'I didn't molest any of the children.'

'But did you have the chance?' pushed Mr Hi-vis

'Yes, did you have the chance?' echoed the policeman, dead serious. 'Answer the question, Dan.'

I exhaled deeply and closed my eyes. 'I suppose I had the chance to molest them if I wanted to. But I didn't want to.'

'He admits it! He's a child molester!' Hi-vis shrieked triumphantly.

'It certainly sounded like an admission of guilt, didn't it?' pondered the hulk-handed testicle.

I couldn't be bothered. I simply could not be arsed. My consciousness was split. In one reality I lay there, gazing at the sky, marvelling at the joys of the world and the beauty of our planet; but I couldn't ignore the knock, knock, knocking of the second reality in which I was being called a child molester.

'Are you the worst policeman ever? I said I *could have* molested the children.'

'That certainly sounds like something a child molester would say,' asserted the policeman.

'I said I *could have* done it, not *I did* do it,' I replied, frustrated.

'So, you didn't molest any of the children?'

'No.'

'First he did, now he didn't,' whined the safety monitor petulantly. 'I just can't keep up!'

'You're certain you didn't molest any children?' asked the officer again, over the top of a notepad.

'Yes.'

'Not even one?'

'Not even one.'

Hulkhands' meaty paw tightened its grip on the pen as he scratched a few notes in his pad. Finally, he looked back at me, his face rearranged into a stern, official expression of authority.

'Well it seems to me that you are free to go, then.'

Relief washed through me like warm, liquid daylight. *Thank fuck.* For a moment I thought there was going to be another line of questioning in a small interrogation room, and potentially another shiny black law-firm car following me around. I relaxed back into the grass, allowing my eyes to locate and focus on a new cloud. A big bald head appeared back in my vision.

'Take care, Savage.'

'Will do, sir.'

He walked away in the company of a rather displeased safety monitor. My mind had only just had the opportunity to refocus on the old cloud, which had very slowly meandered across the sky sunward, when I heard him call out over his shoulder.

'Oh, and Savage: no more shortcuts through the school.'

'Hey?' I sat up. He stopped walking and turned halfway back to me.

'No more cutting through the primary school. You set foot in those grounds again, and next time it won't just be a friendly kerbside chat.'

'But I live there!' I called after him, pointing to my back fence.

'Not my problem,' he called back, turning to go.

'I can't go out my front door!'

'Too bad.'

I stood up. 'How will I get out of my house?' I shouted down the street.

'You're already out!' he said, and I swear I could hear him laughing.

Well, fuck. He was right. I *was* out of my house. How the fuck was I going to get *back in* to my house? *Fuck, fuck, fucking fuck.* I thought he had disappeared altogether until I heard the sound of his deep voice carrying down the street.

'Seriously though, you go in that school and your ass is mine. We'll be watching!' There was another hearty chuckle and the policeman disappeared around the corner.. I'd half expected him to do that two-finger, point at your eyes, point at me thing that people do. I was a little disappointed he hadn't committed to full douche.

So, what happens now? I couldn't cut through the primary school and I couldn't go past my welcome mat. Short of getting air-dropped out of a plane and parachuting into my back yard, there was no conceivable way of getting home. Like Prince Charles getting pegged by Camilla Parker-Bowles, I was royally screwed.

I decided that my best course of action was to wait until I was sure ol' mate Safety Steve and the ballbag-with-chompers were well and truly gone, then sneak through the school and jump my back fence when I knew the coast was clear.

It had become blindingly apparent to me in the last few days that I would have to find somewhere else to live. I had been pushing the thought to the back of my mind, hoping that the whole situation would quieten down and I could go back to living a normal life, but that clearly wasn't happening any time soon. I would start looking for somewhere new to live in the morning; but tonight I needed somewhere to stay, so I had to get back home.

I waited a good fifteen minutes, and, relatively sure they would have gotten to where they were going by now, headed primary-schoolward. They couldn't be watching *all* of the time. I couldn't imagine the local police staking out a primary school overnight on the off-chance that a suspected-but-not-confirmed sex offender might use it as passage to his own backyard. I further reasoned that so soon after they had forbidden my entry, my over-watchers would not be expecting me to breach our 'agreement'. Now would be the best time to strike.

A quick up-down of the street showed it devoid of any police cars, so I proceeded. Approaching the school fence with caution, I made sure there was no-one around. I placed my hands on the top of the fence, and was just about to hop it, when my concentration was broken by a loud 'Caw!' I looked up and, sitting atop a bright red pole, was a crow.

'Caw!' went the harbinger of security-related news.

Like some sort of prophet from above, it went 'Caw!' one more time before flying off. Atop the pole was a security camera, facing out from the front of the school toward the street, its one dark eye silently surveying the area. A rectangular metal sign about halfway down the post declared: These premises protected by Hilterr Security via direct video link to local law enforcement.

Well, fuck. *There goes that idea.* A direct video link to the police station meant he *would* be watching. All of the time. I thought about chancing it that he wasn't watching, but the idea of being officially placed on a sex offenders register was too much. With the recent run of misfortune at McCormack's, and the persistence of the school's safety monitor, there was little room for doubt that there would be a substantial case built against me, even if it was all bullshit. I turned away from the school.

Chapter Nine

Homeless.

I'd always wondered what it would be like to be homeless, but never expected to be in a position where I was forced to find out. I'd always been a bit of a fuck-up. A fuck-up in the nicest possible way, but a fuck-up nonetheless. I just never expected to be a homeless fuck-up.

When I say fuck-up, I'm not talking complete fuck-up; I mean, I wasn't a violent criminal or a heroin addict, but I wasn't exactly setting the world on fire either. I guess I'm just a bit of a floater, if I can use the term without evoking the image of a turd in a toilet bowl. I mean well, but I've never been a high achiever. Work didn't stick for me like it did with other people and I'd always felt that I lacked a certain drive that others appeared to possess.

Anyway, homeless.

That was my reality tonight. I didn't even have any mates in the area whose house I could crash at. We had moved to the area because it was cheap, and Chris grew up around there. I thought about calling Mum, but I hadn't spoken to her in a while and I couldn't quite bring myself to explain to her how I had gotten into this situation. I called Jake.

'Hey man, where are you? I got all of this food and I got back and you weren't here. Did you shoot over the road to knock one out again and get picked up by the cops?' He laughed; I didn't.

'Listen, Jake, I need you—' I began to say, but he cut over the top of me.

'I got lamingtons too! And all of the ingredients to make mashed potatoes... well, potatoes. Did you know that there are like, seventeen types of milk now?'

'Jake,' I tried to say, but he kept going. I thought he must have taken one of his little brothers Ritalin tablets again.

'Yeah, there's soy milk, almond milk, coconut milk, A2 milk, rice milk. Why do you reckon we only really drink cows' milk? How fucking weird is that? Drinking the juices of a completely different species. Surely if you had to drink the milk of any animal it would be a monkey. Think about it, they are heaps closer to us genetically. It makes sense. Maybe we don't 'cause it would be too weird milking them; it's not the same as a cow, is it, where all of the action is so far away from the face? You'd be tugging on the little monkey titties. On the little monkey nipples, looking right into its eyes. It's not really the same as an udder. Udders are all business. Six little teats of business. You following me?'

I wasn't.

'Jake, mate, I need your help,' I managed to get out.

'Sure thing, Dan, anything you need. But first, answer me this, because I think there is a real market for it. If they had it in the fridge at the shops, would you drink monkey milk?'

There were two little heartbreaking beeps, then the line went silent. I looked at my phone, already knowing the answer. It had died. Fucking Jake and his fucking monkey milk. Why didn't I call someone else? Anyone else! My stomach groaned. I realised I hadn't eaten anything (except the bits of ancient milk-bottle I may have involuntarily swallowed) since that crappy dry piece of toast this morning.

I moved away from the school fence for fear of being reported for loitering, but not before flipping the bird to the security camera. I hoped he was watching. I meandered back up the street I had come from, head hanging in defeat, homeless and hungry. For the second time in a matter of days I wondered how my life had gotten to this point.

I tried to pull myself out of the doldrums and turn my practical brain on. Now was the time for action, not self-pity. I needed a roof over my head tonight, and something to eat: they were the priorities. It was starting to get dark.

Maybe the café near the milkbar was still open. Failing that, I remembered seeing a phone booth out the front of the milkbar; like two peas of the same pod, the most disused public convenience of the modern age, out front of the most disused building of the modern age. I could use the small amount of change in my pocket to get in touch with Jake, or even Mum if it came to that.

What I really wanted was some food. I was sure I would be able to think more clearly after a good meal. I'd have a feed, then work out what I was going to do for the night.

The café was about a twenty-five-minute walk from the primary school, or a ten-minute run if you were being chased by a safety monitor, but I didn't feel like running. I took the time to reflect on the day I'd had. Really, I should have just accepted my prison and stayed home, resigning to the life of a house-bound hermit.

When I finally arrived back at the strip of shops, I was greeted by the sight of roller doors, pulled firmly down and latched into place in front of most of the shopfronts. The butcher, the fruit and veg joint and the café were locked up tight. My stomach groaned again. This time it was a muffled roar, like a lion drowning in mud.

The milkbar had no such security as the shops it shared the strip with, just a simple locked door and a 'Closed' sign. No one in their right mind would break into the place anyway, unless they really wanted some lollies you could break glass with and the five-dollar weekly takings. I was so hungry I could eat the lost bird whose picture stared back at me through the glass.

Time to make the call.

I went into the phone booth and inserted a few coins. The little LCD display lit up an olive green; 'Enter phone number,' it read. Right then, it struck me: I didn't know Jakes number. I didn't know my own number. Fuck, I didn't even know my own mum's phone number. I was actually lost without my phone. I didn't have to remember people's numbers because the phone did the remembering for me. Shit, it was the twenty-first century! Remembering phone numbers was a redundant function for the brain. Redundant, of course, until you really needed to know someone's fucking phone number.

My stomach growled again. It was getting more frustrated than me. I was famished. Fuck it. I'd had the thought in my head on the way over but had really hoped it wouldn't come down to it. I reached my hand deep into the bin on the footpath's edge.

I was so hungry.

I felt around until my fingertips came to rest upon their cellophane-wrapped prize. It was like a low-budget claw game. My hand came out of the bin with something sticky on the side of it, but my focus was unbroken. The prize sat in my palm in a loose ball. The blue flyer from earlier that the Uni chick had handed me was glued to the side of the ball, with the congealed remains of the lolly I'd spat into it. I picked it off the side and tossed it on the ground and, unwrapping the cellophane bag, I popped a single stiff milk bottle straight in my gob. It was fairly tough on the old teeth, but I was pretty sure the sugar content would do me some good in lieu of a proper meal. I fed them into my mouth one after another. It was a physical challenge as much as a mental challenge. I ate about half the pack, which was no small feat for my jaw, before stopping myself. It might be a long evening; better to reign in the bottle consumption now than run out early and have nothing to eat later on.

A light breeze blew the flyer along the ground. I watched idly for a moment, trying to remember what it said—something about ethics? I followed after it as it skidded along the path, catching up with it before it tumbled over the kerb. I stopped it with my foot. It stuck to the bottom of my shoe. Peeling it off, I unfolded it and had a proper read this time.

Blackwood Antithetical Cohabitation: a social study read the bolded heading. Most of it had been blurred and distorted by the half-chewed milk bottle I'd spat into it earlier, but I could just make out the main section. 'Are you healthy and between the ages of 18 and 40? Want to be part of an exciting social study? If you answered yes to both, then Blackwood wants to talk to you about Antithetical Cohabitation, a social experiment in temporary, experimental housing.'

It was a note at the bottom of the page, below the contact details, that caught my attention: Rent-free accommodation offered to successful applicants. Looking at it with fresh eyes, Antithetical Cohabitation was looking pretty enticing. I went over and popped my change in the phone booth once more and started punching in the numbers. 'Lucy' was the name against the number on the page. I hit the call button and the phone began to ring. It went on and on; I thought it was going to ring out, until finally a young woman's voice sung out on the other end of the line.

'Hi, you've called Lucy. I'm not here, but I guess you already know that now. Leave a message!' Voicemail.

I hated voicemails. They always got me in a bit of a panic because I never really knew what to say. They always seemed to catch me off-guard, like, you are expecting the person you are calling to answer, so you don't have your script prepared for the scenario where you end up talking to a machine. I think I would have been more relaxed about it if you got more than one go to get it right. I need at least two shots at leaving a voice message, because I always fuck it up the first time. The recording concluded, punctuated by the ever-dreaded beep, my cue to talk. I hung up the phone. I'd try again later.

A few coins jingled down into the phone's discharge bay at the bottom. I hadn't realised how little money I had on me. Just the change from the fiver I'd used to buy the milk bottles now stashed in my back pocket. About three bucks, before the phone call.

I popped another lolly in my mouth and sucked on it. Typically, a milk bottle wouldn't be a lolly you would suck, but for the sake of my molars, I'd learnt that a pre-suck made a world of difference, with that added moisture soaking into it the god-awful lollies were rendered just about bearable. Little victories.

The headlights of a passing car hit my eyes, and I realised dusk was falling. It had gotten to that point of the day when the shadows are longest and the mozzies come out. It would be dark soon.

Fuck waiting, I'd call her again.

I went back into the booth and punched in her number. Feeding the phone another forty cents, I waited. It began to ring. I was more hopeful this time. These days, people are rarely separated from their phones for more than a few minutes. I was actually feeling a little anxious without mine; more so than I'd like to admit. I suppose the anxiety could be partly credited to the fact that I'd recently become homeless. That was still soaking in.

It rang a few more times over, and then the familiar 'Hi, you've called Lucy!' She was so fucking chirpy it was painful. I slammed the phone back on the receiver. No coins rattled down to the bottom this time.

I paced up and down the section of footpath in front of the milkbar. The situation was absolute bullshit. I stuffed another milk bottle into my mouth. I was starting to get worried. It was looking more and more likely that I'd be spending the night camped out in a phone booth outside a milkbar. I had $2.20 in my pocket, which by my reckoning would get me five more phone calls, with twenty cents left over. I didn't want to be calling her at ten o'clock at night, and as the sun was disappearing swiftly over the horizon, I figured I'd better call again.

Once more, I punched in the number and it started to ring. On each 'brr, brr' my hopes grew and I was sure she would answer, only to experience deflation when the chirpy, 'Hi, you've called Lucy!' reached my ear. When her little spiel was over, I took a deep breath and waited for the beep.

'Hi,' I said into empty space. 'My name is Dan Savage and I'm calling about the temporary experimental housing. If you could call me back when you get a chance, that would be great. Thanks.'

Fuck, I thought after hanging up the line. I hadn't left a contact number. What a dumbass. My phone was no good, so I searched around the booth. Do payphones even have phone numbers? I supposed they should, I'd seen them ring plenty of times in movies. I found one printed under the receiver, partially obscured by a piece of gum.

I called her again. 'Hi, you've called Lucy. I'm not here, but I guess you already know that now. Leave a message!'

'Hi Lucy, I just left you a message before, but I forgot to leave my number. I'm interested in talking to you about the temporary experimental housing. My number is—' I scratched at the edge of the gum, squinting, '— five-five-five, two-nine-zero, seven-four. If you could get back to me soon that would be great. I'm Dan Savage,' I added dumbly at the end, after realising I hadn't given her my name this time.

Good. That was good. Now all I had to do was wait. I sat down and got comfortable in the booth. I was down to $1.40 now. Three more phone calls, that was it. I had another couple of milk bottles and wondered what the future might hold. I imagined what it might be like if I got accepted into this experimental housing gig. Maybe I would be partnered up with some absolute babe. Or a nympho.

My mind flashed back to Jenny and the last time I'd seen her. I hadn't thought about her in a while, and I felt a pang of guilt. I wondered what she was doing right now. Probably not sitting in a phone booth eating stale milk bottles. I tried to push her out of my head. I didn't need to add lovesickness to my growing list of woes.

I amused myself for a while by gathering up loose stones that were on the footpath and throwing them a short distance in front of me. I would throw one of the bigger ones, and then try to get as close to it as I could with the smaller ones. It's amazing how easily such an inane activity can provide amusement when you're starved of entertainment. That little game kept me going for a good half hour. The sun had well and truly set by the time I grew bored of my rock game and tried Lucy again.

Voicemail. One dollar, even.

I decided to give it an hour before calling again. I don't wear a watch, so I tried to count for the hour, but gave up around the fifteen-minute mark. I was getting pretty cagey sitting in the bottom of the phone booth, so I got up and stretched my legs, walking up to the end of the strip, making sure not to go further than hearing distance from the booth in case it rang. Probably just wishful thinking.

I peered through the roller door out the front of the butchers. It was that sort of roller door that was made up primarily of brushed metal tubing, so rather than being the solid variety, the door formed more of a cage for the shop than anything. You could still reach your arm through the gap, and I could probably still smash the glass front if I jabbed it with a cricket bat, but I couldn't get in; I guess that's the point.

The butchers advertised 'Quality meats at wholesale prices' and had fluorescent chalk paint all over their window, screaming out low prices to back up their claims. I squinted against the dark, trying to get a look inside, but couldn't see much. It looked like they had packed up their displays for the day.

The whole strip must have gotten a packaged deal on the roller doors (except the dusty little milkbar), because both the green-grocer and the café had the exact same metal caging as the butcher to keep them secure. I moseyed along past the green grocer and had a little lookie-lou in their front window, too. Again, there wasn't much to see. Apparently, grocers pack away most of their produce overnight as well. The potatoes and onions were still out, and that only made me hungrier than I already was.

I kept walking until I hit the café. It was a swanky little place with exposed copper pipework and polished concrete benchtops. Above the front table hung a weathered wooden ladder, dangling horizontally from the ceiling. Hanging off the ladder were a number of green, brown and blue glass bottles intertwined by fairy lights, which had been left on. It was pretty beautiful.

I was beginning to feel a little light-headed from lack of food, so I dug another milk bottle out of my pocket to satiate my hunger. It gave me the sugar hit I needed to keep me going. My eyes wandered up to the chalkboard menu above the front counter, which I instantly regretted looking at. There were walnut brownies and carrot cake on offer, raspberry and white chocolate muffins, banana bread. At this point I would have even gone for one of the paleo-vegan smoothies with quinoa.

Fuck.

I tore myself away from the wonderland of possibilities and headed back up to the phone booth. One more call would leave me with 60 cents in my pocket. I waited what I deemed to be another fifteen minutes and dialled the number. Of course, it went to voicemail. It seemed like I was dealing with the only person in the known universe who is away from their mobile phone for hours at a time without checking it. I left another message, a little more urgent this time: 'Hi Lucy, me again. I'm not sure if you received my last message but I really need to talk to you. Please call me back at any time, and I do mean anytime. I'll be here, waiting. Call me. Dan.'

I was beginning to get worked up. My breathing quickened and my grip tightened on the phone. I immediately dialled again. Surely to fuck, she would hear the phone ringing if she received this many back-to-back calls. Even if she was at the other end of the house, the phone would have to be ringing for a solid two minutes at least.

'Hi, you've called Lucy!' she chirped.

'Argh!' I shouted into the voicemail. I twisted the phone in my hands, biting down on it, then slammed it back into the cradle. 'What could you possibly be doing?!' I screamed into the phone booth. I punched the LCD display, hard. It cracked, and dark liquid splooged out into the screen like black ink. My hand hurt like a motherfucker. I picked up the receiver and slammed it against the telephone box again and again and again until the plastic split and it snapped off at the top, hanging by some thin red and white wires. I collapsed onto the ground, panting, in a heap. I was dizzy, my stomach was eating itself, and I was exhausted from the amount of energy I'd exerted going three rounds with the payphone. I drew my knees up against my chest and held them there, closing my eyes. The day had well and truly got me fucked. I was beaten.

Chapter Ten

I awoke to a tap, tap, tapping on the roof of the phone booth. At
some point in my exhaustion, my body must have finally
submitted and given way to a long, dreamless sleep. The first few
ribbons of daylight peaked over the horizon, a fresh assault on my
bloodshot eyes. It must have been about five a.m.

Tap, tap, tap. Something hard was tapping against the top
of the Telstra orange phonebooth lid. My stomach growled. It was
genuinely painful now. *Tap, tap, tap*. I stared up at the inside of
the booth roof, clutching my stomach uncomfortably. I sincerely
hoped the café opened soon and I could talk some breakfast out
of them, either that or die where I sat, from starvation. Again,
there was a *tap, tap tap* but this time it was followed by a dry
thwack from the direction of the ground just in front of the phone
booth.

My brain jammed up for a second trying to process the vision. A bread roll had fallen from the sky, landing squarely in front of the booth. It was a small dinner roll, the sort you get par-baked from the supermarket and pop in the oven at home. Saliva started to well up inside my mouth, but still I sat frozen. Within an instant of it landing, there was a flutter of wings as a bird came in to land next to it. It put its left foot, claw, whatever, on top of the roll as if claiming the thing for itself, and started pecking at the top of it. It cocked its head and looked straight at me. I knew exactly who this little feathered fuck was. Stephen: the runaway whose mug shot was pasted up on the milkbar window.

He had hollowed out a little handle with his beak at the end of the bread roll by the time I had moved into a crouching position.

'Stephen,' I cooed to the bird, holding a hand out in front of me. 'Come here, mate.'

Stephen wrapped his beak around the little bready handle and, lifting his roll off the pavement, began to hop away from me. I slowly got to my feet, not wanting to startle him, and followed after.

'Stephen' I cooed again, as I left the booth, still squatting. I sidestepped out onto the footpath like a big clumsy crab. 'Come on mate, bring it over here.'

He hopped a little further down the path. I went to follow him, and accidentally kicked one of the rocks from last night's game. It startled the bird and he flapped his wings, fluttering ahead, bread roll in mouth. I thought for sure I would have lost him forever, but he came to land a little way down the street. He dropped the roll and stood on it again, pecking the top. He looked up the street at me, his tiny eye like a black marble in the side of his head, taunting me. I ambled forward, pushing through the delirium of hunger-induced brain fog, reduced to nothing more than the most basic primal instinct: Get food.

I slowed down as I neared the bird again. I crouched down once more so as not to appear quite as predatory.

'Stephen...' His head tilted; so he knew his name. 'Stephen, drop the roll mate. Please.' I edged closer to the bird, holding my breath. He stared blankly back at me. My outstretched hand was maybe a foot away from him.

'Here buddy,' I coaxed, leaning closer still. A sweat broke on my forehead. 'Come here mate.'

I held his gaze as my whole body leant forward as far as it could. He cocked his head. I lunged. My desperate fingertips brushed the crusty exterior of the dinner roll as it evaded my grasp once again. Stephen had been too quick. With my arms stretched to their full extent, unable to protect me, my face scraped along the concrete painfully. I lay flat on my belly, winded.

I craned my neck up just in time to see the mischievous bird flapping its way around the corner. I was all fingertips and toes as

I launched my body up into a starting position, like Usain Bolt before a hundred-metre sprint. The gun went off in my head; I shot off the blocks and tore around the corner in pursuit of my feathered nemesis. As I peeled around the corner I saw him, sitting half way up the street on the footpath, bread roll underfoot, pecking at the crusty top. He looked up and caught my eye. It could have been the lack of food playing tricks with my mind, but I'm pretty sure he nodded at me. I steadied myself for a moment, then crossed to the other side of the street, a strategic tactic that just seemed to come to me. Rather than approaching from the front, in full view of the target, I would cross the road and take a wide arc around the bird, crossing back onto his side of the road once past him, then approaching from behind in a tactical flanking manoeuvre.

I watched him from the corner of my eye as I crossed silently back to his side of the road. He was thoroughly distracted by the bread roll. It was almost offensive what he was doing to the breakfast that should have been mine. Very stealthily, I crept up behind him, walking on the grass nature-strip to muffle my footsteps. He was sat eating his roll out the front of an old brick house, where a fence of wrought iron, broken up by brick columns formed the perimeter of a large front yard, each column topped with a rather uninviting wrought iron spike.. At about the two-metre mark, his head shot upwards. It twisted right around like that girl from The Exorcist. The jig was up, so I threw myself towards him again. Once more I missed, slamming my shoulder into the brick column of the fence. Stephen, the slippery fuck, had fluttered into a dead oak tree in the front yard of the house. I grasped the wrought iron of the fence in my fists, watching him through the gaps. He wasn't getting away that easily.

I hoiked myself up onto a brick column, precariously balancing my body over a wrought iron spike that threatened to penetrate me at any moment. Arms out at my sides, I ran along the top of the fence with surprising agility. I dropped off the top of the fence and into the yard. Stephen remained where he was, roll in mouth—or beak, I suppose.

I approached the tree with a mixture of caution and dead-focus. The old oak tree was probably ten or eleven metres tall, and Stephen was about half way up. I grasped the side of a lower branch and, heaving myself upwards, began my ascent. I managed a standing position on the first branch, then clambered up onto the next highest, my fingers pressing into the soft, cool moss covering the limbs as I pulled myself up. Still, I was too low. Stephen watched on with curiosity from above. Balancing myself with one hand on the trunk of the tree, I climbed a little higher. The bird was perched, bobbing up and down, on a twiggy section at the further extremity of the tree, but would otherwise be within vertical reaching distance. I held onto a branch above and slowly stepped out, heading away from the trunk. I positioned myself directly below Stephen; one quick move and that roll was mine.

I held on to a slightly smaller branch just below the one that the little fugitive was perched upon, to balance myself. As I extended my other hand roll-ward there was a *crack*, and the branch I was balancing myself with broke away from the rest of the tree. My arm flailed wildly, and I swung back into the trunk, catching myself just in time before I tumbled to the ground.

Startled by the commotion, Stephen flew higher up the old oak, nearing the top, where the sturdy boughs opened up onto a nest of twiggy sticks. Not about to give up yet, I steadied myself and followed him higher, keeping closer to the trunk this time. The branches were stronger here. I climbed one, two, three branches higher. The moss covering the tree was drier up here and crumbled off beneath my feet as I continued my ascent. I clung on tight to the trunk as a sheet of moss peeled away. I watched it hit the ground, then steadied myself before climbing higher still. I held out my hand under the bird and pleaded with him.

'Stephen, mate, I'm starving. Drop the bread roll. Please.'

He shat on me in reply. A big milky-green one just under my left eye. I had no response. I just stared up at him. He blinked; I didn't know birds could do that. He blinked again and flew off, up onto a chimney in the middle of the roof of the old house. My heart sank.

There was an internal war between my fear of heights and my desperation for the bread roll. The roll won out. If I got the chance, I would probably eat Stephen too, slap him right in the middle of the roll like a hotdog. I channelled my primate ancestors, and deftly jumped down a few limbs before swinging out of the tree.

With my eyes locked on the little feathered fuck on the roof the entire time, I clambered my way up onto the fence again and tight-roped my way along the top of it toward where it met the side of the house. My vision blurred for a second, and I felt as though I was going to fall. I swayed treacherously on the fence-top. Blinking once, twice, I refocused my vision and managed to steady myself.

Stephen.

I locked my sights back on him and honed in. At the side of the house, I pulled myself up on the guttering. It creaked and groaned under my weight. My hands made contact with the roof-tiles, and I pushed off the guttering with my foot. A substantial groan let out before the whole thing gave way under my weight and tore away from the building. That feeling you get when you go to sit down on a chair and it's a little further back than you thought? I had that, times at least three.

My heart leapt into my throat, and I scrunched my eyes shut, waiting for death. Death was a lot cooler and harder than I would have expected. I opened my eyes to a sea of terracotta rooftiles, still dewy from the night before. I'd fallen forward, landing on my front on the edge of the rooftop. I scrambled to my feet and hands and scampered away from the drop.

I took a perforated breath in, trying to compose myself. Shakily, I gathered up my feet under me and moved toward to chimney, ambling forward cautiously, bent over like a gorilla. I hate being on tiled roofs. I hate being up high in general, but tiled roofs really do it for me. I feel like they are going to slip out from underneath me at any instant and send me hurtling to my death. Mum used to make me get up on the roof and clean the gutters when I was a kid; an act which I'm sure, in this day, would constitute child abuse.

I closed in on the chimney, moving along the ridge of the roof now. I would get Stephen, that fucker, if it was the last thing I did. I grew ever-closer and could just about taste my first bite of the roll.

'Hey!' A cry from below startled me. I was thrown off balance and began to fall backwards in what seemed like slow-motion.

'Nooooo!' I cried in a deep, dramatic, slow-mo fashion. As I fell, three things happened: First, I saw the man that the shout had emanated from—an older, balding man in a red knit jumper; second, Stephen took flight, also startled; third, and most heart-stopping of the lot, the bread roll fell from Stephen's beak as he took flight. It bounced around the chimney rim like a basketball, then fell and began to tumble end-for-end down the peak of the roof. My shoulder crashed down hard on the tiles, and I tumbled end-for-end after it.

The house had been built right up to the property line, so when I tumbled off the edge of the roof, I actually came down with a crash in the neighbour's yard, smashing through one of those crappy shell-shaped pool/sandpit things as I landed. My body was a world of pain. I was sure I must have broken something. I turned over onto my back, and something hard dug into my side. I reached under and pulled it out. The heavens parted as I realised that clasped in my scratched-up hands, like the Holy Grail, was a partially eaten dinner roll.

'Hey!'

I stuffed the roll into my pocket and got to my feet. The old man was yelling at me from the other side of the fence, and a young family had appeared at the back door of the yard I had fallen into. Time to move.

I ran straight for the fence at the side of the property and flung myself over it like a madman. I landed awkwardly on the other side and, getting back on my feet, did it again. I ran straight for the opposing fence and flung myself over that one, too. I fence-hopped three or four houses, before cutting through to the street from a side gate. Crossing it, I ran down a narrow laneway that intersected with another laneway. I took a left. Once out of sight around the corner, I threw myself against a fence, panting. I had definitely cracked a rib. Reaching gingerly into my pocket, I pulled out the roll. *Got the fucker*. I tore into it with abandon. It was stale and horrible, but it was mine.

Chapter Eleven

I'd just about finished the roll, and was feeling much better, when there was a flutter of wings from above. A little blue-faced bird landed in the middle of the laneway before me. Looking into his eyes, I felt a little guilty for eating his roll. It had been a matter of survival, I told myself, and he *had* shat on my face.

He tilted his head and chirruped morosely. When I looked at his face, I swear there was a sadness in his eyes; to tell the truth, he looked fucking heartbroken. I crouched down and, as a way of making amends, held out the last bite of roll to him. He hopped toward me with cautious enthusiasm. I'd have thought he'd stay safely on the ground to eat the bread, but instead he hopped bravely up onto the side of my hand.

I watched him eat. He picked up the crusty morsel with his right foot and raised it to his mouth, crunching on it happily. Tempting fate, I raised him up and popped him on my shoulder.

He didn't seem fazed at all. It was really nice, standing there in the quiet laneway in the sunshine, listening to the sounds of my new mate crunching bread next to my ear. Amid the madness, it was a very welcome reprieve. It was the first time I'd felt properly relaxed in days. I took a deep breath in and out, and even with the sharp pain in my rib, I felt at ease. I wanted to bottle the moment.

My reverie was broken by a distant sound that brought me right back to when I was a young boy at my grandma's house. It was the distinctive *brang* of an old-school telephone, just at the edge of my range of hearing. The sound was so faint I wasn't sure I had actually heard it. Perhaps I'd hit my head when I'd fallen from the roof and was, in fact, experiencing the symptoms of concussion.

I heard it again: *brang, brang!* I looked around for the source of the sound but could find nothing obvious. My eyes scanned the rear of the conjoined buildings that backed onto the laneway. They were old and yellow-bricked with bars on their windows, and some with small, untrustworthy-looking balconies. In faded white paint cracked along a section of brickwork above a roller door were the words 'Bill's Butcher. Deliveries', with a red arrow pointing down.

Everything fell together in my head. I was at the back of the strip of shops. Next to the butcher was a stack of wooden boxes with the odd wilted lettuce leaf hanging off it, and next door to that, a pile of milk crates was stacked haphazardly against the wall. The grocer and the café. *Brang, brang,* went the distant phone. Lucy.

Sorry Stephen. I broke into a run, and the bird tipped off my shoulder in a fluster of feathers and wings. Each stride sent a hot pain shooting straight up from my chest. I held a hand over my ribs as I ran to the end of the laneway. Working my way round the back of the milkbar and out on to the street, I rounded the corner in front of the old shop, which had flipped its sign round to 'OPEN' and legged it toward the phone booth. The broken phone was hanging on its cord, and I wasn't sure how it was ringing, but it was. I slammed into the booth and grabbed the phone just as it finished ringing.

'Hello?' I called down the line. There was no response. Hello?' Just a dead dial tone. I'd missed the call I'd waited all night for.

My heart sunk into my stomach and I placed the phone back on its hook as best I could. Stephen landed on the ground next to my feet, looking up at me. I guess we were mates now. I leant back against the glass side of the booth, my head tipping back against it as disappointment washed through me. I couldn't believe I'd missed the one phone call I'd waited all night to receive, and for what? For a half a dinner roll and a broken rib.

For fuck's sake. What a joke.

I was becoming agitated. My hands had turned themselves into fists without me giving the order, and my breath was coming out of my nose in short, hot bursts. *Walk away,* I told myself. Nothing good was going to come from me hanging around there. I'd probably have to suck it up and walk to Mum's place. It would probably take me all day considering she didn't live nearby at all. I turned to go.

Brang, brang.

I spun around and looked at the phone hanging haphazardly in its cradle. I didn't pick it up it right away. I eyed it suspiciously for a while, as though it might attack.

Brang, brang.

I picked up. 'Hello?' I asked down the line.

This time there was a reply. A light, female voice called back: 'Dan?'

I had to hold the broken top-half of the phone up to my ear separately in order to hear her properly. 'Lucy, hi. I've been trying to get on to you, but I kept getting voicemail.'

Lucy explained that she had been undertaking a digital detox recently. No technology between five p.m. and five a.m. She said it was giving her a much better night's sleep and her thoughts were a lot clearer. It sounded like one of those 'lifechanging' fads that would soon be thrown in the back of the wardrobe along with the *Abswing Pro*.

'Your messages seemed pretty urgent, is everything alright?' she asked.

'Oh yeah, everything is fine,' I lied, as Stephen flew up, settling on my shoulder. He pecked at the top of the phone and I had to swap sides. 'It's just that I'm in a bit of a spot at the moment, and I'm really interested in the housing thing.'

'Antithetical Cohabitation? There is an information session for it this afternoon if you can make it. You'll find out all about how it works, and if you're still interested we'll get you to fill out an application form and a survey, so we can assess your personality type.'

She gave me the details and I hung up the phone.

I spent the rest of the day killing time walking around beforehand. It turned out to be a hell of a lot easier to come across free food during the day. I walked past a dingy little fish and chip shop on my travels, and a quick scavenge through the bin out the front yielded a ball of butcher paper with two potato cakes and a handful of chips in it. A further rummage turned up a plastic bottle with a good two mouthfuls of warm, flat coke. I'd hit the jackpot.

The ache in my ribcage was ever-present, shooting bolts of pain through me whenever I moved too quickly, but I knew not to waste my time going to a doctor. Jake had broken his ribs once trying to jump off a roof into a pool. 'Didn't get enough of a run-up,' he'd said. He hadn't even been close. The doctor told him

there wasn't really anything they could do for broken ribs, and
that he just had to rest up and avoid excessive physical activity. It
hadn't been too much of a challenge for him.

That afternoon, I arrived at the Uni early. Not wanting to
draw too much attention to myself, or make a bad impression, I
coaxed Stephen into the inside-pocket of my jacket, keeping him
out of sight like that old guy from *The Shawshank Redemption*. I
followed signs that directed me to the right lecture hall and went
in. There was a sign-in book at the door, and a young woman took
down my details and directed me through to the adjoining
auditorium, a large space with raked seating and a projector
screen set up on a stage at the front.

Projected onto the screen were the words 'Antithetical
Cohabitation information night'. There was just me and two
others in the entire place: a man shuffling around some notes on
a lectern at the front, and a young woman sitting by herself in the
middle rows of seating. As discretely as possible, I took a whiff of
my armpit and, upon my nose returning the result, decided to sit
a few rows away from her.

I wondered if more people were going to turn up. I had
arrived forty minutes early, or so the woman in the arrival area
had told me. I thought that was pretty good for someone who
had no way of judging the time. Ten minutes passed before a new
face entered, and after that people started slowly filing into the

building. By the time the information session began, there would have been close to forty people there.

'Good afternoon, subjects,' began the man at the front with a chuckle. 'I suggest you're all here to find out a little more about the Antithetical Cohabitation program, so let's crack into it.' He went on to describe the when's, where's, and why's of the experiment.

The *when*: A week from now.

The *where*: one of three student housing buildings within the vicinity of the campus.

The *why*: to study the effect of psychological opposites living together in the same space.

There was a stack of brown recycled clipboards passed around the room with surveys on them, which we were instructed to fill out. Initially, the paperwork came across much the same as what you might fill out when you sign up for a new bank account or a membership at your local *whatever* club, but then it got a bit more involved. I leafed through the stack of pages; there were about seventeen of them. Double-sided.

Fuck, this is going to take me all day, I thought. It was pretty comprehensive and made no attempt to hold back. There were questions about sex, drug use, my relationship with my mother. There were scenarios given in which we were made to show how we might respond to certain situations; for example, 'You are walking at night, and hear a scream from an alleyway; what is your immediate response?' This section of the survey was multiple choice. The options were:

A) *Go for help.*

B) *Head toward to scream and render assistance.*

C) *Keep walking.*

I always struggle with these multiple-choice scenarios, because I have the kind of brain that tells me there is not enough information given to select a singular answer, or that each answer could be applicable given slight variations to the state of events. For example: I'm walking alone at night, just walking along doing my thing when, all of a sudden, I hear a scream emanating from a nearby alleyway. I look down the laneway and I see my mother. Someone is mugging her. My reaction would be to *head toward the scream and render assistance.*

An alternate scenario: I'm walking alone at night, just walking along doing my thing when, all of a sudden, I hear a scream emanating from a nearby alleyway. I look down the laneway and I see two people in circus attire, going for it; just shagging away against a dumpster. In this scenario, the scream was one of ecstasy, not terror. The Clown and the Ringmaster— pun intended—are having a lovely old time, and might be a little offended if I chose to *head toward the scream and render assistance*. They would more than likely be part of the circus-themed-kink scene, and would not at all be looking to be joined in a threesome by a plain-clothed passer-by bent on 'rendering assistance'. In that scenario I would be much better off opting for **C)** *Keep Walking.*

In another scenario I might be walking alone at night, just walking along doing my thing when, all of a sudden, I hear a scream emanating from a nearby alleyway. I turn my head to look down it, but it's not an alleyway at all anymore: it's a giant face, floating, not attached to a head, and the scream is coming from deep within the face's open mouth; somewhere on the back of the tongue, there is a little girl there, holding a balloon. The scream isn't actually coming from her though; it looks like it is, but it isn't. Her mouth is open, and the scream is coming from deep within; somewhere way back, on the back of her tongue, there is another little girl holding a balloon. This continues on, a perpetual rabbit-hole kaleidoscope for me to fall into like I'm sitting in the chair at the hairdressers, staring into the mirror in front of me, looking at the reflection of the mirror behind me, which reflects the reflection of my reflection. The balloon-girl-tongue scream-cycle goes on forever, ending finally at the original source of the scream. I stare deep, deep into the metaphysical babushka, and like dipping your head into a pool of unicorn tears and seeing the meaning of life, my eyes are opened. The source of the scream, way back on the last of the tongue of tongues, is the projection of an alleyway scene. There is a dark laneway, and right at the very end of it in the shadows are a clown and ringmaster, going at it. Just shagging away against a dumpster. I'd probably have to answer **A)** for that one. *Go for help.* A bit much to deal with on your own.

I was the last to complete the questionnaire. Most of the applicants had left the auditorium before I placed my clipboard on top of the stack. I saw Lucy finishing a conversation with an older gentleman at the side of the room. I waved to her, politely flagging her over. I wasn't overly sure how to broach the subject, and was feeling more than a little sheepish bringing it up with her. On the contact details page of the paperwork, I'd had to put down 'Homeless' where it asked for my home address. Under contact number I'd put 'N/A', as my phone would be dead until further notice, and I couldn't recall the number on the inside of the phone booth I intended to sleep at tonight.

I coyly brought this up with her.

'Oh,' she said, when I had finished delivering a heavily edited edition of my current set of circumstances. 'Just a sec, wait here.'

She left me and moved toward the front of the lecture hall, where the old man had begun a new conversation with someone else. She quietly interrupted, whispering something in his ear. He looked over at me, brow furrowed in concern. He leant back a little, palms upturned, and shrugged his shoulders: The international symbol for *I don't fucking know.* He paused for a moment, then looked across the empty space toward me. I pretended not to be paying attention to their conversation. He dropped his arms and looked at Lucy first, then the man he had been conversing with. Leaning in toward her, he said something which I desperately, but to no avail, tried to lipread, before kissing her warmly on the cheek.

She came back over to me.

'I've just had a word with Arnold. He basically co-ordinates the whole study. Given your extreme set of circumstances, he has agreed to let me put you up in one of the temporary accommodation units until we find a cohabitator to pair you up with. He's quite a philanthropist at heart. You're really very lucky.'

Usually, I would never allow someone to turn me into a charity case but, given how accommodation-challenged I had become of late, I welcomed the situation with open arms. I thanked Lucy profusely. She offered to drive me to the unit I was being put up in, and I gladly accepted. First, she had to speak to Arnold again and figure out exactly which unit I was to be put up in. I took her absence as a chance to breathe in.

I flopped down into a chair at the end of one of the rows and stared up at the ceiling the way one might stare up at the night's sky. A hot shower and a good night's sleep would be heaven. When Lucy returned, she took me to her car and we headed off. She drove a little dinged-up, baby-blue Barina. On the way, she told me that I was to be put up in a unit in Clayton.

I'd never really had any reason to spend much time in Clayton, I'd only ever really passed through it, with the windows up. The place seemed to have an equal number of rubbish tips to inhabitants. Sometimes, if the wind was blowing the right way, you would get the pleasant waft of hot jam donuts, but this was just a perfume sprayed from the misting system around the border of the tip to disguise the smell of decomposing waste and scavenging bin-chickens.

Today, I really didn't give a shit. She could have told me I was to spend the night in a unit at the dead centre of one of the tips, and I wouldn't have cared. I was just pleased to be spending the night with a roof over my head.

Stephen gently nibbled the top of my ear for most of the journey. I'm not sure if he was stressed from being taken inside a car, or if he was showing me affection. Maybe he was displaying his upset at being stuck in my jacket pocket for the last couple of hours. Either way, it was nice to have my little buddy along for the ride.

Lucy and I made small talk on the way over to the unit. She was a nice girl who had grown up around the same area as me but was a few years younger. I ran off a few names of people she might know, but she didn't know any of them. The journey to the unit was just short enough for there not to be too many awkward pauses in the conversation, which I was thankful for. The car pulled up in a driveway alongside a block of flats. When she had said that I was to be staying at a unit, I had pictured a small, brick, one- or two-bedroom house with its own attached garage.

'This is the place?' I asked, not impolitely.

'Yeah, it used to be public housing, but it's getting knocked down so the tip can extend out this way.' She pointed to the back of the property where the flats backed onto some parkland, which in turn backed onto the wire-mesh fencing of the tip's boundary. I looked up at the building and wondered why they would even bother knocking it down. The whole place looked like it would fit in perfectly at a tip. The windows that hadn't had bars fitted in front of them were smashed, and the fibro-cement cladding had big holes all through it. What a palace.

Lucy led the way into the building and up an internal stairwell. *Try not to judge a book by its cover,* I told myself as we climbed the stairs. I stepped over a brown stain on the first landing that I was pretty sure was blood. We reached the fourth floor and went down a corridor with doors on either side of it. This area was carpeted and smelled like parmesan cheese. Reaching the door at the end of the corridor, Lucy said, 'This is you.'

She knocked loudly on the door. Obviously, confusion was plastered across my face, because she went on to explain that the place was a known local squat.

'We cleared most of them out over the last few weeks, but it's always good to knock before you go in. They can get a bit cagey when you surprise them.'

It sounded as though she were talking about wild animals.

'There's a bit of a problem with ice around this area,' she said, with an air of casual nonchalance, like she was talking about something no more bothersome than a swooping magpie problem. 'The building was largely populated by addicts. Some of them were prostitutes, too.'

Peachy, I thought.

'There are always those few hangers-on that stick around when a building like this is vacated. Sometimes the original tenants come back, but mostly it's just junkies looking to score or for a place to crash for the night.'

'Will you be staying here too?' I asked.

'Oh, gods no!' she replied. 'Well, good luck!' With that, she turned sharply on her heel to leave. 'Oh, wait!' she said, stopping halfway down the hall. She jogged back to me and placed a phone charger in my hand. 'It's mine, but you can have it. You might need it.'

'Okay...' Her urgency to leave was a bit of a concern. *Like a rat out of a drainpipe,* I thought, as she shot down the hallway, disappearing down the stairwell.

Here goes nothing. I pushed the heavy apartment door and it swung open with a creak. The first thing that hit me was the smell. It smelled wet. Wet with what, I'm not sure. Rain, vomit, urine, blood; these were all good guesses, and possibly all correct. I felt like a wine-taster, trying to decipher the ingredients of a drink by swilling it around in the glass and having a sniff. The whole bouquet of the room was dampness, highlighted with ashy notes of burnt tobacco, and a subtle hint of faeces.

The first few minutes will be the worst, I reminded myself. I'd read somewhere that your sense of smell dulls out with prolonged exposure to a bad odour, like when you go to the bathroom just after someone has dropped a big shit. Initially, the smell is overbearing, but after the first minute or so, your nose has gotten used to the smell and it's not so affronting. By the two-minute mark, you are comfortably going about your business, so to speak.

I stepped into the room.

It was a tiny living area, fully furnished with fully broken furniture. There was a couch that had been plucked straight from the 70's, which had a heavy sag between its itchy-looking orange cushions and lacquered wood armrests. There was a coffee table in front of the couch in the shape of a rounded-off triangle. It had what I supposed was a timber-look laminate on top of it. One of the legs was missing, probably used as a murder weapon in some other area of the apartment. The T.V stand was short one T.V, it having been ripped out of the wall in such haste that the power cord for it was still plugged in, two frayed copper wires sticking up at its end. I turned it off at the switch. I didn't feel much like getting electrocuted.

Carpet meeting imitation-tile linoleum was the division between living area and kitchen-dining. The kitchen was contained completely to one wall: a line of cabinetry, some of the doors still hanging on, and an electric cooker, the kind where you can't tell if they're on or not and always end up burning the fuck out of your hand. A single-bowl, grubby, once-white plastic sink took place at the end of the bench. Some charming junkie had taken to using it as a place for sharps disposal, so that was good too.

At the other end of the bench was a refrigerator that was probably a hundred years old. The only reason it hadn't been stolen yet was the two thick chains securing it to the wall. That, and it looked like it probably weighed as much as an early Ford Falcon.

The dining part of the kitchen-dining area was quite minimalist in its styling. There was a single chair and no table. *Very modern.* A small balcony clung onto the building for dear life, on the other side of a glass sliding door which introduced the scant dining area to the outside. The balcony boasted a breathtaking view of corrugated asbestos roofing, atop a rusted-out shed at the back of the tip.

Fuck me, was about all that was going through my head as I looked around the place. The phonebooth out the front of the milkbar was almost looking enticing at the moment. *Almost.* I was thankful to see two heavy-duty locks on the back of the front entry door. They looked newly installed and would probably be able to keep most potential murderers out.

I thought the bedroom was the room I was least looking forward to seeing, until I saw the bathroom. I opened the door and quickly closed it. I opened it once more, and it still hadn't changed. I took a brave step in and held my breath, looking around.

The mirror, of course, was smashed. Most of it was in the pedestal basin at the corner of the room. The entire styling of the room was off-putting in its own right. The basin, toilet and bath were all an upsetting shade of cool, minty green, with the half-wall of tiles a slightly lighter shade of the same colour. Don't get me wrong, it wasn't the décor of the room that made me so apprehensive to enter; I'm no priss.

The bath. The bath was putrid. The inside of it was black. It had a thick black crust all the way up the inside of it, finishing just below the rim with what looked like a dried-out black froth. It was as though someone had died in a full bath of water, slowly decomposed over time, broken down into a thick black liquid, and then seeped down the plughole, leaving only their slimy black residue behind to be remembered by.

The toilet was broken, the entire bowl shattered and caked with blood. God help me if I needed to have a shit. *Maybe that's what happened to the last guy*, I thought, *cut himself up whilst trying to shit into a broken toilet*. The ceramic was like razors.

After seeing all that, the bedroom wasn't so bad. It was just a double bed with a torn, threadbare skirt draped around its base, and a small, dirty window. The head of the bed sat against the far wall, where a soiled, grey pillow could be seen, disappearing into the void between mattress and plaster. There was a doona that I probably wouldn't use, on top of a bare mattress that I probably wouldn't use. I peeled the doona back from the mattress, revealing a dark, burgundy stain. Probably blood again. I went to flip the mattress over to its better side, but soon realised I'd been looking at it. As I pulled up the mattress to flip it, I got it to about half-way and stopped, face-to-face with a thick, dried smear of shit, caked onto the underside of the mattress. If I had to flip a coin for blood or shit to sleep on, I decided I'd be crossing my fingers for blood. Blood is blood, we all have it, but I'd never seen anything like the shit that was painted across the other side of the mattress. It was horrendous.

I plugged my phone into the charger and sat down on the floor against the wall.

BANG! BANG! BANG!

I woke with a start. I didn't remember falling asleep.

BANG! BANG! BANG!

Someone was bashing away at the front door trying to get in. It sounded like it might have been Thor himself. The hammering continued. My back was glued to the wall where I sat.

'Alex!' came a deep voice from the other side of the door. 'Open up!' The hammering didn't let up. 'Alex!' the voice screamed from outside. *Fucking hell*, whoever Alex was, this guy was desperate to see them.

'Alex!' boomed the voice again. 'Open up, baby!'

I stuck my fingers in my ears and tried to pretend I was somewhere else, somewhere nice, where a heavy-handed man wasn't trying to break the door down. After a few minutes, the hammering and yelling stopped. The guy in the hallway must have given up, thank fuck. I breathed a sigh of relief.

As it turns out, the quiet reprieve was just the calm in the eye of the storm. Almost as soon as relief had flooded into my body, it was drained back out. There was a colossal *'Crack!'* from the front door, the sound that splintering timber makes as a large man barrels through it.

'Alex!' he cried, a wounded bear.

Fuck. I launched myself off the wall and dove straight under the bed, pulling my legs under just in time to be out of sight as the man came thundering into the room. From my low vantage point I could see a big, broad-chested man wearing a red and white singlet and denim shorts. He was absolutely huge: both overweight and heavily muscled. The man must have been forty or so, and his body told the story of as many years of neglect. His loose, meaty gut swung wildly like a liquid extension of his thickset torso as he tore into the room, his big arms aping by his sides like an orang-utan.

'Alex!' he cried once again, storming back out of the room.

Through the open door, I could hear him tearing the place apart. Cupboard doors were being torn off and Frisbeed across the lounge room. The cutlery drawer exploded dramatically onto the lino. I heard a lot of grunting and groaning, followed by an almighty crash. The steaming behemoth had managed tear the fridge from its moorings, and by the sounds of it, thrown it through the window.

'Where is it, Alex?!'

I wondered what '*it*' could be. *Money, drugs, a kitten*? The rampage continued into the bathroom, where Mr. Happy didn't seem at all bothered by the state of the bath. He stood in it and felt his way along the top of the curtain rail. Finding nothing of interest there, he tore the curtain clean off its rings with a rapidfire *popopopopop!* Moving on to the pedestal basin, he reefed it off the wall, throwing it down with a crash as it shattered into a thousand pieces on the grubby tiled floor. I'm sure he was disappointed that the mirror was already smashed when he got there.

He disappeared just out of sight, in the corner of the room where the broken toilet stood. I heard the sound of porcelain on porcelain as he removed the lid of the cistern. The water splashed as he presumably sloshed his hand into it. With a grunt of finality, he left the bathroom, re-entering the bedroom with a dripping plastic bag at his side. The bed dipped down above me and threatened to give way as he planted his arse on it. I held my breath, watching him in the reflection of the mirrored wardrobe door opposite the foot of the bed. The tattered skirt that hung from the base of the old double bed reached almost down to the ground. It had been worn over the years, and eaten away by moths, so the parts of it that didn't have holes already were almost transparent anyway. I prayed the giant man couldn't see me.

He unrolled the plastic bag on his lap and, reaching into it, withdrew something thin that I couldn't quite make out. He held it up to the light coming through the dingy little window and inspected it. The orange cap on the end, which he removed, gave it away. It looked to be a brand-new hypodermic needle. I sifted through the short list of injectable drugs that I knew in my mind, landing on a tie between heroin and anabolic steroids. Given the size of the man, and how angry he had been, steroids seemed pretty fitting; but I prayed it was heroin, so it might knock him out.

A small blue case slipped from the end of the bed, onto the floor in front of me. It was one of those old vinyl pencil cases you used to have in school, with the clear plastic windows on the front so you could put your name in. This one said *BERN*. The zip was open and some of the contents had spilled out onto the floor. There was a book of matches, a couple more needles (looking a little pre-loved), and some clear rubber hose that had yellowed over time. A bent spoon and jet lighter had tumbled onto the carpet, too.

The big man leant down to collect his things, and for a moment our faces were just inches apart, separated only by the thin veil of fabric. I could smell his sweat and his foul breath as he grunted in an awkward position, collecting his gear.

Heroin it was. Well, I assumed heroin, anyway. I didn't know that much about anabolic steroids, but I didn't think you used a lighter and a spoon with them. The plastic bag that Bern had retrieved from the toilet sat on his lap. He withdrew one of several smaller zip-lock baggies from inside it, each one filled with the same light-brown powder. Setting the smaller bag down on the bed, he rolled the larger one back up, stuffing it down the back of his trousers for safekeeping. He moved his massive bulk back into the bathroom and ran water from the tap above the bathtub.

I seized the opportunity go for my phone. Still plugged in at the wall, maybe a meter away from the side of the bed, I chanced it that he wouldn't see. Pulling myself along the carpet on my elbows, I moved as quickly as I could without making noise. Had Bern turned his head even slightly at any point, he would have seen me. Thankfully, the running water and syringe were taking his full concentration. I stretched out my arm, just about to grab my phone, when he turned around. I froze.

His huge body stood upright, and I was sure he must have seen me, but he just held the syringe up to the light again, this time fully loaded with water. The tiny object held his focus while he moved back into the room, plonking himself down in the same spot at the end of the bed, apparently not having seen me. The springs groaned under his weight.

I was too frightened to move for fear that the noise would draw his attention, so I stayed in position, one arm outstretched before me, the phone just out of reach: a snapshot of paralysed desperation. In this position on the blindside of the bed, as long as I didn't move, I was out of sight; so I kept still, half under the bed, half horrifyingly exposed. I tried to quiet my breathing as much as possible with my other hand.

I'd never seen anyone shoot up before, and as terrified as I was, I found myself thoroughly transfixed. I watched as he tapped the powder from the smaller baggie onto the spoon. He squirted some of the water out of the syringe and slowly mixed the powder in with a matchstick. I watched on as he took out his jet lighter from the case and fired it up. He ran it round in small circles beneath the spoon. From my low vantage point, I couldn't see the mixture bubbling away, but I imagined it was.

It didn't take very long before he dropped the lighter on the bed beside him and he dipped the end of his needle into the liquid. Retracting the plunger, he scrutinized the amber liquid that slowly drew up into the body of the syringe. He picked up the yellowed rubber hose and wrapped it tightly around his bicep as a makeshift tourniquet, holding one end firmly between his teeth. The big man groaned as he shifted his bulk up from the end of the bed, standing now before the mirrored door of the bedroom wardrobe. He stared at his own reflection and flexed the muscles in his arm, pumping his hand a few times.

With those huge arms, it wasn't hard for him to find a vein. After a few good pumps, his entire inner-forearm was looking like a street directory. Locating a nice big, juicy vein, he drove the needle home and pushed the plunger back down, emptying the contents into his bloodstream. His mouth released its grip on the hose and it shot from around his arm, flinging into the wall. In the mirror's reflection, I watched the tension drain from big Bern's face, replaced by the warm glow of dopey bliss. A toothy smile opened up.

The big man took a step back and began to sway on the balls of his feet. His body moved around in small, gentle circles, the blissful look never leaving his face. The swaying got a little faster and a little less coordinated as he began to lose balance. He staggered to the side and came crashing down on the corner of the bed. I just managed to pull my head out of the way before he glanced off the mattress, and his colossal form slapped down hard onto the floorboards —and my outstretched arm. I bit my lower lip to muffle the cry that tried to escape my mouth.

Chapter Twelve

Shit.

A hundred and thirty kilos of beefcake had just pinned me to the floor. His head lolled to the side and we were face to face as his eyelids fluttered closed, a look of serene confusion flickering behind the lids before they closed completely over his eyes. Well, shit. The dude seemed pretty out to it, but I still didn't want to wake him up. I wasn't sure exactly how heroin worked. Was he knocked out like an anaesthetic might do, or was it more like a deep sleep, where if I woke him, he might freak the fuck out and beat me to a bloody pulp like he did to the pedestal basin, but with more blood?

I gently tugged at my arm. His eyes flickered. Shit. I tried to roll myself away from him and slowly slide my arm out from underneath but, because most of my body was still under the bed, I couldn't get the angle. I was completely trapped. If only I'd been a little more patient and waited for him to shoot up and crash out before going for my phone... I kicked myself. It seemed like an absolute mile away now, plugged into the wall on the other side of Bern's heaving chest.

Against my better judgement, I rolled myself towards him, until we were almost mouth to mouth. A bubble of drool had formed at the corner of his lips. With my right arm trapped beneath the sleeping giant, I reached over the top of him with my left, stretching as far as I could toward the wall. I could only imagine what might happen if he woke up at that moment, with me effectively giving him a big cuddle whilst he lay passed out on the floor. I shook the thought from my head.

Craning my neck as far as I could, I did my best to get a visual: still too far away. A good foot short. I felt around on the carpet behind the man's undulating bulk for anything I could use. I knocked something small and hard with the back of my hand. Bern groaned and scrunched his face up.

I held my breath. In my haste, I hadn't seen the syringe still hanging out of his inner-arm. I'd given it a good knock, too. I must have waited a good two minutes before exhaling again. Very gingerly, I felt around on the carpet behind him for anything I could reach the phone with. My hand crawled around the dirty carpet for a century, before finally coming to rest on something spongey. I squished it between my fingertips. With apprehension, I raised it up to see what it was. The tourniquet. Great. I never fancied myself as much of a Wild Wild West cowboy type, and felt a little deflated at the prospect of having to lasso my phone, but necessity is the supreme teacher. With my right arm pinned, and losing sensitivity by the second, I had to flick the rubber tubing a few times until I was able to grasp both ends of it in my left hand.

With the ultimate focus, I whipped the loop toward my phone. Missed by a mile. I had another crack at it; then another, this time getting a little closer, slapping the face of the screen. Once more I aimed, and made a shot that was almost as bad as the first. My neck was starting to cramp from leaning over the mountainous oaf on the floor in front of me. I focused myself again, steadied my hand and took a deep breath.

My wrist cracked, and the loop glided through the air, landing tentatively on the base of the phone, on the corner where the charger plugged in. Carefully working the tube until it had a good hold on the base of the phone, I tugged it toward me. The cord of the charger strained against the pull of the tourniquet.

One more firm tug and the phone shot free, skidding across the carpet before coming to rest at the base of Bern's spine, just above his bum-crack. With an almighty heave, and almost dislocating my shoulder in the process, I stretched right around the big man and felt around for the phone, basically on top of the guy. I scratched around on the carpet for a couple of seconds and then bingo, it was in my hand.

Rolling back off the top of Bern, I collapsed in a heap, under the edge of the bed. My whole right arm had gone dead, and I was worried if it stayed stuck under the muscled beast for much longer it might drop off. I held down the phone's power button and the screen lit up. The welcome tone sounded and I stuffed the thing into my mouth as fast as I could to kill the noise. Bern didn't stir.

I opened up my messages and found Jake's number. The text was short and sharp: 'NEED HELP NOW. LIFE AND DEATH.' I realised with a panic that I didn't know the address of where I was. I quickly punched out a second message.

'IN CLAYTON. PUBLIC HOUSING BUILDING AT BACK OF TIP NEAR PARK. TOP FLOOR. HURRY'.

I had another go at getting out from under Bern. My arm was so dead I couldn't even tell if it was moving. I gripped just under the armpit of my stuck arm and twisted awkwardly in an attempt to free it. Gently snoring now, Bern made no effort to assist me. I decided to really test the strength of the drug. Biting down on my lower lip, I gave my arm an almighty yank. A popping noise came from inside the socket of my shoulder, and a white-hot pain shot up through the ligaments. I thought I might pass out. My arm hadn't moved an inch. Neither had the sleeping giant.

I rolled flat on my back, staring up the rusted underside of the bed. Macabre thoughts rolled around inside my skull. I thought about James Franco's character in the movie 127 Hours, and how he'd hacked half his arm off with a pocket-knife after it got pinned to a cavern wall by a rock. I wondered if I could manage that with a bedspring. The thought of parting my right arm from my body didn't thrill me, but having seen what old Bustling Bern had done to the bathroom on his way in, it was a more promising option than being here when he woke up. I wondered if maybe I could talk nice to him and work my way out of it with my mouth.

My thoughts were interrupted by someone stumbling into the apartment. I heard the sound of a splintered section of door skittering across the floor into the kitchen. Jake had made excellent time.

'BERN!' roared the irate voice of a man in the living room.

Not Jake.

The newcomer stormed into the loungeroom, flipping over the 70s couch as he tore through. Here we go again. It was as though this building, this particular apartment, were a magnet for psychopaths.

'BERN!' the man shouted again.

I caught a glimpse of him in profile as he shot past the bedroom door: a tall man in a white singlet, with black jeans held up by suspenders. The top of his head was bald, but the sides sported a wild orange fuzz of hair that tapered down into lambchops, finishing just before the point of his chin. He was another muscled-up beefcake, absolutely ripped, and not nearly as heavy as the bloke currently crushing my arm. He was quick on his feet and looked like he could do some real damage.

As he passed back across the entrance to the bedroom, a beam of light reflected off something smooth and metallic in his left hand. I squinted, and just before he disappeared out of my sightline, I saw what it was: a hatchet. It looked like it could do some damage, too.

'BERN!!' came the cry a third time, now from the kitchen. 'I WILL FUCKING KILL YOU, MY FRIEND!'

I could hear the sound of metal striking metal. It sounded like he was hacking away at the stovetop. There was an unhinged groan from the kitchen, and the hacking stopped. Footsteps came toward the bedroom.

'There you are, Bernie.' The afternoon sun cast a strange light from behind as the man's frame filled the doorway, setting his orange hair on fire, but blanketing his face in eerie shadow.

'I knew you would be here, you greedy cunt.' He leaned casually against the open door, hatchet swinging by his side. He looked even taller, up close. I made myself as small as possible. The man threw his hatchet down. Its blade sunk into the floorboards impressively.

I yanked my arm as hard as I possibly could, searing pain shooting straight through my shoulder again. It could have been from gradual progress, or just the very real fear of being hacked to pieces, but my arm slid free to the elbow—just enough to get me out of sight, for now.

'Where is it, Bern?!' barked the redhead, pulling Bern up into a sitting position. I seized the opportunity to quickly pull my now-free arm under the bed. I was pretty sure he hadn't seen me.

'Where's my shit, Bern?' he demanded of the unconscious man. 'You've obviously had a nice taste already, so I'll ask again. WHERE. IS. MY. SHIT!?'

He slapped Bern hard across the face. Bern responded with a dull groan. The man got angrier, tearing through the house with renewed vigour. If it wasn't tipped over, he tipped it over. If it could be smashed, the big redhead smashed it. I watched a volley of diverse household items take flight before the open door. A badly chipped dinner plate wheeled noisily into the room, making a beeline for the end of the bed; then, as if by its own volition, it hooked left at the last moment, narrowly avoiding collision with the closest bed-leg. I held my breath as the damaged crockery continued its seemingly endless journey before the base of the bed, spinning itself in wide circles. The noise grew with each revolution, and I was terrified it would draw the other man's attention back into the room. My body tensed, and I scrunched my eyes shut as the circles got tighter, and the sound of the plate's chipped edge on the hard boards grew more intense. The circles grew smaller, tighter, louder—reaching an immobilising crescendo before the plate finally slammed down on the floor in front of me.

The footsteps started up again from the kitchen. With the search proving unsuccessful, the redhead quickened his pace as he stormed back into the bedroom, empty-handed. I saw the hatchet ripped from the floorboards by one powerful arm. Bern was grabbed by the shirtfront once more and hoisted back up into a sitting position.

'If you can't answer me right now, and tell me where my shit is, I swear on my mother's grave I will kill you where you lie.'

Bern was catatonic. The redhead made good on his word: there was one sickening, wet crunch, and the big man fell back hard on the floorboards, hatchet lodged firmly between his eyebrows. I involuntarily drew a sharp breath in. Tears leapt into my eyes.

Oh fuck, oh fuck, oh fuck.

There was a dead person next to me. A murdered person next to me. I'd never seen a dead body before. His still, blue eyes stared into me. A thin line of blood trickled down the side of his mouth. My body was no longer under my control. My legs shook so badly I had to hold them down. I scrunched my eyes shut and bit down hard on my lower lip, slowly managing to calm myself. I became still again.

The redheaded man was patting down Bern's lifeless body in search of his heroin. 'Stupid, fat fuck. Look what you've done.' He let out a grunt as he rolled Bern onto his stomach. I was so close I could see the tufts of red hair on the back of the man's knuckles as he ran his hands down the sides of Bern's body in a frisk. A crackle of plastic as his fingers ran over Bern's substantial arse heralded the end of the search. Thank fuck.

My body relaxed a little, knowing that the madman would soon be gone. I couldn't remember the last time I'd taken a breath in. The man got to his feet, whistling softly as he inspected the package. Slowly, he turned to leave. I relaxed a little more.

The sound of Rammstein's music had never struck fear in my heart before, but today it did. A bolt of pure, unadulterated terror ripped deep into my core as my phone buzzed, face-down on the floorboards. The personalised ringtone started out quietly before screaming to life with the signature heavily-drummed intro. I threw myself on top of the device to silence it, but it was too late. The lanky, redheaded psychopath heard it. My covering was hurled off me as the redhead picked up the whole bed by its base, throwing it against the wall.

'WHO THE FUCK IS THIS, BERN?' the tall man screamed at the dead one.

'Please, no!' I tried to say, but the words were sucked back into my stomach as the redhead seized me by the ankles and dragged me across the floorboards. He whipped my entire body round until I was side-by-side with Bern. 'Please!' I screamed, but it was no use. The redhead's foot came down on my throat, pinning me to the floor, crushing down on my windpipe. Fresh tears burned in my eyes. I was going to die on the floor of a crack-house in Clayton.

The redheaded man bent over, and with something that sounded like a gumboot being pulled out of the mud, dislodged the hatchet from Bern's skull. The pressure on my throat didn't let up for a second as the man raised the hatchet up way above his head, a big blue vein pulsating in his temple.

My fingers dug in around the laces of the redheaded man's heavy work boot. I could feel the nails separating from the tips of my fingers as I fought desperately to be free. Hot, wet tears streamed down the sides of my face as the tall man's muscles flexed in the light, ready to deal the fatal blow.

A look of surprise flashed across the redhead's face, and like something out of Alien, a long mess of red and brown shot forth from the front of his neck. Dropping the hatchet to the ground, his hands sprung up to clutch at the object distending from his throat. He staggered, first left, then right, then left again, and right once more, before collapsing on the ground on top of Bern. A dark, syrupy liquid worked its way down the inside of his cheek as the life faded from the man's eyes. One final splutter, and he was gone.

Chapter Thirteen

'Hey.'

My brain struggled to make sense of the situation as I heard Jake's voice from the doorway. 'Found it in the hallway,' he said, motioning to the splintered object skewered through the redhead's neck. I looked at it. It was caked thick with blood and badly broken, but was just recognisable as the missing leg from the triangle coffee table in the lounge. I laughed. It hurt. A little geyser of blood spurted from the hole in the redhead's throat as the last of his life drained out of him.

'I've never been happier to see you, mate,' I croaked to Jake. I grasped my throat. It was hurting pretty badly. I sat up, my head spinning. Jake went and got me some water from the kitchen.

'What the fuck happened here?' he asked, looking around the place.

We stood the old 70s couch back up onto its feet, and I had some water before telling him the story of how I'd ended up in a commission housing building in Clayton. I told him about the primary school guy and the cops and the creepy dude from O&O, about the Antithetical Cohabitation Program, and Stephen, and my night out the front of the milkbar.

'So, where's the bird now?' he asked.

I went over to the shattered sliding door of the balcony and whistled. It was morning now. Strange. The whole ordeal had burnt through most of the night, and the sun was now just rising over the tip. I whistled again, and Stephen flew down from somewhere up on top of the building, landing on my shoulder. We sat in silence for a while, staring at the blank wall where the T.V. should have been.

Jake broke the silence.

'Spliff?' he offered, digging a crumpled joint out of his jacket pocket. It had a small tear in the paper, but we made do.

'We should call the cops,' I said, taking a toke. I winced. The smoke seared my throat.

'I dunno, man. I don't think that's a good idea,' Jake replied. 'The cops already don't like you, and I don't wanna go to jail.' He paused. 'There was an episode of *Breaking Bad* where they dissolved these bodies in acid in the bathtub'

I cut in. 'We're not dissolving bodies in acid, mate.'

I punched in triple-zero on my phone and asked for police. More than likely familiar with the address, and even though I had reported a murder, they took a long time to arrive. The television-less wall didn't get any more interesting.

'I miss my old life. I miss being able to go home. I even miss the monotony of routine.' I sank back into the broken couch, dejected. Jake passed me the joint. I didn't smoke it; I just stared at the wisps of smoke curling out of its end.

'I think I miss Chris, too.'

'No you don't,' he said firmly, taking the joint back. 'You miss the idea of her.' He inhaled, blowing smoke out of his nostrils. 'She was such a fucking snob. You just don't like the idea of being alone.'

He had a point.

'You're better off without her,' he went on, looking over at me. 'Truthfully, I couldn't stand her. She always had it in for me.' He leant in to me with a glint in his eye and a wry smile across his face. 'Joke's on her though. I wanked into her bodywash.'

'What the fuck?' That was pretty fucking weird.

'Yeah,' he continued, 'she was a real cunt to me one day, and I was staying at your place, so when I had a shower, I churned one out into her *Coconut Rush.'*

'That's my bodywash!' I felt dirty.

'Coconut rush?' He laughed, 'Who the fuck wants to smell like a coconut?'

I was completely taken aback.

'What do you use?' I asked, after a time.

'Lynx. Africa.'

I tried to work my way out of my disbelief, but right on that note we were interrupted by the thump of sturdy leather boots coming up the stairs. The police had arrived. They exited the stairwell with guns raised, ready to fire. Jake and I put our hands in the air. Half a dozen of them flooded the room. From the back of the pack came a familiar voice.

'Holy fuck, if it isn't the flasher!' A man with a head like a testicle and the hands of Donkey Kong stepped out from the group. *Why was it always him?*

'Alleged flasher,' Jake corrected him.

'Up off the couch, on the wall where we can see you,' said the officer's strong-jawed partner as she pulled me to my feet. Officer Ballbag went into the bedroom, then came straight back out, holding his nose.

'What the fuck happened in there? Jesus!' He waved his hand in front of his face. There were notepads drawn, questions asked and accusations made.

'Fucking hell, *self-defence* is hard enough, but *defence of another* is an absolute nightmare. There are too many questions asked and the case gets looked over with a fine-toothed comb. I haven't got time to waste working out what happened to those two scumbags. Nah, nah nah, that's not the angle we're going for. Nah, here's what we'll go with: Murder-suicide.'

'Murder-suicide,' I said compliantly.

'You two were never here,' he said, leaning over and wagging his finger at us. 'He killed him, then killed himself,' he said, directing his performance to the other room.

'The fat guy killed the tall guy, then himself?

'Exactly.'

'So the fat guy stabs the broken table leg through the back of the tall guy's neck, then jams a hatchet into his head.'

'Correct.'

'But the hatchet's over there.' I pointed to its location on the floor.

'Well, the other way round then.'

'The tall guy killed the fat guy?'

'Yes.'

'Then himself?'

'That's what I said.'

'How did he stab himself then?'

'Huh?'

'You said tall-guy kills fat-guy, then kills himself. So tall-guy hatchets fat-guy, pulls the hatchet out and throws it over there, then jams a table leg into his own neck. How did he manage to drive a broken table leg through the *back* of his *own* neck?'

Ballbag stood stunned for a minute. 'Very flexible,' he muttered gruffly.

'Okay. So who called you?'

'Neighbours.'

'No neighbours.'

'Then, you did.'

'So I *was* here?'

'Yes, but not in the same sense.'

'In what sense then?'

'You weren't hiding under the bed, you arrived after it had happened. You *weren't here* until you *needed to be* here.'

'Right.'

'You were here,' he continued, 'for a secretive homosexual rendezvous, and you stumbled across—'

'—*homosexual* rendezvous?' I asked.

'Quite,' he replied firmly, before going on, 'You were here for a homosexual rendezvous and—'

'—why does it have to be a homosexual rendezvous?' I pressed. I couldn't see the relevance.

'What else would you be here for?'

'To sell drugs?' I tried.

'You want to submit a witness report to a police station stating that you were here to sell drugs?'

I paused.

I yielded.

'I was here to take part in a secretive homosexual rendezvous,' I mumbled.

'Exactly.'

The police spent a few more minutes taking notes and asking questions, I signed a witness statement from the right perspective, and the meat wagon arrived to take the bodies away. Lucy arrived as they were carrying loaded bodybags through the door.

'I am *so* sorry!' were the first words to leave her mouth. 'What happened?' She looked around the room aghast.

'You put me to bed in a junkie battlefield, that's what happened!' I said to her.

'I am so sorry. This never should have happened.'

The apologies kept on coming as I filled her in on the story. The actual set of events, not the one concocted by the uniformed-testicle.

'Please give me a chance to set this straight.' She left the room to make a phone call. 'Come with me,' she said on her return, leading us out into the hallway and down the stairs. We got to the third-floor landing and she took us to a door at the end of the corridor, directly beneath the horror-show I'd spent the night in. She unlocked the door with a key this time, and with a light push, it swung open silently. We stepped into the room. It was blindingly white. The apartment looked as though it had been newly renovated.

'It's been newly renovated,' Lucy said.

I couldn't believe my eyes. I'd been staying in that dump upstairs, while the whole time there had been a clean, modern apartment right underneath me. I felt an overwhelming sense of having been ripped-off.

'What. The. Fuck.' I started off calmly, anger bubbling away just below the surface. I couldn't keep it in, though, and as I stared about, trying to take it all in, I exploded. 'You had this all along and you put me up in that putrid CRACK-DEN!?'

'Well,' she responded calmly, 'you'd said you were homeless. You obviously hadn't showered in a long time, and by the looks of you, still haven't. We weren't sure it was a good idea to let you straight into the apartment we had just cleaned up for the program. We figured we would set you up in the less desirable suites until we made our decision on whether or not you were to be accepted into the program. It wouldn't have been fair to put you in the nice apartment only to kick you out after a few days because you didn't meet the criteria.'

'I was nearly killed up there!' I shouted indignantly.

'Yes, I'm aware. Sorry about that. Now the program is trying to make amends and extend the olive branch.' She gestured into the apartment's open door. 'Would you like to accept... or make your own arrangements?'

I thought about my options. They weren't great. I didn't have much choice but to accept.

'Great,' said Lucy, the chirpiness returned to her voice. 'You'll be pleased to know we've organised a security guard for the front door, so there shouldn't be any more *mishaps* while you're here. That should provide you with some comfort. You will have the building to yourself until the program commences next week.'

Mishaps.

I asked if Jake could stay.

'Not during the program, but for now, sure,' she replied kindly, before moving to take her leave.

'You gonna be watching us?' Jake asked bluntly, indicating one of two discrete cameras in the corners of the ceiling. I hadn't noticed them.

Lucy frowned at his brashness.

'They won't be switched on until next week, when the program begins,' she said, before adding, 'Everywhere but the bathrooms,' in answer to what was going to be my next question. I smiled at her. We had no more questions, and she had places to be, so we left it at that and she exited down the hallway.

The apartment was an exact mirror of the one above in terms of floorplan, but the similarities stopped there. The kitchen was clean and crisp, with push-to-open cabinetry and soft-close drawers. The cupboards were fully stocked with crockery and cutlery and stout glass tumblers. Unlike the filthy plastic monstrosity in the apartment above, the sink here was brushed stainless steel and it was clean, topped with a chrome gooseneck tap set. The dining area had four chairs in it, AND a table. Even the balcony had had a makeover. It looked safe. It had the same tipward views, but somehow they seemed much lovelier from this apartment.

There was a large, flat-screen T.V. mounted on the wall, in front of a plush red couch which I immediately tried out. It was like sitting on a cloud.

'Hey, check this out!' Jake called from the bathroom. He was standing in the shower, holding the head of the shower-hose. It was a modern, tubular, slimline showerhead.

'Space dildo!' he said excitedly. I flicked the water on and he copped a face-full.

The bathroom was probably the most dramatic turnaround from the hell-hole upstairs. The bathtub was freestanding, with a floor-mounted tower mixer rising up proudly next to it. The tub itself was white, clean and inviting. A small, wall-hung vanity was mounted in the corner, an assortment of soaps and perfumes around the basin. The toilet wasn't smashed: it was clean and it was white; that's about all you can really ask for in a toilet. The flush was good, too.

The bedroom sported a queen-sized bed with crisp linen, running parallel to a large window sharing the same view as the balcony. It still looked so much nicer from this apartment.

'I'm having a shower,' I said. Jake warned me not to go too deep with space dildo. *What a fuckhead.*

I was glad he was here. I heard the T.V. flick on as I stepped into the shower. Dried blood ran off my hands where the nails had begun to lift off the fingertips. They stung a bit under the shower, but they would be fine. I washed my hair, and as I tipped my head back, I drank from the stream of water falling from the showerhead. It was soothing on my sore throat.

I was still coming to terms with what had happened upstairs. I wasn't sure how to process it all. I was physically worn out, but emotionally I felt okay. Perhaps the years of being exposed to extreme violence in movies and online was doing me a favour. I wondered if I should be feeling more. Maybe that would come later. Maybe there was something wrong with me.

I'd always had a weird system for processing emotion. Mum always said to me as a kid, when I was upset, 'Don't worry about it, just think of something happy and move on.' I guess that was a well-dressed version of sweeping things under the rug. Eventually I'd lost the rug and given up on sweeping. I just felt things for a short amount of time, and then moved on to something else.

I caught a whiff of my pits as I rinsed the shampoo out of my hair. *Jesus.* There was a large white bottle with a pump-top sitting in the shower niche. I spun it around. *Coconut Rush.*

'Didn't go too deep?' Jake asked, leaning his head over the back of the couch as I stepped out of the bathroom, a new man.

'Not too deep, mate,' I replied.

'Well, good to see you took my advice. I was worried you'd stick it in so far you'd end up tethered to the bathroom wall.'

I slopped down on the couch beside him. 'You got any more pot?' I asked. It wasn't even really a question. He went down to grab some from his car. I kicked my legs up onto the couch and picked off a broken bit of nail from the end of my thumb. I thought about the Karma Exchange. Something didn't feel right. It had always been a reliable system, and I'd never had any cause to question it before. It had always just, worked. I was questioning it now. I knew I'd made some bad decisions and messed up a few times. Sure, in hindsight, I never should have fucked Jake's sister. If I had my time over, I definitely wouldn't do it again.

Well, maybe I would do it again. Just for old-times sake. I wasn't confident that, if poised with the decision as to whether I wanted to, A) *Have sex with her*, or B) *walk away from the situation, therein avoiding the unravelling of my future,* that I would go for *option B). Option A)* put forward a very strong case against *Option B).* Tash was gorgeous, and obviously the sole beneficiary of the good genes from the Saunders' family tree. There is no doubt in my mind, however, that if had my time again, twice, I definitely would not sleep with her a third time.

It was sleeping with Tash that got this whole big fuck-off karma-ball rolling. If I hadn't done that, then Chris wouldn't have left me and I wouldn't have felt guilty and volunteered to work at McCormacks.

No McCormacks = No Jenny

No Jenny = No getting caught shagging her

No getting caught shagging Jenny = No arrest

No arrest = No restraining order

No restraining order = No homelessness

No homelessness = No need to sign up to an experimental housing program, inadvertently forcing me to bear witness to the gruesome hatchetting death of a heroin addict, and the equally gruesome death of his angry associate. The point is, I tried to do the right thing to balance the scales, and I ended up getting shit on (once, *literally*). Maybe the Karma Exchange could go fuck itself.

Jake came back into the apartment with a half-full sandwich bag of dope swinging at his side.

'What?' he asked, looking at me.

'Nothing,' I said, and asked him to roll me a fat one. We settled down on the big red couch and baked our little tits off, eventually falling asleep on each other. I woke up in the afternoon to a big patch of Jake's drool on my shoulder.

'Wanna get pizza?' he asked. Again, not really a question. We looked up the number for the local pizza shop and ordered. Two large pizzas came with a free garlic bread included.

Half an hour later, the phone rang. Not my mobile, but a proper landline telephone. I didn't even know the place had one. It made me jump. I got up and answered it. It was on the wall in the kitchen.

'Hello?'

'Hello. This is Frank from downstairs,' said a polite male voice.

'Frank from downstairs?' I said to Frank from downstairs.

'Yes, Frank from downstairs.' He said frankly, 'I'm on security. Your doorman.'

'Oh, okay.'

'I've got a guy here who says he's delivering pizzas. Should I let him up?'

'Did he remember the garlic bread?'

'Did you remember the garlic bread?' Frank asked, off the phone. There was a murmur in reply. 'Yes, he remembered the garlic bread,' confirmed the doorman, back on the phone.

'Well, send him up then,' I said, and hung up.

In a post-nap stone-over, pizza was good. Pizza was very good. We didn't really say a whole lot to each other during pizza time. I think we were both pretty content with silence for a bit. I fed Stephen one of my crusts; he crunched away merrily on the arm of the couch.

The rest of the week continued much the same way. We ate bad food and smoked lots of pot. On one of the days Jake said to me, 'You know I killed a guy, right?' I nodded.

'Surely at some point that's got to do something to you, yeah?'

'I guess so,' I said, thinking about my own brush with death.

'Well, when the fuck is that gonna happen? 'Cause right now, I don't feel anything. I jammed that table leg straight through the back of a guy's throat, and I don't feel anything. I'd do it again.'

'You didn't really have a choice. He was gonna kill me.'

'Yeah but, even so, I thought it would have felt different. I always thought if you killed someone, it would affect you for the rest of your life. You'd think that shit would change you.'

'Maybe it will.' I offered.

He smiled and looked away.

Chapter Fourteen

I think in that week I blazed it more than I had in all my years on this green earth. I hardly moved from the couch, unless it was to go to bed, and even then it didn't always happen that way. We'd gotten on a first name basis with Rick, the pizza delivery guy. He hung out one afternoon and smoked a doob with us. He said we were his favourite customers. This came as no surprise; the pizza boxes littering the floor of the apartment certainly suggested we were his more regular customers.

One day, I'm not sure which, the door to our apartment opened. It was so smooth on the hinges that neither of us noticed; nor did we notice the new arrival, standing in the doorway. It was the clearing of her throat that got our attention, which I think was the desired effect. I shifted on the couch to meet the gaze of a young woman standing just inside the apartment. She was of medium height, medium build, with straight brown hair falling down to form a border around a very unimpressed face.

'Who are you?' she asked apprehensively, casting a wary eye around at the state of the apartment. Surrounded by pizza boxes, fast food wrappers and stubbed out joints, our clothes unwashed, and the shower having been neglected for most of the week, we weren't a particularly welcoming sight.

'Jake, Dan,' I said, shooting a thumb at Jake and a finger at myself. 'Who are you?'

'I'm here for the A.C,' she said.

'Works fine,' said Jake, motioning up to the split-system aircon that was pumping out cold air onto us.

'No, I think you've misunderstood.' She was probably right, we had smoked a lot of pot. 'I'm here for the Antithetical Cohabitation Program through Blackwood. This is the room I was given.' I looked down behind her and saw she was toting a wheelie suitcase with floral print.

'Fuck.' I'd lost track of the days. The place was a mess. I got to my feet and tried to pull my shit together and start cleaning up. 'Sorry about the mess,' I mumbled, collecting a stack of dead pizza boxes. 'Must have gotten our dates confused'.

She just nodded her head. Her eyes fell on the bag of pot that had rapidly diminished over the past week. She didn't say anything, but I could see the judgement in her eyes.

'Sorry,' I said again, tossing the bag at Jake, who finally got the idea that he should be tidying up too.

'I'll give you the tour,' I offered.

'No need,' she replied curtly, showing herself through.

Jake looked at me with raised eyebrows. She'd already seen the lounge, kitchen, dining area. There was only the bathroom and the bedroom left to see.

'That's the bathroom,' I called out when she walked into the bathroom. She passed through it into the bedroom. 'And that's the bedroom.'

She came back, still wheeling her floral suitcase.

'There's only one bed,' she stated.

Jake made a purring noise.

All my shit was already in the bedroom.

'You could take the couch,' I offered; then, seeing the look that took place on her face, 'I could take the couch?'

'That would be good,' she said.

Didn't bother me, that couch was the comfiest thing I'd ever sat on. I'd started to worry that from now on, everything that I sat on would be uncomfortable by comparison. I would ask Lucy at the end if I could have it.

'Do you want some pizza?' I offered, always the host. I held out the box to her. There were two slices left over from last night.

'Gross. No, thank you,' she replied. 'I think I'm going to take a shower.'

She went into the bathroom. I heard the click of the lock as she closed the door, then the running of water in the shower.

'If anyone could use that space dildo, it's her,' said Jake in a low voice. 'Up-tight!' he added in a louder whisper, really separating the syllables.

'I'm sure she's fine,' I said, prepared to give her the benefit of the doubt. 'She probably just didn't expect to walk in to two guys and a thousand pizza boxes—and a big bag of weed.'

There was a knock at the door and I went off to answer it. Someone from the A.C. program dropped off a large yellow envelope with the rules and procedures of the program. The new chick, whose name I hadn't absorbed, was still in the shower.

'I'll pass it on,' I told the man who'd delivered the envelope.

'You know he's not really supposed to be here?' He motioned toward Jake. It was pretty rude, actually.

'Yeah, there was a bit of a mix up. He'll be heading off soon anyway,' I replied, closing the door on him.

'Is everyone in this program a dick?' Jake said, after the door was closed. I was beginning to feel that way too, but tried to remain positive.

'I hope not, mate. It's three months.' It already seemed like it was going to be a long three months with this lady. I had hoped to be partnered up with someone fun, but I guess that's not really the idea of the program.

I saw Jake off with a big hug.

'Thanks again,' I said, 'Wish me luck.'

'Good luck. You're going to need it.'

I went to close the door, but his head popped back in.

'Twenty bucks if you fuck her!'

I just shook my head and closed the door before he came out with anything else. I heard the water shut off in the shower, and hurried to pick up the rest of the mess that was lying around the apartment. I piled all of the pizza boxes together and took them down to the bin on the ground floor. Passing Frank on the way through, I gave him a nod. I'd never actually seen him yet and realised, slightly embarrassingly, that aside from the balcony, I hadn't set foot outside of the apartment since I arrived. I looked up at it from the driveway. It was still the same dilapidated heap of shit that I'd seen on my first day.

When I got back up to the apartment, my new roommate was out of the shower and dressed. She had moved all of my things from the bedroom and stacked them neatly beside the couch. I decided to try and redeem the situation and see if we couldn't start fresh.

'Hey, I think we got off on the wrong foot earlier. I didn't realise you were coming today. I'm usually actually pretty clean,' I said.

'No, you're not,' she responded, matter-of-factly. I was taken aback. That was a bold call for someone who'd never met me before.

'You're my opposite,' she continued. 'I selected options in the survey that would have me described as a tidy person. Had you done the same, we wouldn't have been paired up. *Opposites.*'

She was pretty smart.

'I think I've got a fairly good idea of who you are,' she said, with a supreme air of superiority. I couldn't help but hate her.

'Someone dropped this off while you were in the shower,' I said, handing her the envelope. She looked disapprovingly at the torn edge of the envelope. Probably compiling a comprehensive list in her head of several tidier ways to open an envelope. 'I didn't have much of chance to go through it.'

She opened it up and started reading to herself from a staple-bound document of maybe ten pages.

'We have to go and do our first shop together,' she said at length, looking up at me. 'The first payment is in the envelope, but the rest from here on out will be made into the bank account of choice. Here, you've got to fill one of these out.' She handed me a document that looked like one of those tax file declaration forms you fill out when you start a new job.

'Payment?' I queried, looking the form over. I hadn't realised we were getting paid.

'Well, they didn't actually use the word *payment.* It's called a reimbursement for our time. Three hundred dollars a week.'

Holy shit in a handbasket. Money for nothing.

'Three hundred dollars between us?' I asked.

'Each. Didn't you go to the information session?'

'Yeah, I did, but I was a little tired that day. I didn't sleep well the night before.' I thought back to my night in the phone booth, and meeting Stephen, who was now nestled warmly in the pocket of my jacket.

'Tired?' she asked with raised eyebrows.

'I don't just smoke pot all day. I was tired. And you don't know shit about me like you think you do.' I knew what she was implying.

'Right. Whatever you say.' She turned back to the papers. 'Anyway, we've got to do our first shop. If we are going to be living here together for the foreseeable future, we will need to stock up on all of the basics, as well as whatever we are going to make for dinner tonight. Have you got any recipes that you like to cook?'

I wasn't much of a cook. I'd grown up in a household that wasn't very adventurous in its culinary practices. My favourite meal was something called Asparagus Chicken. Mum's specialty. There wasn't a fresh ingredient in the entire dish. It involved a pre-cooked chicken-in-a-bag from Safeway, curry powder, a litre of milk, and a bag of grated cheese to top it off with. The other ingredients in the dish were something called Cream of Mushroom (a thick, grey, gelatinous mess that stood up in a perfect cylinder when you tipped it out of the can. Thankfully it was canned, because it was an ingredient that was obviously left over from the 80s, when casseroles were all the rage) and tinned asparagus. When Chris had first sampled the culinary wonder, I remember her telling me, not so much with amazement as disappointment, that she didn't realise you could get asparagus in a can. I didn't realise you could get it fresh.

Another hangover from the 80s, apricot chicken, was the reason in our house for a dinnertime anomaly called Jam Chops, another one of Mum's brain-children. My mum was never one to let a lack of the appropriate ingredients get in the way of meal. If it wasn't in the fridge or pantry, mum would find a way to substitute it with something else. Her version of apricot chicken was pretty basic: some chicken fillets, apricot jam (easier to find in the supermarket than apricot nectar), and another blast from the past, French onion soup mix. She would cook the chicken a bit, then slather it in apricot jam and throw it under the grill with dehydrated French onion soup mix sprinkled over the top.

One fateful day, the day jam chops were born into this world, mum decided that despite having almost none of the ingredients, we were having apricot chicken for dinner. Substitution time. Upon checking the pantry, mum realised we had no apricot jam. Not to worry, strawberry jam will do fine. Now for the chicken. On checking the fridge and finding it devoid of any edible fowl, mum returned to the kitchen bench, despondent. What could you possibly use as a stand-in for chicken?

Ah. An idea had worked its way into her cooking-brain. She went to the deep freezer and pulled out a plastic bag full of meat. In the microwave went six lamb chops to defrost. What better to play the part of a chicken than a lamb? Once the chops were fully thawed, Mum painted a thick coating of strawberry jam onto the meat and sprinkled her famous 69 cent packet of dehydrated French onion soup mix on top. I never worked out if it was a soup mix made from French onions, or if it was just a plain onion soup made in France. I suspected neither.

Into the grill went the strawberry-coated meat. Surprisingly, they weren't terrible. No-one outside of my immediate family agreed with me, but they hadn't grown up eating all of her other improvisations, like the time she made a carbonara into a curry because I told her I didn't like pasta—but I digress.

But while we're on the topic, bombshell! In case you missed it, I don't like pasta. No one gets it, and I've never met a single person like me, but I just can't stand the stuff. We went to Italy for a family holiday when I was younger and my report back was that it was a nice place, but the food was terrible, all except a little restaurant by the Trevi fountain that did an alright chicken and chips.

'I'm not much of a cook really,' I replied, 'but my jam chops aren't too bad.' She looked at me sidelong. 'Never mind.'

'Well, I make an excellent spaghetti bolognaise,' she informed me, smiling proudly.

'Great,' I said, rolling my eyes.

'What?'

'Nothing.'

'No, what?'

'Nothing, honestly. What else does that thing say?'

Her eyes returned to the page. 'It is only the two of us who can stay here. We can each have a visitor in the apartment for up to two hours per week. Nobody stays the night, and we aren't allowed to spend the night anywhere else but here, unless it's an emergency, like a hospital visit.'

I'd already zoned out. It wasn't the most interesting manifesto I'd ever heard. I went over to the couch and plonked down on it as she continued to read.

'No drugs.' She paused and looked at me.

'Of course.' I didn't think of pot as a drug, anyway.

'No violence,' she went on.

There was half a bit of pizza crust that I'd missed, stuck down the side of the couch. It took my attention. I pulled it out of the all-claiming gap. Quietly opening my jacket, I fed a little to Stephen. He whistled happily from my pocket in reply.

'What was that?' she snapped.

'Stephen. He's my little mate,' I said, letting him out onto the couch. He took the crust and flew up onto the curtain rail to finish it off.

'Ahhh!' cried the unnamed woman, diving for cover behind the kitchen island. 'I just said, *no pets!*'

'Really?' I hadn't heard, but then again, I'd pretty well given up listening to her after she'd said the bit about no drugs, in her uppity way.

'He's just a bird,' I said.

'I'm ornophobic!'

'You arsehole!'

'It means I'm scared of birds!' Stephen sat up on the curtain rail, oblivious, crunching his crusts. 'Like, petrified, terrified, mortified by birds!' She spoke directly into the floor.

'He's just a little bird, lady,' I said in his defence. I couldn't see any reason to be afraid of him, unless of course you were on your last legs and he had his eye on your dinner roll; then he was a fierce competitor, and certainly something to be feared.

'Get him out!'

'But—' I started to say.

'It says no pets. Get him OUT!' her voice was booming into the kitchen floor.

I complied. I opened the sliding door to the balcony, and Stephen flew dutifully up onto the one above us. He seemed to prefer it up there, anyway. I closed the door, and the only sound to be heard was the panting of the woman on the floor.

'You okay?' I asked.

'Just give me a minute,' she replied. 'And don't you ever call me *lady* again.'

'Well *pardon* me,' I said, 'but you never told me your name, even though I have been the thorough gentleman, introducing you to myself, my friend Jake who has now taken his leave, and my friend Stephen, who you screamed out of the building.'

There was a pause, before the woman slowly pushed herself up from the floor to a sitting position. 'It's Melinda,' she said at last, having recovered from her intense hyperventilation session. 'Who names a bird Stephen?'

'I don't know,' I shrugged. 'That was his name when I met him.'

She looked at me strangely, but said no more on the topic. Ignoring my outstretched hand, she pulled herself to her feet and grabbed the orientation document back off the bench.

'We have to keep a journal, too. I don't know if you missed that as well?' she asked, a note of sarcasm matching her raised eyebrow and slight smirk. I *had* missed it; and there was that smarmy attitude, rearing its ugly head again. She took the journals out of the envelope and set one down on the arm of the couch, next to where I had resettled myself. I flicked through the journal with scant enthusiasm. It was a simple paperback booklet, the cover made from recycled cardboard. Inside were blank pages with dates at the top.

'We are to record our experiences and feelings in them.'

'Great.' I wondered if it was acceptable to write '*She is a cunt*' on each page.

'We should probably go and do our first shop,' she said. 'Do you know where anything is around here?'

'Just the tips, mostly.'

I told Stephen he had to stay where he was. I don't know if he understood or not, because, you know, how do you tell with a bird? We went in Melinda's car. When I told her I didn't have a car here she rolled her eyes and said, 'Typical.'

It took a bit of driving around, but we eventually found one of those small, local community-run supermarkets.

'Just the essentials first,' she said, pushing the trolley down the first aisle, 'then we can assess our budget.'

We had six hundred dollars between us. I didn't see how we could go over budget, but whatever. We went down an aisle with chips and chocolates on either side. I went to grab a bag of chips, but she held my wrist to put them back.

'Just the essentials,' she repeated firmly. We turned the corner and headed down the spices and tinned goods aisle.

'So what exactly is your idea of an essential?' I asked her.

She picked up a yellow and black packet from the shelf. 'Cornmeal.'

Cornmeal. *Cornmeal.* I'd never even heard of the shit, and apparently it was *essential.*

'I'm gluten intolerant,' she said, setting it down in the trolley. *Of course she was.*

She loaded us up on all sorts of herbs and spices—most of which Jake and I had in the pantry at our place, but had never opened. There were things like Star Anise, which I was sceptical on, having never seen the fucking thing before in my life. Then she would grab a more mainstream spice like paprika, a spice Mum always said was 'Just to colour, not to flavour' a dish. I had to put my foot down when she picked up a vial of saffron. It was about fifteen dollars and its contents were something like four eyebrow hairs. I'm pretty sure she put them in anyway when I wasn't looking.

Once we'd bought a fucktonne of spices I would never look at again, Melinda decided we could start to look at things that weren't *just the essentials.* She had kept a running tally of the prices, and let me know that we could have fifty dollars' pocket money each if we kept our extraneous expenses down to one hundred dollars.

Her *essentials* had come to four hundred dollars.

I bit my tongue. At least we only had to do this once. I did buy chips. And Maltesers. I got some hamburgers, too. Melinda was vegetarian, so she could just go fuck herself on burger night. If I was going to eat her gluten free pasta tonight, she could sort herself out on burger night. I used the rest of my money to buy a slab of beer. There was no way I was getting through the next week with her without a drink. In hindsight, I probably should have gotten something stiffer.

When we got back to the apartment, Melinda immediately started unpacking all of the groceries, finding homes for them in the cupboards and fridge. I would have helped, but I needed to take a shit.

I ducked off to my porcelain sanctuary on the other side of the wall and got comfortable. I couldn't believe how much crap she'd already unloaded over the bathroom vanity. There was a toothbrush and toothpaste, perfectly aligned; moisturiser; cleanser; toner; antioxidant hydramist—whatever the fuck that was. There were skin-masks and eye-masks and a nailfile and all sorts of garbage. I didn't even have a toothbrush.

I finished my business and went back into the kitchen.

'Put the fan on,' she snapped as soon as I entered the room. I went back and put the fan on.

'Did you spray?'

Fuck me. It was like living with Christina again. I went back into the bathroom and saw that she had even packed her own air-freshener for the loo. Lavender. I hated lavender. I gave it a few short pumps and left the room.

'Seat down?' she asked.

You've got to be fucking kidding me.

'It was a shit. If the seat was up I would have gone in,' I snapped back.

'I meant the lid. There is no excuse for being unclean. You close the lid, and it keeps the bacteria in. *Everybody* knows that.' She rolled her eyes. It sounded like horseshit to me, but I went back in and closed the lid. *Not worth the argument,* I told myself.

'Okay, what can I put away?' I asked.

'Nothing, it's done. I've put everything away already,' she replied coldly.

I felt like we were a married couple, fast-forwarded thirty years to when the love had well and truly drained out of the relationship, its position filled by disdain and contempt.

'Well, can I give you a hand with dinner then?'

'I really think it would be best if you didn't.' *Fuckin' Jesus.* She was in a right mood.

I took myself outside to see Stephen; I'd feed him some potato chips and see if he liked them. Turns out ringnecks like salt and vinegar chips. After crunching away at one for a while, I was worried the salt might be a bit much for him. I let him quench his thirst at the rim of my beer can. He didn't like that very much. After a few little drops of beer he wouldn't stop shaking his head and fluffing up his feathers.

'Last drinks for you, mate,' I told him. 'You're not a very good drunk.'

Jake had pre-rolled me a few joints to get me through the next few days. I took one out of my top jacket pocket and lit it up. I knew Melinda would have something to say if she saw me, so I cupped my hand around it and blew the smoke out the corner of my mouth. At least I was smoking outside.

The last burst of purple exploded across the sky as the sun finally set over the tip. It was pretty beautiful.

Almost as if on cue, the sliding door was pulled open abruptly. I was only a few drags in.

'Excuse me! Is that a marijuana cigarette?'

I had to stifle a laugh.

'No,' I replied.

'Because it smells like a marijuana cigarette. I know what they smell like, you know.'

'I can assure you it's not a marijuana cigarette,' I said, and she seemed to relax a bit. 'It's a joint.'

Her face went red with anger. 'I knew it was a marijuana cigarette!' she spat, pointing at me.

'Not a marijuana cigarette—a joint! It's fine,' I laughed.

'This is no joke. It says in the guidelines, no drugs,' she said sternly. 'Put that thing out.'

'Pot isn't really a drug—'

'It's illegal!'

'Hardly.' I laughed again.

'Just put it out!'

I took a long deep drag, and then flicked it off the railing. She was furious. If anyone needed a joint, it was her. She stormed back inside. I thought I'd give her ten minutes to cool off, so I hung out with Stephen a little longer. He'd sobered up a bit now, and wasn't shaking as much. I gave him a kiss on the top of his head and he responded by biting my lip playfully.

After the ten *cooling off* minutes had passed, I tentatively entered the house again. Melinda had her back to me at the dining table.

'Your dinner is on the bench.'

I took it over to the couch and turned the T.V. on. She sighed loudly, disapproving. I didn't bite. *Top Gear* was on and Clarkson was going to blow up his house or something.

I managed a few mouthfuls of the terrible tasting dinner. Gluten free pasta and vegan mince were among the list of things I didn't want to put in my mouth, along with cocks and Brussels sprouts; not necessarily in that order. The dish, on the whole, tasted like it had been peeled off the inside of someone's work-boot. I was seriously considering throwing it in the bin and ordering a pizza, but I didn't want to risk the fallout.

Melinda went to bed early. I don't think she was much of a *Top Gear* fan. As soon as she left the room I went to the balcony and tipped the pasta straight over the edge. Good riddance.

Maltesers would be my dinner tonight.

#howtofuckacantaloupe

At some stage prior to Jeremy Clarkson's house being demolished, I fell asleep on the couch. It was a pretty reasonable sleep, apart from being woken up by the sound of someone on the telly trying to sell me a soft serve machine a little past two a.m. It actually looked pretty good. It made soft serves out of frozen fruit. The family in the infomercial seemed rapt with it. I was tempted to call up and order it but decided instead to just turn the T.V. off and go back to sleep; not before going to the sliding door and getting Stephen, though. I couldn't have him sleeping outside in the cold. He could snuggle into my chest for the night and I'd put him back outside in the morning. He was pretty happy to be back in the house; I could feel the chill of the cold night air on his feathers. We drifted off to sleep together on the couch.

I awoke to the sound of a cement mixer set to one million the next morning.

'What the fuck is that?!' I yelled over the back of the couch.

'Vegan hemp smoothie,' came Melinda's reply from the kitchen. I peered over the couch and saw her pouring almonds into the top of her Nutribullet.

'Jesus. What time is it?

'Six forty-five.'

Six forty-five is no time to be doing anything. With Stephen secured under my jacket, I went out on to the balcony for a cigarette.

'That better not be marijuana or I'm calling the Uni,' she called out as I took the first drag of the morning. I held the packet up against the glass. It was just a cigarette.

'I'm going for a run,' Melinda said as she downed the last of her smoothie. I politely declined the offer to join her. I wasn't sure if she was making amends for our uncomfortable first day, or if she was just being a smartass, having made the correct assumption that I wasn't a runner.

My first journal entry was made that morning. The first page had yesterday's date at the top, and the instruction to 'write about your day.' I did.

Today was a difficult day, I wrote. *I find Melinda very hard to be around. We did our first shop and blew all our money on shit I've never heard of. When we got home, Melinda made a dish out of some of the alien ingredients. I tipped it off the balcony for my own safety.* I wasn't sure how to finish it, so I just wrote *The End.*

Breakfast for me was another packet of chips. I wondered if I should put them in the Nutribullet to make them healthier.

Chapter Fifteen

'I'm going to cook you dinner tonight,' I said to Melinda, after a couple of very uncomfortable days of living together. She obviously had no intention of making things more convivial, so I took it upon myself to be the first to try to ease the tension.

She eyed me skeptically. 'What is it?'

'A surprise,' I told her.

The roast, even though it was my first go, was a success. The potatoes were crispy and golden, the lamb was delicious. Even Melinda's faux-pork didn't smell half bad. I couldn't work out how they did the crackle.

We set our plates down on the counter, mine licked clean, hers with just the dinner roll sitting on the edge. It was still a bit of a point that I had forgotten to get gluten-free. I had a hard enough time sourcing fake pork, I couldn't remember everything. It didn't bother me, though; I knew a certain someone on the balcony who would be more than happy to take on the dinner roll, in its full gluteny goodness.

'Dessert?' I offered, stacking our plates next to the sink.

'Is it gluten-free?' She asked, not completely rudely.

'I think so. Fruit fondue.'

The study organisers had really gone all-out setting up this place. I'd found a fondue fountain at the back of one of the cupboards earlier in the week. I hadn't seen one since my childhood, so of course I had to put it to use.

I loaded some chocolate into the top and added cream. I'd gotten a touch carried away at the shops and bought way too much fruit. I cut up some pineapple and banana and set out fresh strawberries on a plate.

'I haven't had fondue in *ages*,' she said.

'Me neither.' Finally, we had something in common, even if it was just a shared timeframe for the absence of liquid chocolate in our lives.

I tried a strawberry. As expected, it was delicious. It was my firm opinion that you could roll a strawberry in shit and it would still be better than most other fruits. Strawberry was king. I skewered another with my fondue fork, dunked it in the fountain and popped it in my gob. Heaven.

I could hear my phone ringing. Rammstein. I looked around but couldn't see it anywhere.

'Where's that coming from?' I asked Melinda.

She had a mouthful of pineapple. 'The balcony, I think,' she managed awkwardly.

It was. I opened the door to go outside and was immediately confronted with a close aerial pass from Stephen. His wing clipped my ear as he barrelled into the room, making a beeline for the kitchen island.

The dinner roll.

Melinda screamed and swatted him away. He turned to avoid the flailing hands and flew into the lounge area before circling back in a renewed attack. He divebombed the plate, but the fondue-fork being waved around by Melinda was too dangerous, so he completed another circuit. On his way round again, he approached with caution, keeping his distance. He flapped his wings, hovering just above the dining table, gearing up for another divebomb attack on the roll.

The rest happened so quickly.

I had my eyes on Stephen, ready to shepherd him back outside when the opportunity arose. From the corner of my eye, I saw Melinda's forearm straighten.

'NO!' I cried. A flash of silver whizzed past me.

Stephen's little body was thrown against the wall, like it had been yanked backward by some invisible cord. He hit it with a *THUNK*, but never fell to the floor. A long, thin fondue fork had him pinned to the plaster. It had gone all the way through his chest and out the other side. His head lolled. His wings went limp.

'Stephen!' I cried, running to him.

I grabbed the handle of the fondue fork and wiggled it up and down, working it out of the plaster. It had embedded itself in deep. I pulled him off the wall like a feathered kebob and held him in my arms. I'd heard once that if someone has been stabbed and the knife is still in them, it's best to leave it in until medical assistance can be rendered. I assumed the information was transferrable to speared birds. I set him down on table, his head rolling from side to side with each movement I made.

'You'll be alright mate, you'll be alright,' I told him. He didn't make a sound. I put my ear to his chest.

Nothing.

My eyes prickled.

'You killed him,' I whispered, slowly turning to face Melinda, 'you killed Stephen!'

'There weren't supposed to be any pets,' was all she could manage, wide-eyed and trembling.

I grabbed some things and gently picked up Stephen's lifeless body, then left the apartment. I couldn't stand to look at her. I called Jake, and we had a little ceremony for him in the park, burying him under a tree alongside Melinda's leftover dinner roll. It's what he would have wanted.

'He was a good bird,' I said, in a eulogy of sorts. 'He never meant any harm to anyone, except maybe the time he shat in my eye. I believe all he wanted from life was to be outside, and to enjoy the crunch of a stiff dinner roll. He died doing what he loved.'

'Getting skewered through the heart with a fondue fork?' Jake asked skeptically.

'No, eating a dinner roll,' I shot back.

'Yeah, but he didn't really get to eat it, did he? It's right there.'

'Okay, he died about to do what he loved most.'

'Doesn't quite have the same ring to it, does it?' said Jake. 'Why don't you just say, "buried alongside his greatest joy, here lies Stephen."'

It was actually quite poetic. I carved the words into the base of the tree where his shallow grave was, then threw a few handfuls of dirt over the bird, patting it into place. 'Rest easy, old mate,' I whispered to the ground. I turned to Jake. 'I don't feel like going back up there yet.'

We tried out the Clayton RSL for a drink; '*a wake for Stephen*', Jake had said. Really, I was just treating it as an excuse not to go back to the apartment. I wasn't ready to look Melinda in the face yet. Jake said he would shout the beers. I had no choice but to accept, having spent most of my money on tarragon and cornmeal.

We settled down in the little beer-garden courtyard with a couple of pints, neither of us intending to stay there for a long time; however, one pint turned into two pints, two turned into four, four to eight and before you know it, I was rolling around in the backseat of a cab on the way back to the apartment building.

I got home just before daybreak, stumbling through the front door of the apartment. I struggled with the key in the lock for quite some time, and when I entered the room, I was greeted by the sight of Melinda in a robe, arms crossed. I think I'd woken her up.

'You stink.' It was a funny sounding apology.

Staggering past her, I pushed my way into the bathroom and opened the lid of the toilet. Too drunk, I jumped the gun, pissing before I'd properly gotten out of my pants. I copped a spray on the t-shirt and a lot missed the bowl initially. The sound gave it away. Sounding more like pissing onto sand than into water, I looked down and saw that I was urinating into the basket of fresh toilet paper rolls. I took squinty, one-eyed aim at the porcelain and shifted my body. The noise changed from the dampened sound of urine falling onto a soft surface, to the much louder splatter against a hard surface, finally stopping at the liquid-on-liquid waterfall that we were here for. I let my ears be my guide, as the beers had told my eyes to take the night off. The whole activity finished with the standard, guttural *quack* of a fart, signifying 'close of business.'

Covered in piss is not the way I usually choose to spend my morning, so I headed for the shower. On the four-step journey I lost my way, stumbling on nothing in particular and losing my balance. I wobbled unsteadily on one foot; then, losing the battle, was sent staggering into the wall hung vanity. I caught myself on the basin, knocking all of the products off with a clumsy sweep of my arm as I tried to stand myself back up.

'Everything okay in there?' came Melinda's voice from outside the door.

I dug up what I thought to be a more sober voice and answer shortly, 'Yep.'

I slowly turned myself around in front of the vanity and re-joined the original venture to the shower. Stripping my clothes off was a task-and-a-half. The situation would have been a lot more manageable if the room would just stop fucking spinning for a minute. I tripped over my jeans twice whilst trying to take them off. I flung my undies into the basin and my t-shirt to the other side of the room, before moving over to the shower. I opened the glass door and slipped in (literally, not figuratively), turning the water on after catching myself on the soap caddy hanging from the showerhead. Loofas and oatmeal face scrubs flew in all directions.

'You sure everything is okay in there?' came Melinda's voice once more from outside the door. I was certain her concern was for her products, and not my own welfare.

'Fine,' I managed, steadying myself on the mixer. The water went red hot.

My body sucked back against the glass like a gecko. I reached around the scalding stream to flick the mixer to a less mutilating temperature. I settled for somewhere down the low-end. The cool water cascading down my body was refreshing, and a welcome change from scalding heat.

Swaying evenly from front to back, I thought about Stephen. He was just a bird, but his death had sincerely affected me. I hadn't even gotten this upset when my Grandpa died. I pictured Stephen's last moments. The scene replayed in my head for the hundredth time that night. Melinda, with all the skill of a highly trained knife-thrower, gearing up to launch her attack. I'd been as helpless as Stephen, as the narrow fondue fork soared through the air. There was nothing I could do. I shook the scene from my head. It was only making me angry. I squirted some shampoo into my hand and got back to the business of showering. About fifteen minutes later, there was a knock at the door.

'Are you done in there?' Melinda asked, impatiently.

'Just about,' I replied, rinsing the foam from my body and stepping out of the shower. I threw on a towel and left the bathroom, passing her on my way out. We made eye contact as we passed each other. I locked my eyes on her, and she looked away.

'I hope you didn't use all the hot water,' she said uncomfortably. I just slipped past her and went into the lounge room, crashing out on the couch.

I thought about leaving the program. I didn't ever want to have to see her again. Every time I looked at her, I was reminded of what she'd done. I genuinely thought about leaving, and I would have, but I had nowhere to go. It was the program or the phonebooth: those seemed to be my only two options.

Chapter Sixteen

Coming back into consciousness on the couch around midday, I spent most of the afternoon watching cartoons and avoiding conversation with Melinda as best I could. She must have been feeling bad for Stephen somewhere inside herself, because she brought me some water and a Berocca a little after I woke up.

'For your head.' She had said, frowning.

It was the first nice thing she'd done since the program started, and the effervescent drink did make my head feel a little better. We had a vegetable medley for dinner; Melinda cooked. It was okay. She made some hot chips to go on the side of my plate and brought it over to the couch. She seemed to be really making an effort. After dinner was finished, she took my plate away. Although I knew she was trying to make things better between us, I couldn't bring myself to acknowledge it. I couldn't feel comfortable around her. I needed some air.

The sun was setting over the tip in a brilliant explosion of orange. I closed the sliding door behind me as I stepped out onto the small balcony, taking one of Jake's joints out of my top pocket. I lit up. It had dried out a little, but he'd rolled them tight, so it didn't burn too fast. I inhaled deeply and held it there.

One of the rollers clicked on the sliding door as it opened behind me. Melinda appeared at my side, two cans of beer in her hand.

'Here,' she offered, leaning gently on the railing.

I took the can and had another puff on the joint, staring straight ahead into the distance. She opened her beer and took a sip from it. I did the same. She made a strange, involuntary noise after the first sip, but said nothing. I don't think she liked the taste. A few moments passed, and we stood in silence watching the last of the sunset. Melinda was the first to speak.

'Can I?' she asked.

I was a little surprised at the question, but what the hell. I passed her the joint. She held it awkwardly between her thumb and forefinger. I watched her as she cautiously raised it to her lips, inhaling tentatively. Her cheeks exploded like the guy off the Listerine ad. She coughed raucously into the side of her beer can, trying to cover her mouth. I couldn't help but laugh at her. She coughed for a solid twenty seconds, then handed the joint back to me, taking a desperate swig from her drink.

'Thanks,' she coughed.

I had the last of it, then flicked the dead end into the coffee mug ash tray on the outdoor setting.

'I'm sorry about your bird,' she finally said.

I scratched something at the corner of my eye. 'Stephen.'

'I'm sorry about Stephen.'

I didn't say anything.

'I didn't mean it, you know. It was like a reflex. I didn't mean to kill him.'

Part of me knew this already. I didn't like Melinda, but she never struck me as the kind of person who would intentionally hurt someone, or something.

'I was just scared.' Her voice trembled. 'I really didn't mean to hurt him.'

I turned to her. Tears welled in her eyes, threatening to spill down her cheek. I swallowed on a dry throat.

'It's okay,' I told her. I patted her on the back awkwardly. I've never really known what to do when people are crying. I put my arms around her when she turned to me, sobbing into my shoulder.

'I'm really sorry.'

'It's okay,' I told her again, putting a hand on the back of her head. 'It's okay.'

We held our embrace for a couple of minutes, before awkwardly breaking apart. She went inside and washed her face. I finished my beer on the balcony. When I went back inside,

Melinda had fallen asleep across the end of her bed. I pulled a blanket over her and closed the door behind me before settling in for another night on the couch.

I woke up to the light streaming through the open curtains by the balcony. It was quite a pleasant way to rise. It was nine o'clock already. Melinda had obviously decided not to make her demolition smoothie this morning before she left. I went to the kitchen in search of my own breakfast, finding some eggs in the fridge. I cracked them into a hot pan. We didn't have any bread in the pantry, so I thought I'd run the gauntlet and have a crack at a couple of slices of the gluten free stuff we'd bought. It was undersized and dense, but I figured it would do the trick once I stuck it in the toaster for a while.

The smell of eggs in a pan must have woken her up, because just as mine were about halfway done, the door to the bedroom opened. I hadn't realised she was still home.

'Morning,' I said, as she stepped out of the room.

'Morning,' she replied, a little sheepishly.

She wasn't wearing any pants. I'd never seen her without pants before. I'd only ever seen her fully clothed and ready for the day, or one time, before bed, in a thick woollen robe. She wasn't wearing any pants and I wasn't sure where to look.

What she did have on was a dark grey singlet-come-nightie. I decided it was just a big singlet playing the part of a nightie, because it barely covered the black underwear she was wearing, which I saw as she stretched her arms upwards, while walking into the kitchen.

'Would you like an egg, Melinda?' I asked.

'Call me Mel. Everybody else does.' She didn't have a bra on, either. 'And that'd be great.'

I commented on her sleep-in.

'I forgot to set my alarm. I sat down on the edge of the bed, and before I knew it, asleep. I think it was—' she paused, leaning in, '—the drugs.'

I laughed. She certainly seemed more relaxed. I dished her eggs up onto a plate, smiling.

'Pot can make you a bit sleepy.'

We ate together at the kitchen island. She still didn't have any pants on, and I couldn't help catching a cheeky glimpse of bare skin as she swung her legs on the stool. She actually did have very nice legs.

Jake sent me a text telling me he'd drop my van round today. I was getting sick of having to ask Mel for a ride every time I wanted to go somewhere. He told me he'd come around midday.

'That's cool, I've got lunch with my mum today, so I won't be here anyway,' Mel said when I let her know Jake would be coming around later.

After breakfast we went for a walk together. Now, normally, I'm not much for walking, but Mel asked me if I would like to come with her, and I decided I would. It was the most pleasant she'd been to me the entire time we'd been living with each other, and I wanted to keep that going. If we could be on good terms for the next couple of months, the program might actually turn out to be enjoyable.

Mel showed me along her usual route. It trailed through the park, around the back of the tip, along a main road and into another, much larger park. We completed one entire circuit of the open space before heading back. I learnt a lot about Mel on that walk. She had three sisters, one with a disability. She'd grown up in a strict Christian household and her father was a minister. She told me she hadn't much of a relationship with him. I told her I hadn't much of a relationship with my dad, either. She liked exercise and was part of a squash club. I wasn't overly familiar with it as a sport, but it sounded pretty fierce.

'You should come one time,' she said. I told her I would think about it.

We concluded our walk and headed back up to the apartment, exchanging pleasantries with Frank the doorman on our way through. Mel was heading out, so she had the first shower. I lay down on the big red couch as she stepped into the bathroom. She must have used a little extra force in closing the sliding door that divided the kitchen and bathroom, because when it hit the wall it bounced back open a touch, leaving a small strip down the edge of the door where the bathroom light poured out onto the kitchen floor.

I looked away.

'Hey, Mel,' I called out, wanting to bring her attention to the openness of the door, but she had already started the water and couldn't hear me. I looked back at the door and quickly shut my eyes. I'd caught her bending over, pulling activewear down her legs. Curiosity got the better of me and I opened one eye. She'd unzipped her long-sleeved sports-top and taken it off, moving onto the white singlet beneath.

Before I knew it, I was looking at the back of my completely naked housemate as she stepped into the shower. She had a much better body than I'd initially thought. She was toned and athletic. I pulled myself away from the scene and went out onto the balcony. It didn't feel right. I lit a cigarette and waited out there until she was finished.

'Shower's free,' she said a few minutes later, sticking her head out the door. I went in and had a shower while she got ready for her lunch.

A short while later, I heard my van pull up downstairs, Meatloaf blasting through the open windows. Jake arrived at the apartment as Mel was leaving. They passed each other in the doorway with a casual 'Hey'. The door closed behind Jake.

'Did you two fuck?' he asked, straight off the bat.

'No—definitely not!' I said. 'Why?'

'She was smiling. Like, an actual, proper smile.' He grinned. 'She struck me as the kind of person who avoids smiling for fear their face might crack.'

'We had a good night last night; that's it,' I told him.

'You did fuck!'

'That's not what I said. We had a beer together and smoked a little bit of pot. That's it.'

Jake didn't believe me. 'There is no way you smoked pot with that prude!'

'Swear on my life, your honour,' I said, hand on heart.

'Fuckin' hell!' He laughed. 'Make sure you stick that in your Study Journal! 'Got a beer?' He started digging through the fridge. It had just gone midday.

'Down the bottom,' I told him.

He pulled out two cans and asked, 'What's with all the fruit?'

'It's from the fondue the other night.' Thinking about it gave me a hard lump in my throat.

'Oh, shit. Sorry, man.'

I told him to forget about it and grabbed a beer out of his hand. We changed the conversation, but Jake kept glancing down at his phone throughout, distracted.

'Everything okay over there, brother?' I asked him. 'You haven't got a porno playing on that thing, have you?'

'Can you believe these arseholes?' he said, holding up his phone to me. It was open on YouTube.

'What?' I asked, confused.

'One million, five million, six million!' he said, flicking through the videos.

'Six million what?' I pressed.

'Views!' He declared. 'Six million views.'

'So what?'

'I was reading about this shit all last night. These guys get paid some serious money for people watching their videos, especially when you start getting up into the millions of views. YouTube sticks an ad at the start or in the middle and the more views you get, the more they pay you. Look,' he showed me the phone, 'this dude here got a million views from reviewing a videogame. A fucking videogame! That's cash banked.'

He was getting pretty worked up. I didn't understand why he was telling me, but I had a feeling I was about to find out.

'Forty-nine million views for a cat playing the keyboard! And I don't even know if that's the original!' he cried out. 'Twenty-five million views for this dude singing a song about vaginas! *We* could sing a song about vaginas!'

And there it is. He wanted us to make a video for YouTube.

'We split the profits fifty-fifty and watch the cash roll in!' he enthused. Jake was a good one for a get-rich-quick scheme. He seemed to come up with a new idea for a business or some way to make fast cash every few months. About six months ago he came to me with the idea of building and renting out small, one-person caravans, despite having zero experience in caravan construction, construction in general, or caravans. He'd done up some sketches and showed them to me. They looked like coffins that you towed behind your car.

Now, I had no doubt that we could sing a song about vaginas, but I dismissed the idea almost right away because I knew it was never going to happen. Jake was very big on ideas, but very small on action. I went along with his rant just to appease him.

'The real market is in *how-to* videos. That's what's popular at the moment.'

I went to the fridge for another beer.

'Here,' he went on, 'how to whittle a spittoon, how to restore an old bike, how to upcycle your pubic lice.'

'How to fuck a cantaloupe,' I added, spinning round and throwing one at him in a surprise rugby pass. It hadn't made it to the fondue. He caught it awkwardly.

'A cantaloupe?' he asked, laughing.

'Well, what fruit would you fuck, if you had to fuck a fruit?' I asked him. He shrugged his shoulders.

'Definitely not a pineapple,' he said, leaning into the open fridge. 'Ouch. Okay, so how *would* you even fuck a cantaloupe?'

'Well, you'd have to put a hole in it of course, unless you wanted to stick it up your arsehole. You'd need a lot of lube. I don't know about you, but I haven't got an arse like a bucket.' I cut the fruit in half. 'Feel that.'

Jake stuck two fingers into the seedy pulp at the middle. 'Brilliant,' he said, eyes shining.

'You'd want your hole to come down through the top into this seedy bit, I reckon.' Before I knew it, Jake had set up a camera, and I was down to socks and jocks. *Better for the viewers,* Jake said.

How to Fuck a Cantaloupe was born.

Step 1: *Purchase a cantaloupe from your local cantaloupe purveyor.*

Step 2: *Cut your hole. I find a power drill works best for this. Select a drill-bit to suit the size you need. Today we are going for a 32mm forstner-bit for a snug fit. If you don't have a drill handy, a knife will do the trick; just take care to make the entrance as smooth as possible.*

Step 3: *Weather dependant, you may want to warm your cantaloupe up a little. I find thirty seconds in the microwave gets it up to a bit over body temperature, so it feels nice and warm inside. Any longer and you might end up with a microwaved party-pie situation, except it's not the roof of your mouth that's peeling off.*

Step 4: *Fuck your cantaloupe. Find a private place where you are free from disturbances and shag that melon.*

*** *** ***

'Are you sure about this?' I asked Jake, taking my pants off. 'I don't know if people will get it.'

'They'll love it!' He said, 'Grab another melon.'

I took a fresh cantaloupe out of the fridge. I don't know how many people I thought I was catering for to warrant two entire cantaloupes for a fondue. *At least it's getting used*, I thought.

'Do you think they'll get that it's a joke?' I asked. I didn't really want to do the video, but Jake had a way of pleasantly twisting your arm.

'Who cares! If they don't get that it's a joke, then that's on them. We are either going to make some cash on this video, or, worst-case-scenario, we don't, and we've wasted three bucks on a rockmelon. *Boohoo*.' He had a point.

We chatted about how we were going to shoot it and came up with a rough script on the back of a cereal box. I came up with the bit about the microwave.

'Okay, so what's next?' I asked.

'We shoot. Just as we discussed, we'll shoot it all in sequence, and I'll break it up into steps when I'm editing. Just talk through what you're doing, and I'll make you look good afterwards. And don't fuck it up—we've only got one cantaloupe.'

No pressure.

Fruit. Drill. Heat. Fuck. Those were the steps written on the back of the cereal box, just out of frame. I plonked the melon in front of the camera.

Fruit.

Next, I lined up the drill with the top of the melon and plunged it through to the centre.

Drill.

I microwaved it for 30 seconds. It was actually starting to feel pretty nice inside.

Heat.

Fuck.

'Do I actually have to fuck it?' I asked Jake. He paused the camera.

'It's for the project, man. We want it to seem authentic.'

'It's a satire though. It's not meant to be authentic. And I'm not fucking a piece of fruit on the internet.' Jake reluctantly agreed to me not fucking the fruit.

'Just a shot of you holding the fruit in front of yourself then,' he said, compromising. I said 'okay'. 'But you have to take your jocks off. It won't look as good otherwise. Don't worry, I'll angle the camera, so we don't see your Johnson.'

Johnson. For the sake of decency, I went into the bathroom to strip off. Jake and I had seen each other naked a million times, but it seemed the right thing to do. I came back out into the kitchen, cantaloupe in place.

'I'm ready for my close-up, *Mr Demille*.' I said suggestively.

The camera's red light went on.

'And that, ladies and gentlemen, is how you fuck a Cantaloupe.' I said, taking a little bow. The apartment door swung open.

'What. The. Fuck?'

I turned and saw the horrified face of Mel, standing in the doorway. I was too stunned to move.

Another voice warned, 'Language, dear!', then closely followed it up with, 'What in the world?' as she stepped into view. The owner of the voice wore a floral summer dress and sun hat, and bore a striking resemblance to Melinda. *The mother*, I presumed. Jake was still filming. I could hear him laughing behind the lens of the camera. I snapped out of my trance and hobbled as rapidly as I could to the door, taking special care not to move the melon too much. The women in the doorway had seen enough, they didn't need to cop an eyeful of the plums too. I closed the door firmly on the mortified pair, apologising profusely.

'I'm sorry, you'll just have to come back later. I'm kind of in the middle of something,' I told them, in the same way you might tell a Jehovah's witness to return later on.

'What's going on?' came Mel's voice from the other side of the door.

'Nothing,' I told her, 'you just got here at a really bad time.'

She continued to bang on the door but I wouldn't let her in. Eventually she gave up, and I heard their footsteps trailing off down the hallway. Jake shut off the camera and burst out into a fit of laughter, rolling over the back of the couch in hysterics.

'Holy fuck!' He exclaimed. 'Did you see the looks on their faces?'

'I don't think they're our target audience,' I said dryly, cantaloupe still poised in front of my knob. I put the melon on the edge of the kitchen island and went into the bathroom to get dressed again. When I came back out, Jake was cutting it into slices.

'You're gonna eat that?' I asked him.

'You didn't actually put your cock inside it.'

'It did touch my cock though.'

'Yeah, on the skin. I'm not eating the skin, duh.'

Once it was all sliced up, he arranged the slices into a creative mandala of cantaloupe and took a photo. 'Step five: Share with your friends. The perfect summer treat.'

Chapter Seventeen

We sat on the couch and watched the video back. It wasn't bad. I got a few laughs out of it. Jake was rolling around out of control. I think Jake may have been the target audience: mid-twenties, easily amused, enjoys the effects of marijuana.

'This is brilliant!' He said, on the final shot of the video— me, with a cantaloupe covering my genitals.

'Turn it off now.' I said as the video kept rolling.

'This is the best bit!' He said as the camera panned across to the apartment door, and the horrified faces of mother and daughter.

It was almost worse living it for a second time. Almost. I had no idea what I was going to tell Mel. Things had been pretty good lately and I didn't want to scare her off. I made Jake promise to edit the last part out. I didn't find it as raucously funny as he did, and I didn't want Melinda and her mum to be associated with *How to Fuck a Cantaloupe.* He begrudgingly agreed.

He must have played that video on a loop the whole way back to his house. I pulled my van up to the kerb at the end of his street to drop him off.

'Can't go any further, sorry bud.' I said, looking down my old street.

Jake sorted me out with a little more pot to get me through the next week, then started walking home, still chuckling along to the footage playing on the little flip-out camera screen, as I rolled away from the kerb. When I pulled up to our building, I saw Melinda's car parked in the driveway.

Fuck. I was hoping to be back before she was. I entered the apartment, closing the door slowly behind me. The coast was clear. All I wanted was to go to bed and not have to deal with it, but since my bed was the couch in the middle of our loungeroom, *not having to deal with it wasn't* really an option. Melinda came out of the bedroom anyway, so I guessed it was time to deal with it.

She walked past me to the loungeroom.

'I don't even want to talk about it.' She said, raising a hand up next to her head.

Oh no. Not the hand. Chris used to give me *The Hand.* The hand was not to be taken lightly. The hand meant business.

'Let me explain.' I said to her, having absolutely no idea of how to explain the situation she'd walked into earlier. She just put her hand up again, blocking me out. 'It's not what you think,' I pleaded.

'It's not what I think? It looked to me like my mum and I walked in on your friend filming you having sex with a piece of fruit, so tell me: how exactly is it not what I think?'

It was exactly what she thought. She raised a very good point.

'Look, I don't care what sort of weird shit you guys get up to in your own time, but please don't bring it into my life.'

'It wasn't weird.' I lied. 'It was for the internet.' The explanation didn't make things any better.

'Like I said, I don't care what sort of weird shit you two get up to, keep me out of it. And did you really have to *eat* it?' She added.

The cantaloupe mandala was still on the kitchen counter, half eaten.

'It was only Jake who was eating it,' I told her. That didn't make it any less weird. Maybe it would have seemed more reasonable if I told her we shared it, I don't know.

The next few days were as awkward as you'd like. We hardly made eye contact with each other, and it seemed like all the good work we'd done earlier in the week had been undone. We barely spoke to each other out of embarrassment, mostly on my behalf.

'Are the apples safe?' Mel asked hesitantly, the day after the fact. That was one of the few times she spoke to me. I think she was worried if she talked to me too much it might trigger me to stick my dick in something, as though I were some sexually-charged animal, fuelled by conversation. She didn't go near the bananas.

On the third day, I was having some serious reservations about going ahead with the video. If I was uncomfortable around one person who had seen me naked with a piece of fruit, I didn't think I'd cope well with the world having access to the footage. I called Jake.

'Too late,' he said casually, when I told him how I felt, 'already launched.'

Shit.

'Can you take it down?' I asked.

'Take it down? Are you kidding? This baby's up to a thousand views already!'

'A thousand? When did you put it up?' I asked.

'About an hour ago.' It sounded like a lot of views to get in an hour. 'People are loving it. This might be the best thing we've ever done.'

I was skeptical, but I let it go. Out of interest, I logged into YouTube and typed in 'How to fuck a cantaloupe.' The video was on top of the list, just above 'How to build a recycled milk carton coffee table'. 1050 views. I watched the video again. If it was taken the wrong way, it could definitely be perceived as a genuine instructional video. I hoped that I wasn't going to be responsible for people all over the country dipping their wicks into rockmelons.

Considering her initial tour of the apartment had been cut short at the front door, Mel was having her mother round again. I made the call to get out of the house for a while.

I tidied up my belongings into a neat-ish pile at the end of the couch, making some sort of effort to save face. I didn't want Melinda's mum thinking I was a fruit-fucker *and* a slob.

'I'll be out for most of the day.' I told Mel on my way out, an attempt to reassure her that her Mum wouldn't be confronted by my presence at any stage. I hit the road in *Van Go*—the old girl who should probably have been the *old boy,* considering her punny namesake, but I didn't really like the idea of travelling around inside a man, so she was the *old girl.*

I wasn't sure where I was heading. Having no plans made for the day, I found myself cruising aimlessly down the road, listening to a mix-tape I'd bought from a church op-shop a couple of years ago. Van Go never got the digital upgrade she so deserved, so we were still running a cassette player from the 1980s. K.C. and The Sunshine Band were carrying on inside my rattly speakers. I wound down the window to get a bit of wind in my hair. *'That's the way, uh-huh uh-huh, I like it.'*

The meandering drive inevitably took me back to my hometown of Scoresby. It hadn't changed in my twenty-four years on this earth, and It wasn't likely to change for another twenty-four. I went past my Mum's place, the house I grew up in. A simple brick house with a small front yard bordered by a simple, easy-to-manage garden. My initials were still set in the concrete of the footpath out the front of the house. I had been about twelve when I did that. I remember Mum being worried sick that the council workers would know it was someone from our house, just from the initials.

'Who would be stupid enough to put their own initials outside their own house?' I reasoned with her. It was sound logic, and I liked it. I was stupid enough to do it, but if I was ever questioned about it, that was a great defence. She was a good woman, my mum. I told myself that would call her tonight. We hadn't spoken in a long time.

My journey continued on for a few more tracks and a few more suburbs before I passed a house with brick columns separating short spans of wrought-iron fencing. There were wrought-iron spikes atop each of the columns. I sped up a little when I saw a fat man out the front, watering his driveway.

Going around a corner, the road opened up to a street with a Milkbar, a café, a butcher and a green grocer. A beat-up phone booth stood alone on the corner. It seemed like ages ago now since I'd spent the night there. I pulled into the parking out the front of the café. *Breakfast would be nice.*

A rusted cowbell clanged on the door as I entered, taking a seat by the window beneath a chandelier of coloured glass bottles. The place was about half-full. There seemed to be a theme amongst the majority of the café's patrons. The common trend was women in activewear and runners with brightly coloured laces, and men in gaudy-patterned short-sleeved shirts done all the way up to the top, wearing fedoras and rounded Lennon sunglasses. I was a little on the outer in three-quarter cargo shorts and a grubby t-shirt.

A few minutes passed, and I flagged down one of the waitstaff. I assumed he was one of the waitstaff, but it was hard to tell in this place given the very lax dress-code. He wore a fun Hawaiian shirt and chino shorts, carrying the laid-back ensemble all the way down to his feet, where he sported a pair of blue thongs. In fact, the only reason I guessed he was a member of the waitstaff was that he was carrying a notepad and pencil. For all I knew, he could have been writing a novel.

He came over to the table after I signalled to him politely. The waitstaffperson/novelist wore his hair tied back in man-buns. *Plural.* He had one on each side of his head. I was about to have my order taken by the Princess Leia of hipsters.

'How can I help?' He asked. Either he worked there, or he was a very polite author.

'I'd like to order some breakfast, thanks.' I told him.

'Coffee or tea to start with?' he asked, raising pencil to pad.

'Coffee, thanks.' I said.

I'd begun to develop a taste for it since living with Mel.

'Great.' He said, leaning in expectantly. I'd been distracted by his buns.

'Oh, just a cappuccino.'

'Milk?' he asked.

'Sure.'

'No, what sort of milk? We've got regular, soy, coconut, goat, skim, almond, rice...'

'Got any monkey?' I asked, jokingly. He didn't get the joke. 'Just regular thanks,' I said, and then added, 'from a cow.'

'And what about the beans? We've got dark, medium and light roast. All single-origin and Fairtrade of course.'

Breakfast was turning into fucking pop quiz.

'Just whatever everyone usually gets,' I said. He decided on medium. I really didn't give a shit at this stage.

'And what about the dusting?' he inquired. I had no idea what the question meant. 'The dusting on top of the cappuccino. We do dark chocolate powder, a milk chocolate, white chocolate, or carob.'

I asked for the milk chocolate.

'And lastly, did you bring your own cup?'

I had to look around the room to make sure I was actually still in a café. 'I was hoping to use one of yours,' I said. *Did I bring my own cup?*

It was all getting a bit too much for me. Thankfully, he had completed taking my order, and stuck the pencil back in one of his man-buns. I wondered how they got anything done around here if they had to play *Twenty Questions* every time someone wanted a bite to eat. He toddled off to the lady at the coffee machine.

I hoped the breakfast menu was more straightforward.

The dual-bunned guy came back past a moment later, dropping a menu off in front of me. It was a simple white piece of paper on a miniature brown clipboard. Aside from the cursive headings, the whole menu was in Courier New font. It may as well have been in Wingdings; I hadn't heard of a single thing on the menu. He told me he would give me a couple of minutes, then come back and take my order. I was definitely going to need them.

Fermented Beetroot salad with goats cheese and walnuts.

Fuck me. Fermented Beetroot sounded like something that belonged in a bin, not a salad. I just wanted some bacon and eggs. There were other things, like *Olives in Brine* and a *Trio of Radish*, which sounded like entrees, but were listed under the Mains section. My mind boggled, looking at the alien menu. Man-buns appeared at my table.

'I just want some eggs!' I told him, at an unreasonable volume, a little worked up from time spent trying to decipher the menu.

'Certainly,' Replied the man, 'Duck, Quail, or Pheasant?'

'That's it!' I shouted, flipping the little clipboard off the table as I stood up. 'I've had enough!'

A sea of ironic haircuts and designer fishing hats turned to look at me as I stormed out, almost bowling a lady over as I burst out the door onto the street.

'Dan?' Came the voice of the woman I'd just about skittled. I turned around.

Holy fuck.

My mouth went dry, and my hands felt as if they had started to swell. Staring back at me from the doorway of the world's most infuriating café was an absolute sight for sore eyes: Jenny. She ran over and wrapped her arms around me.

'Shit, Dan. I haven't seen you since –' She started. 'How've you been?'

'I've been alright.' I said to her, taking a step back from the embrace. 'And you?'

'I'm doing great!' She said, beaming. 'Jake said you weren't living there anymore?'

'You spoke to Jake?' I said, perplexed.

'Yeah, I came 'round a few days after, *you know*... He didn't say anything to you?'

'Apparently not.' I answered steadily, baffled as to why he hadn't mentioned it.

'I dropped off a little note with my contact details on it. I just figured you didn't want to talk to me after everything that went down.'

I couldn't believe that Jake hadn't told me about the note. Well, I *could* believe it, Jake was probably blazed off his tits when she came around. He had a tendency to forget important things from time to time, anyway.

'I haven't stopped thinking about you.' She said.

'Me neither.' I told her.

We just stared at each other for a while.

'Want to grab a coffee?' I asked, then quickly added, 'Not from in there. I don't think I'm allowed in there anymore.'

She looked at me quizzically, then her face fell. 'I really can't, sorry. I'm on my way to work. I was just grabbing a quick cup on the way.'

'McCormack's?' I asked. She nodded.

We exchanged phone numbers and agreed to catch up soon. My heart was aflutter as I walked away. *Jenny*. I couldn't wait to see her properly. To catch up on everything that'd happened since we'd last seen each other. I grabbed a box of muesli bars from the milkbar before getting back in the van. They were only just out of date.

I called Jake.

'You spoke to Jenny?' I asked him, straight up.

'Hey?'

'Jenny. From McCormacks. You spoke to her?'

'Oh yeah! Jenny. What about her?'

He was stoned, and I was already getting frustrated.

'Did you speak to her?'

'When?' He asked.

'I don't know. Like, ever?'

'Yeah, of course. She came to our place a few weeks ago. Didn't I tell you?'

'I think I would have remembered.'

'I'm sure I told you. I came 'round the other day and I gave you this note she wrote you. Oh...' he trailed off.

'What? What *oh...* ?'

'It's still in my pocket.' He said, putting the pieces together. It didn't surprise me one bit that Jake hadn't washed his pants in a month. 'Sorry dude. I totally gapped it. I completely forgot.'

I hung up the phone.

Pulling out of the café-front parking, I had one last look at the group of shops before taking off down the street. There were still a few hours to kill before the apartment would be Melinda's-Mum free. I thought I'd blow a couple of hours at the movies. Go see 'The Fast and the Furious 15' or something.

When I got to the cinema the place was packed. Some new teen vampire drama had come out, and there were psyched-up adolescents everywhere. I joined the back of the ticket line. I must have had a snot hanging out of my nose, because the girl in front of me kept looking over her shoulder. I wiped my face on the sleeve of my shirt. She looked at me again, a confused expression passed across her face, then looked away. She whispered something to her friend. Her friend glanced back. She turned around completely this time.

'Excuse me, do I know you from somewhere?' She asked, pretty abruptly.

'No, I don't think so.' I said, looking her over. She had a pretty face with freckled cheeks and glasses with thick black rims. I was pretty sure I would have remembered her if we'd met before.

'It's just, you look so familiar...' she said, inspecting me closely.

'I'm sorry, I really don't think I know you.' I asked her name.

'Caitlin.' She replied. Nope, nothing. 'What's yours?' she asked. I told her.

'Savage...' She said, pondering. 'Savage...Sounds familiar, but, I don't know...'

'Next waiting, please.' Came the voice of a chunky man with a greasy face standing at the ticket counter. It was Caitlin's turn. She turned away, puzzled, to buy her ticket.

My turn came around and I still hadn't worked out which movie I wanted to see. Pressure landed my decision on a remake of Jumanji. *Whatever*. I was only there to kill some time. I'd liked the original when I was a kid. This one had Jack Black in it, so I guessed it would be okay, although he hadn't really done much worth talking about since *School of Rock*, except maybe *Kung Fu Panda*. I took my ticket and headed over to the candy bar to buy some popcorn and a drink. I'm glad I bought some popcorn and a drink, because I remember thinking earlier in the day that my wallet was just too heavy.

Large coke and popcorn in hand, heading up the stairs to where the cinemas were; I must have been about halfway up when I heard it: a high-pitched voice shouting from the bottom of the stairs. I spun around to hear,

'Hey! I remember where I know you from! You're that guy who fucked the cantaloupe!'

'Holy shit, *he is too!*' Came another voice from about halfway between Caitlin and me, a teenage boy this time.

'He did what?' Asked a freckled girl at the top of the stairs.

'He fucked a cantaloupe,' said another girl who was with her. 'Here, I'll get it up for you,' she offered, pulling out her phone. I put my head down and kept walking toward the cinema, passing the pair leaning over a phone screen at the top of the stairs.

'Oh my god!' The freckled girl shrieked.

I hastened my stride. I got to the guy checking tickets outside the corridor where the cinemas were.

'Holy shit. Are you that *How to Fuck a Cantaloupe* guy?' He said.

I had to get out. As more and more people recognised me from the video, their heads popped up from behind popcorn and choc-tops, locking eyes on me like a flock of domesticated turkeys on a tub of three-grain scratch, I freaked out. Spinning round, taking the stairs two at a time, I tore through groups of people trying to get to me.

'You rock, my man!' Said some long-haired yahoo as I passed him.

'You're fucked up, mate.' Said another blurred face on my way through.

'Did it feel like the real thing?' Said a boy in front of me at the bottom of the stairs. I paused. He couldn't have been any more than eleven, standing next to his puzzled father. I considered suggesting some safe-search options to the bewildered adult, but there was no time. I pushed past them.

First pulling, then pushing, I burst out of the glass doors at front of the building, panic-sweat dripping from my forehead. A little lightheaded, I stumbled out onto the paved street at the front of the cinema, gulping in greedy lungfuls of air. Shaking, I looked back over my shoulder to see if anyone had followed me. There must have been a hundred people pressed up against the long bank of glass doors, staring at me, or filming with their phones.

It was eerie.

I straightened up, taking long strides back to the carpark. Digging my phone out of my pocket, I made a call.

'Jake,' I said as he answered the phone.

'Look man, I'm really sorry about all that Jenny stuff—' he began.

'Forget it. I don't care about that anymore.' I'd gotten a glimpse into my future and I didn't like it. *'How to Fuck a Cantaloupe,'* I continued. 'It's got to go.'

I jiggled my key in the van's door. I was ever-jealous of the people of the world enjoying the magic of central-locking. Every time I had to unlock my van, the key threatened to snap off in the lock a little more. I punched the door-panel next to the lock with the side of my hand whilst turning. It submitted.

'I've just been mobbed at the movies.' I said to Jake, speaking over the top of his objections.

'Do me a favour.' He said calmly. He was always calm. 'Open up YouTube.'

'I don't care about that!'

'Just open it up.'

I complied. I typed in the words 'How to'. This time YouTube finished my sentence with 'Fuck a Cantaloupe' as a suggestion. I hit the suggestion. The video loaded up. My mouth popped open.

100,000 views. *Holy shit!*

'Exactly.' Jake said, in response to my silence.

'That's a lot of views!'

'Fuckin' oath that's a lot of views.' Jake said. 'We will hit the mil in no time. The fucking thing's only been up there for a few hours. And it's not just the money from YouTube I'm interested in, I've been thinking about it; people are going to want to talk to us. This is going to be big.'

I wasn't sure I wanted it to be big. I wasn't sold on being the face of cantaloupe-fucking. I told Jake my concerns and he quickly dismissed them. I pressed them on him a little more. We came to a compromise.

'Look, leave it for an hour or two, think on it. If you are still convinced that you don't want it up by the end of the day, I'll delete it and you can get on with living your usual, boring life.' He said.

I needed to get away from the world for a while. I took the van down to the park where Mel and I had gone for a walk a few days before. I couldn't remember seeing a single person when I was with her. It wasn't far.

On the way there I was stopped at a set of traffic lights when I looked over at the car next to me. There were a couple of kids sitting in the back seat, maybe twelve and thirteen. One of them pointed at me through the glass and nudged the other, presumably his brother. The boy's eyes lit up and he started waving. I pretended not to see them. His brother started tapping on the window and carrying-on, trying to get my attention. I looked over again and the window-side one had his head down. The lights changed just as the boy looked up, slapping a white piece of paper against the inside of the window. 'We like you better than Logan-Paul,' it said, in the childish scrawl of Texta. I didn't know what a Logan-Paul was.

I pulled up into the car-park a few minutes later, turning the van off as I looked across the open reserve. I got out. There was no one around. I breathed in. It felt like it had been a long time since I had breathed. I started walking, making the conscious decision to leave my phone in the van. Two walks in one week. I was beginning to worry that it might become a regular thing, walking.

I ventured out into the park and walked for a good forty-five minutes without seeing a single person. I didn't think about the video, or Melinda, or her mum, or Jake or anything. I just walked. Even with the Clayton wind blowing the wrong way, it was bliss.

I smoked a very mild joint beside a pond, watching the ducks paddle around. A *driver*, Jake called it, when you wanted to take the edge off, but you still had to drive after. Lying back on the grass, staring up at the little flecks of nothing that slowly pinball their way through your vision when you aren't focused on anything, I slipped into a warm daydream.

Jenny and I are walking down a remote beach in some forgotten part of the world. The sun is shining, and the wind blows back our hair. If there is anything closer to paradise, I haven't seen it.

Jenny walks a few paces ahead of me. I watch the way her body shifts in the flowing white dress she has on, as she floats along the beach. She turns to me over her shoulder, smiling with her eyes, her beautiful white teeth on show. I'd never realised how perfect her teeth were. She starts jogging along the sand, her light gown billowing out behind her.

I chase after her.

She turns her head, laughing playfully as she runs, encouraging me to follow.

There was a sharp sting in my left arse cheek.

'Fuck!' I cried, snapping out of paradise. Something had bitten me on the arse. I scrambled to my feet, pulling down my shorts at the back to inspect my burning arse-cheek. There was no sign of the perpetrator. From the path behind me came a squeal.

'Ahh!' Cried a small Korean girl in a soft pink dress, at the sight of my red arse. Her mother grabbed her hand tightly.

For fuck's sake. I thought. I wasn't going to let this happen again.

'No, it's okay. I've just been bitten.' I said to the little girl, taking a step towards her. I turned to show her the bite. She screamed again. 'I've just been bitten by something.' I repeated, now to the mother. 'Here, see.'

'Stand behind Mummy,' the girl's mother instructed her, terror brimming in her eyes.

I pulled up my pants. 'Look.' I said 'All gone. No problem. All good.' I dusted my hands off to show that it was finished with. I held my hands up in the air, empty palms facing outwards in an attempt to show I meant no harm.

The mother clutched her daughter tightly by the wrist behind her.

'Look, I'm going to go this way now,' I told them, pointing down the path. 'I'm going to leave, and everything is going to be okay.'

I moved slowly in the direction I had pointed. 'Everything is alright, yes?' I asked the mother. She nodded grimly. 'No need for police, right?'

She shook her head, the way someone might if you had a gun to it.

I wasn't convinced. Keeping my hands up, I painted the friendliest expression I could muster on my face. It's funny how closely the 'I'm not a predator' smile resembles the 'I am a predator' smile. I backed away until they were just two tiny figures in the distance, then turned on my heel and ran back to the van. I must have set some sort of record for most cases of wrong place, wrong time by now. I left the park quickly, wheels spinning on the gravel driveway as I took off.

I got back to the apartment in the late afternoon. 'I saw the video.' Melinda said to me after I'd been pottering around sorting out a very late lunch in the kitchen. Dry crackers with slices of tomato and cheese on top. *Get some vegetables back into me,* I'd thought.

'Oh,' I replied. There wasn't much more of a response I could give.

'And,' She went on, 'I thought it was kind of...funny.'

'Really?' I asked, a little shocked.

'Yeah.' She added rapidly, 'It *was* meant to be funny wasn't it? It's not a proper instructional, yeah?' She looked worried.

I assured her that it was satirical.

She smiled at me and touched my hand.

'You're a funny guy, Dan.' She said and smiled genuinely. I wasn't sure what to make of it.

'Thanks.' I said uncomfortably. Her hand was still on top of mine. She moved it away.

'Mum didn't really see the funny side.' She said, 'Maybe it's a generational thing. She's never really had much of a sense of humour.' She was looking at me strangely. Staring right into my eyes.

My phone rang. I tore myself free of her gaze and looked at it. Jake. I answered.

'How do you like the sound of a thousand bucks?' was the first thing he said.

I liked the sound of a thousand bucks very much. Raising an apologetic hand to Melinda, I took myself out onto the balcony.

'Where have you been all morning man? I've left you, like, twenty messages,' he complained.

'I left my phone in the van. I went for a walk.' I told him.

'Yeah, well, while you were out taking in the sights, guess who went viral?'

The statement could have meant a couple of things, coming from Jake. He went 'viral' once when we were living together and couldn't walk properly for a week. He sorted it out with some ointment, but we were warned not to mix our bath towels up for a while. I was pretty sure he was talking about the video this time.

'What exactly is *viral*?' I asked him.

'One million. We've clocked the million, mate!' There was a silence on the line for a couple of seconds. 'One million, fifty-five thousand and two, to be precise.'

It seemed like a lot.

'Are we celebrating?' he asked excitedly. I didn't see any reason not to.

We agreed on the Irish at 7. It had been a little while since we'd had a good session there. When I arrived, Jake had already secured a booth down the back and had a pint on the go. It was medium-busy; not out of control, being a Wednesday night.

I stopped off at the bar on my way to the back of the venue. A disinterested-looking woman with bright pink lipstick that didn't match her flat demeanour greeted me dully. Her hair was scraped back into a greasy, high pony-tail. A piece of chewing gum passed from one side of her mouth to the other as she asked,

'What can I get ya, darl?'

'Pint of VB, thanks,' I replied.

'No worries, darl.' Her thin arms raised a glass to the beer-tap. 'Eight-sixty, darl,' her mouth said. Her eyes said, *'kill me'.*

I paid her and took my drink to the booth Jake was at. He raised his glass to mine in greeting. 'One-point-five,' he said, big smile plastered across his face.

'Holy shit!' I fell into the booth, mind reeling.

Phuc, the owner, came out from the back with an ash tray and set it down on the table for us. Jake pulled a cigar out of his pocket. It didn't suit him at all.

'What? We're celebrating, aren't we?' he said.

Jake talked excitedly about the future, between puffs on the fat cigar. 'We are gonna be huge, man. Everyone is going to want a piece of us. It's going to be massive.'

'Has someone contacted you?' I asked

'Not yet,' he said, 'but they will. You just wait. This is going to be huge.'

I thought Jake was getting a bit ahead of himself. I just nodded and took a sip of my beer, the head now just a thin skim of foam on top.

'Excuse me?' said a voice at the side of the booth. It belonged to a tall man with a checked, short-sleeve shirt and a hunching neck. 'Are you the guy from the video?'

'I'm not sure what you're talking about,' I said to him.

'The... the *cantaloupe* thing,' he said, whispering the word cantaloupe as though he were asking me if I were a scat-porn star.

'Never heard of it,' I said, 'sorry'

He hung his head a little further into the hunch and walked away despondently, shaking his head and muttering to himself, 'I could have sworn...'

'Why would you do that?' Jake asked, looking annoyed.

'I had enough of that at the movies today,' I told him. 'I'm here to relax.'

'You are here to celebrate,' Jake corrected me. 'And that doesn't include snubbing-off fans.' He whistled at the gangly dude in the checked shirt and flagged him over.

'Yeah?' said the guy, arriving at the booth.

'Forgive my friend's poor manners before, sir,' Jake said, suddenly acquiring a ridiculous formal tone. 'He's still getting accustomed to his budding fame, and has been feeling a little overwhelmed by the influx of attention we've received; but yes, he is in-fact the guy from the *How to Fuck a Cantaloupe* YouTube video.'

I gave him a little wave.

'I knew it!' he said, pointing at me. 'I never forget a face!' He was shaking with excitement. 'Can I buy you drink?' he asked.

'Pint of VB would be nice,' I conceded, looking at my near empty glass. 'Thanks.'

He rushed off over to the bar. I saw him pointing at me excitedly as he ordered the drink. The woman behind the bar looked equally disinterested as before. The man returned quickly, nearly tipping the beer over with excitement as he set it down on the table. He slid into the booth, right next to me, sidling up real close. *Okay, so this is getting a little too familiar for me.* Our legs were touching and I was pretty much backed up against the end of the booth. I had to lean away as he opened his mouth to speak to me. I was so close to his mouth I could see the redness of gingivitis where his gums met his big teeth. His breath didn't smell bad, but it was hot.

'Y-your v-video, he stammered, his hands shaking and voice quivering with excitement. 'It was perfect.'

It was a comic instructional for fucking a piece of fruit; I'd say it was funny, maybe, but I wouldn't call it perfect.

'I-It's ch-changed my life,' he continued, a shiny wet patch appearing on his bottom lip.

'Always happy to hear from a fan,' Jake said, smiling and raising his glass like Leonardo Di Caprio on the poster for *The Great Gatsby.* I nodded rapidly in agreement, squashed up so hard against the end wall of the booth that I thought I might become a part of it.

'How exactly has it changed your life?' I asked, not really sure how it could have.

'M-my s-s-s-self-esteem is through the r-roof.' He said, taking a long sip of his beer to quell his excitement. 'I used to come here every w-week.' His buggy eyes flicked between mine and Jake's as his long neck swung his head between the two of us like a crane. 'I t-tried to p-p-pick up g-girls to t-take home.'

I pictured a deep hole with a rope and a bucket being lowered in. *It puts the lotion on its skin.*

'I a-almost always went h-home alone.' The *almost* worried me. 'I s-spent so much m-money on buying girls drinks, and n-nothing. Now all I need is a c-cantaloupe and a m-microwave.'

Oh god.

'And it's all th-thanks to you.'

'Well, look, ah...'

'Mack,' he said.

'Mack. We're really happy you found the video... useful...' I said, 'And I'm sorry if this is a little brash, but we're actually meeting some people here soon so, ah, if it's not too much trouble...' I wasn't sure how to finish what I was trying to say.

'Oh,' he said awkwardly, shuffling in his seat, 'oh, okay. Yeah, cool.' He stood up uncomfortably and stretched. 'Well, I-I'll just be o-over there,' he said, pointing at the far end of the bar. A look of sadness took hold over his face for a moment, but was quickly replaced by a probably-forced, toothy smile. 'I-it was really nice m-meeting you guys,' he said, hunching right over to shake our hands before taking his half-finished pint and lumbering over to the bar.

As soon as he was out of earshot Jake said, 'What the fuck.' And we started laughing.

'The dude genuinely fucks cantaloupes,' I said, flabbergasted.

'Seems safer than him taking girls back to his place,' Jake replied. I leaned out of the booth to look at the guy. There he was, sitting on a stool at the end of the bar, looking straight at me. He waved. I waved back uncomfortably. Before long, Jake was back to telling me how we were going to be the *next big thing,* and I was back to staring at him through the bottom of my pint glass as I knocked back a fresh beer, which was going down a treat, and was an excellent accompaniment to the anxiety that was trying to rise up inside me each time Jake mentioned how huge we were going to be. Each time the fear stirred in my gut, another wash of V.B would dump down on top of it.

I didn't want to be famous. Sure, money would be a nice thing to have, but I wasn't sure I wanted all the attention that went along with it. Perhaps I just didn't want to be famous for sticking my dick inside a piece of fruit.

That was probably it.

'One-point-seven million views,' Jake said amidst some rant or other about superstardom.

'Can we talk about something else?' I asked him. He seemed hurt. 'It's all we've spoken about all day. I just want to think about something else for a while. Just five minutes.'

'Okay.' He said. 'What did you want to talk about?'

'Anything at all, as long as it's not cantaloupes.' I said, smiling weakly.

There was movement at the side of the booth, and two figures appeared in its entrance, giggling: two women in their early twenties, wearing almost matching outfits of low-cut blue singlets and khaki shorts. One of the girls, the taller one, had a red cap on that said *Noosa*, with the embroidered image of a sun setting behind a palm tree on the front.

'Hi,' I said to them. They looked at each other and started giggling again.

'What's the joke?' I asked, unsure.

'No, nothing, nothing,' they said, and burst out into a new fit of laughter. The taller one nudged the shorter one, and giggle-whispered in her ear.

'No, you ask him,' said the shorter one, flicking her eyes to me, then darting them swiftly away. I think I detected an English accent.

'Ask me what?' I said.

They giggled again.

'My friend wanted to know—' she paused, tittering nervously, '—my friend wanted to know—' She couldn't get it out without giggling shyly and looking up at her friend. She tried one more time. 'My friend, Sarah here, wanted to know—'

'—Are you the cantaloupe guy?' the one in the hat interrupted excitedly.

'He doesn't want to talk about that,' Jake said dismissively. The girls looked disappointed.

'No, no, it's okay,' I said to them, but mostly to Jake.

'But you were just saying before that—'

'Jake, seriously, it's fine,' I said to him through gritted teeth. I smiled up at the girls. 'It's fine.'

'So, you are the cantaloupe guy?' asked the little one, excitedly.

'The one and only,' I said, flourishing my hands dramatically. 'Dan Savage.'

'Can we get a photo?' Sarah, the tall one, asked. Before I had a chance to respond, she was climbing into the booth, stretching her long legs out in front of me to sit down on my left knee, mobile phone poised for a selfie. The shorter, less hatty one, followed suit, sitting down on the opposing knee. I had foreign butts on my legs and four breasts in my face and I didn't mind a bit.

'Can you take it?' Sarah asked, handing the phone to Jake.

'Sure,' he said, seeming more than a little deflated with the division of butts. He took the photo.

'Another one!' Sarah said excitedly. The next one she leant in and whispered in my ear, 'You're so funny, Dan.' As she said this, she slipped her hand down the back of my jeans. My eyes went wide as she grabbed my arse cheek. The phone's camera clicked, and the girls begged for one more photo.

'Okay, but this is the last one,' Jake said.

The girls pressed their lips against each of my cheeks and got a photo kissing me, the meat in their lady-sandwich. Sarah's hand still well-and-truly down the back of my pants, my eyes just about popped out of my head as Jake leant forward to take the photo. A high-pitched sound, which I'd never before heard come out of my body, issued forth as the camera clicked. Sarah giggled and kissed me on the cheek again before standing up.

'We were just going to go and grab some dinner, boys,' she said, 'but I'm sure we'll see you round.' She winked at me as they left the booth, arm-in-arm.

'That's not fair,' Jake said to me, watching them go. 'I'm half of the video. I filmed it and edited it. Where are the girls fawning over me?'

'She put a finger in my arse!' I said to him, still in shock from the event.

'Really?' he asked.

I nodded, feeling a little ashamed. 'In the last photo.'

'Why do you get all the fun?' He rolled his eyes. I think he was genuinely jealous. She hadn't got the whole lot in, but as the flash went off, she definitely had the tip past the threshold, at least to the base of the nail.

'I'm pretty sure that's rape,' I said to him, 'It's rape isn't it? Did I just get raped?'

Jake didn't share my concern. He finished his beer and went up to get us a couple more. A guy in a footy jumper and shorts walked past the booth, talking loudly on his phone. He stopped and looked straight at me.

'Holy shit,' he said into the phone, never breaking eye contact. 'You know that dude with the cantaloupe? He's here.' There was a moment's pause whilst the recipient responded. 'Yeah, I'm staring right at him. Holy fuck!' He raised his glass to me. 'Dude, you're awesome,' he said, before turning to the bathroom.

It was a pretty good feeling, being called awesome by a total stranger. It felt much better than an unexpected acrylic nail in the rectum. Jake got back from the bar with two more pints.

'What are we up to?' he asked.

'Oh,' I said, unlocking my phone. I hit refresh on the video. 'One-point-nine.'

'No shit! We've had two-hundred-thousand views just in the time you've been here.'

'It's pretty unreal,' I said to him. 'Another guy recognised me while you were gone.'

'You know why?' he replied, 'Because it's a fucking awesome video. I even showed Phuc when I was getting a beer.'

'What did he say?'

'He didn't get it at all. Language barrier got in the way. I think he thought I was telling him *how two Phuc's can't elope*, and then when he saw you with a melon on your pecker, he didn't know what to think.'

The next beer went down uninterrupted. Jake talked about making a sequel. I told him it felt too soon. He had big aspirations for the video. At one point he was talking about a contact he'd made in the poster industry. I must have tuned out. I didn't know what we were going to do with a poster.

'What are the posters for?'

'Publicity! It will get our names out there!'

Buying posters for publicity seemed a lot like digging a swimming pool with a Wizz Fizz scoop. I couldn't think of anything more public, or faster to get the word out, than the Internet. Posters were very analog. I finished my drink and went for another at the bar, making the conscious effort to keep away from Buffalo Bill at the end as I waited to be served.

'Excuse me?' Came a voice over my right shoulder, 'But are you Dan Savage?'

I was caught off-guard. I'd started to get used to people recognising me from the video, but this guy was calling me by name. *Social media*, I guessed.

'Err, yeah,' I said, turning around to a guy in a black jacket and t-shirt standing behind me.

'Do you mind if I get an autograph?' He held out a pen and a cardboard coaster advertising Furphy's Refreshing Ale. 'It's all I could find,' he said, shrugging and smiling pleasantly.

I'd never done an autograph before, and my signature was pretty boring. It was essentially just 'D.Savage' with a little scribble through it. 'Who do I make it out to?' I asked.

'I'm Dave.' He said.

To Dave,

Keep it real.

Dan.

It was all I could think to write. I added a couple of extra loops to my signature at the bottom to make it more interesting. Dave was stoked.

'My kids love you!' he said, in an abject display of bad parenting.

'Thanks,' I replied, unsure how else to respond.

'No, no, no, thank *you*,' He said, waving the freshly-signed coaster as he walked away from the bar.

'What, are you like, *famous*, or something?' said the woman with the scraped-back pony-tail behind the taps.

'Not really,' I said to her. I tried to order a beer, but she cut me off.

'He seemed pretty happy to get your signature,' She said, raising a heavily-harvested eyebrow that had had to be drawn on in spots.

'It's nothing, really. Just an internet thing,' I said to her. She squinted at me.

'Can I grab a pint of Vic, please?' I asked, trying to fill in the gap as she scrutinised me with her eyeballs.

'I thought I recognised your face,' She said. Throughout the entire conversation, her tone of voice and overall facial expression hadn't moved from bland disinterest. 'You're in that watermelon-fucking video.'

'Cantaloupe,' I corrected.

'A what?'

'It's cantaloupe-fucking. I'm in a cantaloupe-fucking video. It's not a watermelon.'

She looked horrified. Her chewing gum fell out of her mouth. 'You fucked a cantaloupe?'

'Well, I didn't actually fuck it, but we made it look like that,' I said, glancing away.

'So, you didn't actually fuck a little horse?' she said.

'What?'

'You just made it look like that, yeah?'

The penny dropped.

'Oh. God. No, you're thinking of an antelope,' I said, realising the terrible mistake she'd made. 'And they're more like deer than a horse, really.' I went on, 'What I fucked was a melon, not a deer. Like, a rockmelon. The video is called 'How to Fuck a Cantaloupe.''

'Oh,' She said, her face returning to its usual state of deadpan boredom. She started pouring my beer. 'Why didn't you call it, 'How to fuck a rockmelon', then?'

Eager to escape the conversation, I told her I didn't know, and started to head back to the booth. There was a commotion at the front of the pub. I turned around to see a horde of men entering the pub excitedly.

'I told you he was here!' came the cry of a man at the front edge of the pack, ushering the rest of them in. It was the footy guy from before, and it looked like he had brought half the team with him. They made a beeline for me, throwing their arms around me and scruffing up my hair as they surged around me for a photo. Drinks were handed to me left and right.

Things got messy. Very messy.

Typically, I never gelled with the footy-boy crowd, not for any reason other than that it was a clique that I wasn't part of, nor would I become part of. I sucked at sports, and football was something that I never managed to get into. I sometimes wondered if I'd missed out on the camaraderie, the brotherhood that grew from team sports, but then I was reminded of all the running that was involved and decided that the juice wasn't worth the squeeze.

If I'd missed out, I certainly made up for it that night. I may have had my misgivings as they barraged through the front door, but I had to hand it to them, they knew how to let their hair down. I called Jake over and we did shots at the bar with the whole team. I turned around after about shot number three and the place was pumping with bodies.

'We rang around,' said one of the footy-boys— I think his name was Troy. 'Everyone wanted to come and meet you.' And so they did. Jake and I were passed from person to person to person, making new five-minute-friends throughout the entire evening. Phuc brought out a bottle of champagne and two glasses for us. I tried to give him some money but he said, 'You're famous now! You don't pay tonight, Mister.'

I didn't pay for a drink for the rest of the night.

After the champagne hit our lips, the rest of the night turned into a wild blur. The thump of the music, the flash of coloured lights and the sweat of bodies pumping in the hot space all blended together with the smoke machine and alcohol. I remember two girls pouring champagne down my throat and on my head, before I was hoisted into the air by some big men. They bounced me up on their shoulders in the middle of the crowded dancefloor. Everyone chanted my name. I fell back on top of the crowd, caught by their awaiting hands, and they threw me up and down in the air in time with the music.

That's about the last thing I remember from the night.

Chapter Eighteen

Waking up, bleary-eyed, under the coffee table in the apartment, I scrunched my eyes together and opened them again until things started to come into focus. Turns out I'd vomited under the couch.

Where are my pants? I thought, as I felt the carpet scratch against my genitals.

My head!

My head was pounding. I could feel my pulse palpably beating away inside my temple, as though something were trying to break free from my skull. I rolled away from the couch, and the pile of vomit beneath it. I'd deal with it later.

I found my pants. They were firmly buttoned up around the waist of a young, dark-haired girl on the floor next to me. It appeared that she had lost her shirt.

'Morning, lover,' she said to me as she turned over, her bare breasts rolling from one side to the other with the twist of her body.

'Hi.' I had no idea who she was.

Suddenly, I became very self-conscious of my limp penis sagging down against my thigh. I followed her gaze and quickly covered up, cupping my genitals in my hands.

'Not as enthusiastic as last night,' she said, with a light laugh, stretching.

'I'm sorry, did we—' I went to say.

'Yep,' she finished for me.

Wow.

'Jane,' she said, in answer to my next question, extending a hand to me.

'Of course,' I said. 'I knew that.'

What a lie.

'Can I have my pants back?' I asked.

'What will I wear?' she replied.

'Where are your pants?'

'You *were* drunk. You really don't remember, do you?'

If I could forget having sex with her, I guessed I could forget just about anything. She tilted her head to the balcony. I had a blurred flashback.

I'm standing on the balcony, kissing a pair of wet lips, my hands running up the smooth skin of her back. She is pale and beautiful. Her fingers curl themselves around the hem of my t-shirt, and she lifts it up over my body, handing it to me.

'Throw it,' she says.

I can't say no. I throw it over the edge of the balcony.

The fuzzy recollect didn't make a lot of sense. I wasn't missing my top, she was. I looked down. I was wearing a very tight, black t-shirt with a pink cat on the chest. *Her* top. She laughed as I tried to make sense of it.

Another hazy recall:

I am laying her down on her back on the tiny table of the outdoor setting. Her fingers busily unbutton the front of her jeans and she slides them halfway down her thighs. I pull them the rest of the way off and throw them over my shoulder. They fold in half and catch on the railing of the balcony, before slowly sliding off over the edge like a black denim snake. A look of shock passes over her face as the pants slip over the railing. It is quickly replaced by a smile as she begins to laugh. She curls herself upwards and grabs a hold of my lower lip between her teeth, pulling me down over her.

I looked over at the balcony once more. This time I noticed the table was broken, the flat top of it snapped clean off.

'Shit.'

'Don't worry, they are just pants,' she said. 'I'll just keep yours and we can call it even.'

I only had one pair of pants.

'I've only got one pair of pants,' I said to her.

'Who only has one pair of pants?'

Me, evidently. I wasn't much for forethought, and since living in the apartment building, I hadn't done any clothes shopping. I'd asked Jake to bring me some of my things from the house, and he'd brought me one of each of the necessary items of clothing: One pair of pants, one t-shirt, and one pair of underwear. I hadn't really had the need to buy anything more than that.

'Here,' Jane said, reaching into the back pocket of her/my jeans, 'you can wear these if you want.'

She flung a pair of knickers at me. They were pink, with black edging right the way around them, perfectly co-ordinated with her t-shirt. She laughed as I held them in my hands, staring at them. *Fuck it.* I rolled onto my back and pulled one leg up. She made an unusual noise. It wasn't my best angle. Poking my left leg through the undies, then my right, I pulled them up until they sat uncomfortably in position, not quite making it all the way to the top of my pubic bone.

I looked ridiculous. It was obvious now that female underpants were not designed to house male genitalia. The whole situation reminded me of cryo-vacked deli-meats. I don't think she'd expected me to actually put her knickers on, but faced with looking ridiculous or swinging in the breeze, I took ridiculous. She laughed, a lot.

'Shh!' I said quickly, remembering Melinda. 'I don't want to wake my room-mate. I'm not really supposed to have sleep-overs.'

She raised an eyebrow. 'Is your room-mate your Mum?'

'It's a long story.'

I got up and went out to the balcony, looking over the edge. My topless friend appeared beside me. I could see my t-shirt straight away, it was on the windscreen of Melinda's car. I couldn't see Jane's pants anywhere.

'You gonna climb down there?' she asked, leaning forward over the edge. It was quite a sight to take in. I leant forward with her, and then I saw it. The pants had slipped off the railing of our balcony and fallen down to the railing of the balcony directly below. I felt as though I didn't really have much of a choice. I looked down. It wasn't that far away, and I'd always been a pretty good climber as a kid. I hooked my leg over the railing, sort of straddling it.

'Whoa! I was joking,' Jane said, grabbing my arm.

'It's not that hard,' I said. 'I've got this.'

I looked down. My vision blurred, then came back into focus. I was actually way too hungover for this.

'You're insane!' she said, letting go of my arm.

I lifted my other leg up over the top of the railing to join the other one. As it was mid-arc I heard, 'Dan?' I looked up, startled by the new voice. My eyes met with Mel's. She was standing in the kitchen.

'Whoa!'

I lost my balance. My leg flew over the railing, completing its arc, but not landing alongside my right foot. The force of the swing flung me around, and I had that feeling that you get in your stomach when you miss a step coming down a ladder—except this ladder was very high.

My stomach dropped out of my arse as my fingers slipped from the railing and I was sent tumbling backwards over the edge of the third storey balcony. I was certain I was going to die as I completed a full backwards somersault, my arms flailing, reaching out and catching only air. I heard a shriek from above as I dropped out of sight.

They say when you have a traumatic experience, close to death, time slows down, and you get to experience the last moments of your life frame-by-frame, like some dramatic *arthouse* scene, each second stretched out before you like an enormous piece of elastic representing your life. In this instance, that was not the case. Everything moved so quickly, and so unexpectedly that I only had a fractured fragment of a second to prepare myself for death.

I scrunched my eyes shut tightly.

Thwack!

Death hurt my elbow. Not really my elbow, but the inside of my elbow. Like, the crease on the inside of your arm between your shoulder and your wrist. Armpit number two, I'd always called it.

My hand gripped cold steel. I opened my eyes. I wasn't dead. As I'd fallen, my body had spun around and I'd smashed my inner arm on the metal railing of the balcony below, hooking me on the hand-rail. I looked down. The view past my black-and-pink-knickered pelvis and pasty legs was terrifying. I was dangling by one arm, three storeys up from the hard asphalt car-park below.

My eyes huge, I took two rapid breaths in and swung my leg upwards to the handrail. The muscles in my core burned as I used all of my power to complete the manoeuvre. My heel clunked down on the handrail painfully, right where Jane's pants hung, and slipped off, flicking the jeans over the railing. They wrapped around my other foot on their way down. I tightened my elbow's grip on the railing and strained my core again, passing the jeans up to my free hand with my feet. Hooking a finger into one of the belt-loops, I yanked them upwards, stuffing a good portion of the waistline into my mouth to free up my hand.

Sweat cascaded off my forehead, stinging my eyes. I watched as a bead rolled off the side of my jaw and fell through the air like a salty raindrop, splattering on Melinda's windshield; *my* path of trajectory if I didn't get my shit together. My elbow feeling like it was about to explode, I used the final vestige of my strength to swing the leg up once more. This time my heel passed over the railing and I was able to hook the back of my knee, my leg-pit, over the steel. I grabbed on with my free hand, clinging to the handrail like an upside-down koala.

I could breathe again. I looked up at the two girls leaning over the apartment railing.

'Melinda; Jane,' I said, by way of introduction. 'Jane, my housemate, Melinda.'

I threw myself completely over the railing to the safety of the balcony. I picked up Jane's jeans and swung them over my shoulder as I looked ahead. On the other side of the glass door, I was met with the faces of a bewildered couple eating breakfast at the table just inside. I let myself in.

'Wow, same layout as ours,' I said as I walked past the pair, picking up a piece of toast from the table on my way through. I grabbed the handle of their front door, before turning to them. 'Dan Savage, from upstairs.' I said. 'You might have heard of me.' I closed the door behind me and stepped into the hallway. They hadn't uttered a single word.

Chapter Nineteen

'Can I please have my pants back now?' I said to Jane, as I re-entered the apartment. Melinda looked like she might faint. Jane took the pants and went into the bathroom to change.

'You aren't supposed to have people over,' Mel said as she examined my arm. 'You could get us kicked out of the program.'

Typical of her to be worried about breaking the rules. I'd nearly fallen to my death only a little while earlier, and she was worried about *the program.* 'I think it's okay,' she said, letting go of my arm. It hurt like a bitch. 'I don't think its broken or anything, but you should probably get it checked out properly.'

Jane emerged from the bathroom and handed over my pants. I got changed and came back out to join them in the kitchen. I handed Jane a scrunched-up pair of knickers, which she put back in her pocket.

'They looked better on you,' she said coyly.

'Oh.' I'd almost forgotten I was wearing her t-shirt. I whipped it off and handed it over to her. I was more than a little surprised when she reproduced the action herself, removing the t-shirt Mel had loaned her, in the middle of the kitchen.

'Nothing you two haven't seen before,' she said in response to our surprise. 'Are you still taking me home?'

'I guess,' I said, not recalling agreeing to it in the first place.

'You promised me last night you'd take me home in the morning.'

'Koo Wee Rup?' I repeated as she jumped into the passenger side of Van Go.

'Yep.' She said firmly, then smiled.

'Koo Wee Rup?' I asked again, astonished. She nodded amusedly.

The only things I knew about Koo Wee Rup were that it was a shithole town on the edge of nowhere, and that it was at least an hour's drive from where we were. We'd need to fill up before we left.

We pulled in to the petrol station clunkily after a short, yet incredibly painful trip from the apartment. My arm was killing me, and the uncooperative gearbox that had been thrown into Van Go when she was manufactured wasn't helping. Every change of gear was agony.

As Jane filled up, I went inside to pay. I had to wait until she had hung up the hose before I could complete the transaction. I needed to get smokes, so I asked the guy for a pack and he asked me for I.D. I hadn't been asked for I.D. since trying to buy beers when I was sixteen, and even then I wasn't asked often. I'd always looked a few years older than I actually was. The guy behind the counter looked over my licence.

'Dan Savage. Like the writer?' he asked.

'No,' I responded bluntly.

I wondered if one day people would be saying to the writer Dan Savage, 'Dan Savage, like the guy who fucked a cantaloupe?' The thought made me very happy. I was about to pay when a pack of jelly-snakes were thrown down on the counter.

'And those, too,' came Jane's voice over my shoulder. 'Thanks.'

I paid for the lot and we got back into the van. The gearstick looked up at me menacingly.

'I think you are going to have to work the stick,' I said to Jane, with a childish smirk at the way it sounded.

'Cool,' was her response; she didn't even flinch.

I started the van. 'Okay, first,' I said, putting my foot on the clutch. She wrestled the stick into position. 'That's the hardest one,' I said as we pulled forward slowly. 'She puts up a bit of a fight, but it's easier once you're past second.'

The road was clear as I approached the end of the service station's driveway, so I went for it. 'Second.' She pulled the gearstick downwards, with a little more ease this time.

'Third,' I said, as we built up a bit of pace.

We wrestled through the streets and gears until we were on the freeway.

'Thank God!' Jane said as we began to coast along the open road in fifth gear. I heard the crinkling of plastic next to me as she opened up the pack of snakes. I looked over as she popped one into her mouth. They were the *Natural Confectionary Company* ones.

'The yellow ones are my favourite,' she said, biting one in half.

It sounded like a lie. Nobody liked the yellow ones. They were only just above the orange ones in the herpetological-confectionary hierarchy.

'Nobody likes the yellow ones.'

'Well, I do,' she responded, throwing the other half into her mouth. 'I love 'em.'

Traffic was pretty light and the drive passed easily as we chatted about nothing in particular. I liked Jane. She was easy-going, uncomplicated; we seemed to just click.

We turned onto a dusty, old dirt road that looked like the opener of a scene from *The Deliverance*. She pointed at a house toward the end of the street, and I had to double check it was the right one. It was an old weatherboard house in need of much love. The boards were split and grey from the heat, and the white paint had all but peeled off. The front yard was thick with weeds and grass growing to waist-height.

'This is me,' she said, leaning in for a kiss on the cheek. I couldn't believe she lived in such a dump.

'Is there anything I can do for you?' I said dumbly. I felt as though I ought to be collecting canned foods for her and her family. She just looked at me funny and opened the door. Getting out, she shut the van door firmly behind herself, turning to lean in through the open window.

'Here. You can keep 'em,' she said, throwing me her scrunched-up knickers. 'They did look better on you anyway.'

I sincerely doubted that.

She turned and headed down a narrow gravel pathway that cut its way through the overgrown jungle of a front yard. I hung the knickers from my rear-view mirror. I'm not sure why.

When I finally got back into reality, my phone blew up. I had a shit-ton of missed calls from Jake. I tried to ring him back, but his incoming call cut over the top of mine.

'Hi mate,' I said. 'What's up?'

'Five million, that's what's up!' he yelled down the line. 'Get yourself dressed in something nice, we're on The Project tonight.'

Five million. Jesus Christ.

'What project?' I asked.

'*The* Project,' he replied. 'Like, formerly *The 7pm Project,* now just *The Project* but everyone still calls it *The 7pm Project.* That project.'

Holy shit.

I put my foot down and punched it all the way home. I think I got back in half the time. At the apartment I started going through all of my stuff, looking for things to wear. It was all rubbish. It was only two o'clock, so I still had plenty of time to go and get something else to wear. We weren't *shooting*, as Jake had said, till seven o'clock. I'd expected we would be going into some studio in the city, but Jake said they were just going to cut to us live at the apartment. I wasn't sure if that would be cool with the A.C. Program's guidelines, but Jake's place was off-limits to me, so we had no other option. I hadn't told Mel yet.

I got back in the van and shot down to the shops. I figured I'd get some really nice pants and a really nice top from *Jay Jays*, something that said *professional*. I got some really cool whitewashed-denim jeans, tailored with rips in the knees, and a t-shirt that had a picture of a cartoon dog that had been run over, with the word 'bugger' written underneath it. By the time I'd finalised my selection and paid, it was around 3.30. I was feeling pretty nervous.

Jake had once told me that if you have to do something that scares you, you should have a wank first. He'd told me that before exams when we were in school, and I'd performed spectacularly poorly. I'd definitely been more relaxed, though. I decided it would probably be a good idea if I got back to the apartment and had a quick wank before we started shooting, just to calm me down a bit. On the way back to the van, I got a call from Jake.

'Yello?'

'Where are you?' He said.

'Just picked out some new threads,' I told him.

'We can't get in. Everyone is waiting.'

'What do you mean? We've got like 4 hours.'

'They need to set up, you dickhead. It's not just some dude with a camcorder walking in and shooting us. There are lights and audio things to do.' He sounded annoyed. How was I to know? I'd never been *shot* before.

'Well, I'm on my way back anyhow,' I told him. 'I'll be there in fifteen.'

I got back to the apartment and there was a big white truck blocking the drive. *Studio Ten*, it said on the side. I parked on the street and went up. It was bedlam. There were people everywhere, mostly dressed in black, and at least half of them wheeling trolleys with black and silver boxes on them. I let them in and they immediately started moving shit around, like a frenzied collection of nosey ants. They unplugged appliances and our TV, making room for their own equipment to plug in. Furniture was dragged into the kitchen to make room for their lighting stand, which faced toward the bare wall next to the T.V.

Two guys started hammering nails into the top of the wall, to which they attached a rolled-up green-screen.

'I'm not sure if you're allowed to do that,' I said to them, but before I had a chance to say any more an arm linked through mine and a woman steered me toward the kitchen.

'It'll be fine,' she said, 'I've already cleared it with your partner.' Jake waved at me from the balcony.

'Right.' I said.

I looked at the woman. She had a flatcap on and round sunglasses with yellow lenses. Her hair was tied back in a pony-tail. She looked as though she'd accidentally wandered out of a Jazz-club.

'I'm Amanda,' Amanda said, shaking my hand. 'I'll be running things. If you have any problems or questions, see me first.' She handed me some pieces of paper, stapled at the top corner.

'Here is a copy of the script. It's not word for word, but it gives you a rough idea of the way the interview will go. I suggest you familiarise yourself with it, but don't think too hard on it. We want your answers to come across natural, like a conversation.' She spoke really fast. I found it difficult to keep up. My eyes were so busy with all the ants running around my apartment setting up their T.V equipment. The place was nearly unrecognisable. I just nodded along as she spoke.

'Hair and makeup is at six-thirty, so you look fresh, and Jodie from wardrobe will be here in half an hour to sort you out,' she said, looking me up and down.

'That's okay,' I told her, 'I've just bought these.' I indicated my cool new outfit. Amanda frowned.

'Jodie from wardrobe will be here in half an hour,' she said again, decisively.

There was too much going on, and I was feeling pretty overwhelmed. I went out and stood next to Jake on the balcony. He was smoking a joint.

'I told you they'd start calling,' he said.

I took the joint out of his hand and had a small drag. It was no wank, but it would have to do.

'What happened to your table?' He asked, looking down at the broken outdoor setting. It seemed like ages ago now.

'Long story,' I told him. 'Good story, but long story.' I thought about Jane's breasts. They were magnificent. I took another drag on the joint.

Half an hour passed by quickly, and Jake and I were interrupted by an abrupt rapping on the glass. A woman with wild orange hair that shot out in untamed curls stood on the other side of the door. She pointed at Jake and curled her finger toward herself, beckoning him to come inside. He sat the cigarette he'd started smoking on the railing and obliged.

He was gone for about fifteen, maybe twenty minutes. When he returned, he was wearing a navy suit-jacket casually unbuttoned over a plain white t-shirt, brown pants, and boat shoes. A pair of gold-rimmed aviator sunglasses hung from the neck of his t-shirt. It had to be said, he looked fantastic. He didn't look like Jake, but he looked fantastic.

'You're up next, mate,' he said, pointing inside. 'She's set up in the bedroom.'

Mel would've been fuming if she knew that her bedroom had been taken over by a film crew. I'd give her the heads-up when I got the chance. I followed Jake's direction and went inside to the makeshift dressing room. The wild-haired woman introduced herself as Jodie *from wardrobe.* She had a range of outfits for me to try on, laid out on the bed. I explained to her that I'd just been shopping, so there was really no need. She eyed me up and down, responding only with 'Mhmm.' She handed me a light shirt with tiny flowers all over it. 'Try this on.'

'I really don't want to,' I told her. I was already comfortable in what I was wearing. She pushed, and I refused once more. I hadn't spent fifteen dollars on a t-shirt not to wear it. When it became clear to her that I wasn't in the mood to negotiate, she radioed Amanda, and the production manager appeared in the room almost instantly.

There was a tense back-and-forth between me and Amanda, with Jodie throwing her own opinion in the mix throughout. They eventually gave in and let me wear the *Bugger* t-shirt, so long as I agreed to wear their stupid Fedora hat, as well. I begrudgingly accepted their terms. I couldn't see what the big deal was with what I was wearing. It was a nice shirt.

The afternoon flashed by in the blink of an eye, and before I knew it, I was next to Jake in the kitchen having my makeup finished off. We were rushed over to some chairs set up in front of the green-screen. Amanda counted us in.

'Five, four...' The rest of the countdown was non-verbal. I guess it's a *shoot* thing. Amanda held up three fingers, and silently mouthed the word 'Three', then two fingers, one.

'And joining us from their home in Clayton are Dan and Jake, creators of the viral sensation...Well, I can't even say the name of your video!' It was the cheery voice of Carrie Bickmore, appearing on a tiny T.V. screen in front of us.

Jake and I waved back and smiled dumbly.

'Hi,' Jake said.

'Hi,' I followed.

We'd never been on television before. I hoped it wasn't obvious.

'Hi guys!' It was Carrie again. 'So, you two are the creators of the viral video, let's call it, *How To* Blank *A Cantaloupe.* I'm sure our viewers at home can, well, fill in the blanks!'

She was very bubbly. There was a clip from our video playing in the background, me in my undies, putting a cantaloupe on the benchtop.

'So, tell us guys, what gave you the idea for your video?' Said Carrie, tactfully evading the offensive title.

I stared blankly into the camera. I had no idea what to say.

'Well, it was Dan's idea actually,' Jakes voice piped up from beside me. 'We were just talking about how so many people had found success from posting instructional videos on Youtube, and he came up with the idea for *How to...blank... a cantaloupe.'*

'Hi guys, big fan here,' came the distinct, croaky, sometimes-deep-sometimes-high, maybe-one-ball-dropped-and-the-other-one-didn't voice of Peter Hellier. 'I just wanted to say thank you. Thank you for answering the question men have been asking for decades, maybe centuries: How do you blank a cantaloupe? I've often wondered to myself, whilst strolling down through the fresh fruit section of Woolies, how exactly do I blank a cantaloupe?' He was having a bit of fun. It got a good laugh from the audience. 'Seriously though,' he finished, 'I think you two are geniuses.' Jake laughed along with him and said thanks.

'Thanks.' I heard the word leave my mouth but wasn't sure I'd created it.

'You know what, I'm actually not so sure,' came a third voice. It was Waleed Aly, another panellist on the show, known for his persistence and hard questions. 'What about the moral implications?' He asked, staring down the barrel of the camera, his dark eyebrows like Michelangelo's *The Creation of Adam,* painted across the ceiling of the Sistine Chapel; perpetually reaching out to touch tips with one another, but never quite making it. Struggling, as if being held apart by some unknown cosmic force, or rigorous morning routine.

'I'm not sure what you mean,' Jake responded.

'Well, it's all well and good to make a video for a laugh, and to turn a profit, but YouTube is an all-age platform. What about the children who might view this video and think, okay, that's what I do with my fruit now, this must be okay. And what about the parents of those children, and the impact this will have on families—have you even considered that?'

I unfolded the piece of paper in my lap. He wasn't sticking to the script at all.

'And furthermore, what about things such as food wastage? In a world that is striving to be more environmentally conscious, you encourage people to turn perfectly good food into waste, instead favouring the self-indulgent pursuit of carnal gratification.' It was a bloodbath, but he hadn't finished yet.

'Is this just another case of Gen-Y-ers taking the easy road and making some bold, outrageous, *offensive* video for a few minutes of internet fame and a bit of cash? I mean, come on guys, don't you have more productive things to be doing with your time?'

There was silence.

'Dan? We haven't heard from you yet. What have you got to say?' Said Ali, his dark eyes boring into the lens.

I heard myself answer.

'You're a fucking douchebag,' I said.

The shocked face of Carrie Bickmore appeared on the small television in front of us. Amanda looked furious.

'Ah, well. That was unexpected!' said Carrie. 'Moving on to other news, a woman who makes tiny wheelchairs, specifically for chickens, will be joining us on the other side of this break. Don't go away!'

'What were you thinking?' came Amanda's voice from the right of me as she stormed through the makeshift set.

'You were specifically instructed not to swear.'

Jake just looked at me.

'What the hell is all of this?' A voice at the door. I looked over. *Shit.* It was Mel; she didn't look happy.

'We are not supposed to have multiple guests in our apartment. It's breaking the rules of the program.'

'She's right,' I heard myself say. 'You're gonna have to get out.' Nobody moved. 'Come on,' I said, clapping my hands, 'Move it. Get out of here!'

It took a while, but they scrambled all of their shit together and got out whilst Jake spoke to Amanda in the hallway. Her arms were shooting out in all sorts of directions as she spoke to him, before storming off down the corridor into the stairwell. Jake came back in.

'So, we're not getting paid,' he said.

I'd expected as much.

'He *was* being a bit of a douchebag,' Jake said, smiling.

Douchebag. It was a good word. Not one that I would typically use often; in fact, I'm not even sure I'd used the word since the early 2000s, but it so succinctly summed up what I was trying to say—with the added tang of *fucking.*

Fucking douchebag.

I wonder if they would have dumped us if I had have just called him a douchebag, and left the fucking out of it. I guess we'll never know. Truthfully, I didn't think Waleed was a douchebag most of the time. I generally liked him. I usually agreed with what he had to say, and, for the majority of the time, he had some pretty worthwhile opinions, but when he stared down the barrel of the camera and started getting into us, I couldn't think of anything else to say. He was being a total douchebag.

Jake and Mel were talking in the kitchen. Everyone else had left.

'You guys were on *The Project?*' she was saying.

'For all of two minutes,' Jake replied, 'before old mate bigmouth over here, who hadn't said a word through the whole interview, arks up and calls Waleed a douchebag!' He was laughing, but I could tell he was a little disappointed. It was really the first time we'd had equal recognition for the video, and I know Jake would have been dying for the opportunity to get his face out there.

'I love Waleed!' Mel was saying. 'Why did you call him a douchebag?'

I walked past her and got a beer out of the fridge.

'Because he was being one.' I said, and went out onto the balcony. I opened the beer and took a sip. My phone dinged.

I unlocked it.

Facebook notification.

I was one of the few people I knew who wasn't completely absorbed by Facebook. It wasn't a big part of my day-to-day life. Truly, I could take it or leave it. I hardly ever posted on it, and I'd often go weeks at a time without thinking about it. It looked like I had a bit of a backlog: nineteen new notifications and twenty-seven friend requests.

I opened one of them up. A friend request from a man named Mark Hardman. I didn't know any Mark Hardmans. I don't even think I knew any Marks. I used to know a Mark when I was in primary school. He came over to my house one day and ate all of our toothpaste; it was bubblegum flavoured. I don't think this was him, though. Out of all the Marks in all the world, he was the only one I'd ever known, and I didn't know him anymore, and his last name wasn't Hardman. It was Campbell. And I didn't remember Mark Campbell having a small swastika tattooed between his eyebrows back in grade four, but hey, people change. I still don't think it was him though. I hit the 'Decline' option.

Maybe it was harsh of me. Perhaps Mark Hardman was a really nice guy. Perhaps we could have been friends. His tattoo selections stacked the odds heavily against him; however, I felt a little guilty declining the possibility of growing a friendship with Mark Hardman solely on face-value. But when your face, and your values, are inked permanently with that off-green tattoo colour that would have once been black, boldly displaying one of the most widely recognisable, albeit crudely-drawn, anti-Semitic emblems of history, chances are you are not going to be everyone's cup of tea. He probably did it himself. Given the unsteady lines, I'd say that was a fair and reasonable deduction. Maybe he actually was a nice guy, and he'd tried to brand himself with the Buddhist symbol that the Germans had reversed to become the Nazi Swastika. Maybe he had tried to do that, but he'd been looking into a mirror whilst doing it and ended up looking like a Neo-Nazi skinhead. Perhaps I'd gotten the situation all wrong, and his head was shaved down to the scalp because he was a Buddhist monk, not a fascist.

I went back into his profile and scrolled through his photos. The word *God* underneath an image of Hitler wasn't doing him any favours. I stuck with my decision and moved on. Another friend request: this one was from a man named Malcolm, with no last name. He didn't have a picture of himself on his profile, just a sign that had been altered to read 'Black lives *don't* matter.'

Jesus.

I flicked through the rest of the requests. They were much the same. I called Jake outside.

'Did you just get an invite to join *The Real Nationalists* on Facebook?' He said as he opened the door. I had.

'I think people liked what you said about Waleed.'

'Oh, for fuck's sake. I called him a douchebag because he was being a douchebag, not because he's black, or...brown. In this day and age, can't you call someone with dark skin a douchebag without being accused of racial implications?'

'I don't think anyone has called you racist,' said Jake, scrolling through his Facebook feed.

'No-one has called me racist, but racists are calling me friend, and that's just as bad,' I told him. I do not like being associated with the far-right, *fuck off, we're full,* breed of Australians.

I legitimately had a friend request from Pauline Hanson. Shit the bed.

I closed my phone. I didn't want to look at it anymore. I took a long draught of my beer and tried to relax. Jake's phone rang and he went inside to take the call, passing Mel on the way in.

'I'm going to bed,' she said, 'I haven't been feeling well all day. Can you make sure he goes home tonight? I really don't want to get kicked out.'

I told her he'd be gone soon.

'We've got an interview with *Triple J* in the morning,' Jake said, smiling from ear-to-ear. He'd just come back onto the balcony. I was dumbfounded. After that train-wreck of a TV appearance, one of my favourite radio stations still wanted to speak to us.

'I guess if people didn't know who we were before tonight, they definitely do now.'

Chapter Twenty

I woke up the next day and my phone had blown up. Not literally, like Samsungs occasionally did, but figuratively, like iPhones didn't. I had over a thousand friend requests and a whole bunch more notifications. It was mental.

Jake arrived out the front and tooted his horn. I met him on the street and we got into my van. I always preferred to drive, never really knowing what level of stoned Jake might be at any given time. I'd decided to give the *Bugger* shirt another run, since it had really missed out on its day in the sun yesterday. We got to the radio studio twenty minutes early, found a park and went in. After signing a couple of forms on arrival, we were directed in to a waiting area.

'Are we allowed to swear?' I asked the woman at the reception.

'Try to avoid the C's,' she said to me, smiling. 'Douchebag is fine.'

I didn't know why *Triple J* was allowed to air profanities and commercial radio stations weren't. I guessed it was because they didn't have to worry about upsetting companies advertising in the breaks like the commercial ones did.

The actual *Triple J* studios are in Sydney, but through the magic of radio, we were connected to *Breakfast with Ben and Liam* from the ABC Melbourne studio. It was just us in the room, and a dude who made sure the mics were working.

The interview went well. Much better than *The Project.* It was over pretty quickly, and we laughed the whole way through it. I left with a happy heart. There was no way I'd be misconstrued by *The Oz Patriots* group this time.

After the interview with Triple J, I received a strange phone call. I was waiting for Jake to finish taking a shit so we could leave the studio, when my phone rang. I didn't recognise the number, but I hit 'Accept' and put it to my ear. I didn't even have a chance to say hello before the voice on the other end started talking.

'Dan! Theodore Schilling here, but you can call me Ted. I'm about to make you an offer you can't refuse,' he said in a strong voice that commanded attention, 'are you familiar with *Ted's Melons?*'

'Yes,' I said. Everyone knew Ted's Melons. He was all over the T.V., the radio, and had a few well-placed billboards too. Ted's Melons was an absolute institution.

If there's a story that's worth the tellin',

It's the one about the humble melon.

Why not ask my wife Helen?

She'll say, 'Get your hands on big Ted's Melons!'

The jingle was catchy, and Ted was an out-and-out caricature of a man. Dressed like a 1930s oil tycoon, complete with the big white cowboy hat and boots, he would dance around the T.V. screen with a melon under each arm. Of course I knew *Ted's Melons.*

'I hope you're in the mood for making money,' he went on, 'How does eight hundred sound?'

'For doing what, exactly?' I asked. Jake usually handled the money side of things, so I wasn't sure whether eight hundred dollars was good money or bad money.

'A photoshoot. One day. We want you to become the new face of *Ted's Melons.*'

'I'd have to talk to Jake about it,' I told him, 'he normally handles the money. And eight hundred does seem a little low if you want me to be the face of something.'

'You are a hard businessman,' said the oil-tycoon doppleganger. 'I like that. Look, I'll make you another offer, but only because I think your video is hilarious, and we've already seen a fifteen per cent spike in cantaloupe sales since your video was released. I can go as high as eight-hundred-and-fifty-thousand, but not a penny more. What do you say?'

Eight-hundred-and-fifty *thousand.*

He'd been talking in *thousands.*

I accepted his offer right away.

How To Fuck a Cantaloupe gained traction fast. The next few weeks were filled with interview after interview. Jake was already talking about making a sequel.

'Maybe one for the ladies?' he said. '*Carving Cocks from Cantaloupes.*'

He really liked the cantaloupe theme.

'We could call it *Cockmelon*, for short,' He beamed.

I decided not to tell him about the *Ted's Melons* deal. Ted had made it clear over the phone that he would only be requiring *me* for the job, so I made the call that it'd just be unnecessary to cut Jake in on the contract. I was the face, anyway; and besides, he was already making good money from all of the interviews, of which there was an abundance.

The video was going gangbusters. Our personal Facebook pages, as well as the dedicated H.T.F.A.C page Jake had set up, were swamped daily with messages of praise and appreciation. Jake said it would be a good idea to *expand our platforms*. He uploaded the video to Instagram, where he told me our *hashtag* was *trending*. He may as well have been speaking German, for all I understood of it.

I was yet to confirm it, but I'd heard on the grapevine that *Club-X* even had to open up a fresh produce section in some of their stores to keep up with demand. We had developed an intense following. People loved us. It was becoming more and more difficult to walk the streets without being mobbed. The public couldn't get enough.

However, for every brilliant idea, there is going to be a small minority that are offended. As it turned out, not everybody was thrilled with our video, and our minority was very vocal.

I awoke early one morning and made plans with Jenny to go down to the local café I'd discovered in recent weeks. We were going to grab some breakfast and head out to the beach before it got too crowded. The weather had been pretty warm over the last week, and it was set to hit high-thirties again. A day down at the foreshore would be perfect. I pulled up in front of the dingey-looking cafe and went in. It wasn't much to look at, and calling it a café was probably a bit generous, but they did a half-decent bacon and egg roll, so that was something. I liked the place because it was one of the few quiet havens left in my manic life. If the old Polish women running the place knew about the cantaloupe video, they didn't let on.

I quietly deliberated whether I was going to get a strawberry or chocolate Big M from the fridge while I waited for my brekkie-roll to be made. Easily bypassing *Egg-Flip*, I settled for the chocolate flavoured milk drink. I'd made the mistake of buying an Egg-Flip Big M once before, and like putting your penis in the opening of a soft-drink can, it was a mistake you only made once.

Jenny sent me a text saying she was running a bit behind, so I was in no rush. She would meet me at the café, then we would go from there to the beach. I let my eyes wander absently around the joint. The black and white linoleum tiles were beginning to wear in the doorway, and one of the fluorescent lights in the fridge flickered incessantly. Next to the fridge was a black wire stand with newspapers in it. I picked one up. The story on the front was about the impending birth of yet another Royal Baby. I don't know why people get so excited about royal babies. With the cloudy gene-pool it's coming from, it's just going to look like a cabbage anyway.

Underneath the cabbage-baby-to-be speculation, there was a black banner with big white letters that read: *How To F*ck A Cantaloupe—is it really a laughing matter?*

I opened the paper to page three, and there, spread across half a page was my head, and the title of the article: *How To Rape A Cantaloupe: just another man's conquest of sexual non-consent.*

I couldn't get past the heading.

You have to be shitting me.

#howtofuckacantaloupe

I quickly folded the paper in half and paid for it, along with my roll and Big M. I thanked the lady behind the counter and left. Back in the van, I flipped the paper open and began to read over the article.

What may seem a harmless video at first, tells a much darker tale of man's views of women as nothing more than a sexual object.

What the actual fuck? There were no women in the video whatsoever. I read on.

On the surface, the video may appear to be just a man giving an instructional film on the lesser-known pleasures of rockmelon, but when you begin to analyse the footage, and the subtext of the video, it is clear that the melon is just a substitute for a woman.

She was half-right.

And if we take this knowledge, and apply it to the video, watching it back without the fog before our eyes, what does Dan Savage do to the melon, to the woman? He puts a power-tool to her. He drills a hole inside of her, shaping her into something to suit his purpose, forcing her to become something else, the same way men have been forcing women to be something other than themselves for centuries; the cleaner, the carer, the painted doll.

Oh God.

And where does consent come into it? Not important, apparently, in Dan Savage's eyes. In a world where we are taught that no means no, what of the sexual partners who can't vocalise 'no'? What then? I watch the video once more, and I don't hear 'No', but I certainly don't hear a 'Yes'. We should be practicing enthusiastic consent, not absence of objection; and in Dan Savage's film, the silence is deafening, and so is the truth: the only one enjoying themselves in this video is Dan.

I swallowed a lump in my throat. It was hard-hitting stuff. I thought of the last line in the article: 'The only one enjoying themselves in this video is Dan.'

I *was* the only one in the video, *wasn't I*?

I'd begun to question myself. I had to sip my Big M to calm me down. It was delicious.

WHACK! A hand slapped the driver's window hard, and I just about jumped out of my skin. I spilled some of my chocolate milk in my lap.

It was Jenny.

'You scared the living shit out of me.'

She just laughed and jogged around to the passenger door. I leant across and opened it from the inside. The passenger door, notorious for playing up, had decided recently that its handle on the outside would now be purely decorative. I tucked the newspaper underneath an old jacket as she leant in the door, throwing a beach towel in the footwell.

'I'm just gonna grab a coffee. You want anything?'

I smiled and held up my brekkie roll. 'I'm good, thanks.'

I watched her as she walked over to the café. She was beautiful.

My head still spinning from the article, I tried to wrap myself around the situation. It was one of the first real negative pieces of feedback I'd received since we launched the video. I wasn't sure how to take it. I was pretty certain it was all bullshit and there was nothing to it, but the article had been so well-written, and so convincing, that I wondered if maybe I *was* just another man that was part of the problem.

I started the van as Jenny got in.

'You alright?' she asked. 'You look a bit off.'

'Fine,' I replied, looking over at her, mustering my most convincing smile. She looked radiant. She had on some oversized sunglasses and a big floppy hat. Underneath her loose-fitting singlet I could see the edge of her red bikini top.

'Fuck,' I said.

'What?'

'Forgot my bathers.' *What a dickhead.*

'How'd you manage that?' she asked. I didn't know. I was wearing denim shorts. They'd be no good for swimming. 'Can't you just go in your undies?'

Normally that would be fine, but it was washing day, so I wasn't even wearing any. Under my ripped denim shorts, I was flying commando. I told Jenny and she laughed.

'We'll have to go past the apartment,' I told her, pulling out of the carpark. I drove back to the apartment. Jenny made light chit-chat about McCormack's, and I tried to pay attention, but the newspaper article was still niggling at the back of my mind. I hardly touched the bacon and egg roll on the way.

When I pulled into the driveway, there was an explosion on the van's windscreen. A big, white, liquid explosion. Jenny gasped in shock.

'Hey!' I cried, leaning out the window.

I was met by the image of three women with aggressive haircuts standing in front of my van; one of them was holding a picket-sign, but it was facing the other way and I couldn't read it. I saw the cause of the explosion, lying just on the windscreen, balanced precariously on the wipers. A now-empty Egg-Flip Big M carton. As the milk cleared on the glass, I saw the green hair of the woman at the head of the pack come into focus. I wasn't sure if she had thrown the drink *at* me, or if she was simply trying to get it away from her lips as quickly as possible, and I'd just pulled into the firing-line. I flicked the wipers on, and her face became clear.

She was livid.

I couldn't blame her, they were disgusting.

'It's okay,' I said, leaning out the window again. 'Don't worry about it. I know, they are disgusting.'

Egg-Flip really did suck.

#howtofuckacantaloupe

The woman with the picket-sign at the back spun her sign to face me and I realised I'd misread the situation. It said: *Cantaloupes Can't Consent.* And as a footnote: *We love Egg-Flip Big M's.* What kind of sick breed of human was I dealing with?

'What's going on?' Jenny said to me. 'What's this all about?'

'This,' I said, and handed her the newspaper. 'Wait here,' I told her, getting out of the car. I approached the women slowly, my hands in the air.

'Look. This has all been a big misunderstanding,' I said, 'I just made a video for a laugh. I'm not a rapist.'

'Rapist!' Came the fierce response, but not from any of the three women before me. It came from a balcony near the top of the building.

I looked up.

'Rapist!' came the cry again. It was Mel. She was leaning over the railing of the balcony above us, waving something in her hand. 'You raped me! You are a rapist!'

'Excuse me,' I said, stepping gingerly around the very unhappy looking women. Once past them I ran up to the building's entrance, saying a quick 'Hi' to Frank on my way through, then ran all the way up to the apartment. I opened the door and poked my head around the corner. I pulled it back just in time to avoid being hit by a large ceramic pot. It smashed against the edge of the doorframe.

'Mel, hi. It's me,' I tried, cracking the door slightly.

There was another great *SMASH* on the back of the door. She knew who it was.

'What's going on?' Jenny appeared beside me.

'I have absolutely no idea. She's lost her mind,' I said to her.

'What's going on, Mel?' I called out through the crack in the door.

'You raped me!' she screamed from inside the apartment. 'You raped me! You are a rapist!'

'I'm not a rapist,' I told her. 'I promise.'

If she did think I was a rapist, I doubt a promise from me would mean a great deal. I opened the door a little more. A coffee mug appeared in front of my head. It was upside-down and in the air. It was travelling very quickly. Luckily, this one didn't shatter, because the impact of the throw was cushioned by my face. It hurt. A lot.

I stumbled through the door, seeing stars, and put the coffee mug on the back of the couch. I'd somehow managed to catch it before it hit the ground. Jenny rushed to my side and held my arm, steadying me. The volley of crockery had stopped with the introduction of a direct hit. A look of shock was plastered across Mel's face. I don't know what outcome she had been hoping to achieve from hurling kitchenware at me, but she seemed surprised by the result.

She threw something else at me. I flinched as it bounced off my chest and dropped to the floor, much lighter than a coffee mug. I looked down. It was a pregnancy test. Two blue lines were visible through a small window on the side. I didn't know what the symbols on a pregnancy tester typically meant, but from the drama she was creating, I assumed two blue lines meant *pregnant.*

'What's this?' I said dumbly.

'I'm pregnant!' she said. 'It's yours—you raped me!'

'You raped her?' Jenny asked, taking a step away from me.

'I didn't rape her,' I replied, turning to Mel, 'I didn't rape you.' If I did, I didn't remember it, and I was pretty sure rapists would remember raping. 'I definitely didn't rape you,' I reiterated.

'You must have,' she said, arms folded. Her voice had dropped a few decibels now.

My head was throbbing, but I was thankful nothing else was being thrown at me. I went to the fridge and got a bag of frozen Potato Gems out of the freezer, icing my head with it. Jenny hovered in the doorway, visibly conflicted as to whether she should comfort the potential rapist or console the potential victim.

'Okay,' I said, gathering my thoughts. 'When did I rape you?' I held the Gems to my forehead. It was an unusual question.

'You tell me,' she said.

'You don't remember being raped?' Jenny asked her.

Being a forgetful rapist was one thing, but I was pretty sure being raped was something a person would remember.

'You must have done it while I was asleep.'

'Wouldn't you have woken up?' I asked.

'Gently,' she said, looking away.

'Huh?'

'You raped me gently. You must have gently raped me.'

I wasn't sure you could gently rape someone.

'Why do you think it was me?'

'It couldn't have been anyone else,' she said, still looking away out the window.

'Why not?'

She said something quietly, and I couldn't make it out.

'Sorry?'

'I'm a VIRGIN!' she said. 'I *was* a virgin, until you raped me. Gently. And it couldn't have been anyone else because I haven't shared a house or fallen asleep near anyone else in the past month. I haven't lived with any boys ever. Except my dad, and he wouldn't do it because he's a minister!'

It was a lot to take in.

'Maybe it's a bad test?' Jenny offered.

Mel told me to go in the bathroom. I opened the door and looked in.

'I did four of them.'

So she had. There were four pregnancy tests face-up on the bathroom vanity, all displaying their own individual 'positive' symbols.

I was pretty sure I hadn't raped her.

It felt nice to be safely in a different room to Mel, free from the fear of flying crockery. I rested my back against the tiled wall. It felt cool on my skin. I looked absently around the room, trying to make sense of it. My heart stopped. I left the bathroom and came face-to-face with Mel in the loungeroom.

'I have to go,' I said, turning and moved quickly past Jenny and out the apartment door. Mel yelled after me, but I threw myself into the stairwell, taking the steps three at a time. I pulled my phone out of my pocket as I got down to the bottom floor and went outside.

The group of women picketing in the driveway had doubled. They saw me and started heading my way. I ducked back inside. I wasn't sure where to go. A door marked 'maintenance' appeared in front of me, so I took it, pulling the door shut behind me. The tiny room was full of mops and chemical drums.

Jake answered his phone on the third ring.

'Eight-point-five million,' he said straight up.

'Something bad has happened,' I said down the phone.

'It's never good news when you call, is it?'

'I wanked into her bodywash,' I said.

'Whose?'

'Who do you think? Mel's. I wanked into her bodywash.'

'Priceless!' he laughed into the phone.

'No, not priceless. Not priceless at all. She's fucking pregnant.'

'I don't think it works like that. I don't think that's possible.'

'I didn't think it was possible either, but what do you know? She's pregnant! She's got an actual human baby in her and she's pretty sure it's mine!'

'How deep was she washing?' Jake asked. I didn't respond. He seemed to be missing the point. 'When did you do it?' he asked. The scene replayed in my head.

I've just gotten in from the pub. Blind. Drunk. I've been out with Jake, drowning my sorrows. It is the night Mel skewered Stephen with a fondue fork, and the wound is still raw. The two small indentations in the plasterboard behind the kitchen table silently taunt me.

My memory skips ahead.

A blurry flash of me falling against the bathroom basin. Skincare products skittle onto the floor. Covered in my own piss, I head for the shower. Finally at the right temperature, warm water cascades down my back. An idea forms.

'Just a minute,' I call back, unscrewing the pump-nozzle on the bodywash.

It was a vague, drunken memory, but it had definitely happened. I felt sick. *What the fuck was I going to do?*

I sat down on a twenty-litre drum of bleach and tried to think my way out of it. I came up with nothing. I sat there,

defeated, for I don't know how long. I couldn't really go anywhere
else. With the aggressive cantaloupe sympathisers baying at the
door, and the end-result of the worst decision I've ever made
waiting for me upstairs, I stayed put on my bleach-drum, feeling
sorry for myself.

My life was over.

Finally, after what could have been hours, I summoned the
energy to act. I'm not proud of what I did. When I look back on it
now, there is not a single moment I regret more in my life; I was
cowardice and solipsism made flesh.

I ran.

There was a back entrance on the opposite side of the
building from where the protesters were. It was a fire-exit and
wasn't accessible from the outside. I'd seen it when I was
exploring the building on one of the first nights Mel and I had
been living together. At the time, it was a good excuse to get
away from her.

I ran headlong to the fire-exit, thinking of nothing else but
getting out of there. I slammed down the heel of my palm on the
bar that ran horizontally across the door, launching myself
outside. An alarm sounded immediately. It was deafening. I
ignored it and kept running. Tearing open the door of the van, I
threw myself in, stabbing the keys into the ignition. The engine
groaned and struggled to turn over.

'Come on!' I yelled at it, slamming my fists on the dash.

'There he is!' shouted an angry voice from nearby. I'd drawn the attention of the protesters. They ran toward the van, the green-haired one leading the charge. I turned the key some more, nearly snapping it off in the barrel. I could feel the metal begin to twist in my fingers as the engine finally coughed itself into life. The wheels spun through a cloud of blue smoke, the smell of burning rubber filling the air as I tore out of the driveway. Something hit the side of the van with a thud.

Another Egg-Flip, no doubt.

I was scared. Anxiety had taken up residence in my chest and was squeezing tightly. I didn't know where to go or what to do. I just drove. I'd made some pretty big mistakes in my life, but this was definitely the biggest. I don't even think I could classify it as a mistake. Certainly, the outcome wasn't intentional, but the act had been deliberate. *What the fuck is wrong with me?* I'd pretty much ruined Mel's life, and as much as I couldn't stand her most of the time, she was a good person. No-one deserved what was happening to her. I tried to push everything out of my brain, to think about something else. Anything else would do.

I turned the radio up loud. I didn't have a plan, and I wasn't sure where I was going, but after an hour of driving I ended up at Mum's house. I had no idea what I was going to say to her, but she was the only one I could think to turn to at this stage. I knocked on the door.

There was no indication that anyone was home. I was about to leave, when I heard the pantry door close in the kitchen. I knew that sound well. The doors were tall and the pantry was deep, and whenever someone closed one of the doors the soundwaves would ripple through the entire house like an atomic bomb.

I heard footsteps coming up the long hallway.

The door opened.

'Hi Mum,' I said. Tears welled up in her eyes and she threw her arms around me.

'Daniel! It's so good to see you.' She held me tight, then took a step back to assess me. 'Are you well?' she asked, looking me up and down.

'Can I stay here for a little while?' I asked.

She frowned.

'Why? What's happened?' she asked suspiciously. 'Are you in trouble? Oh! Did you have a fight with Christina?'

'What? No.' It *had* been a while. 'Actually, yes.' That would do for now.

'What happened?' she asked, her eyes wide with worry.

'I don't really want to talk about it. I just need somewhere to stay for a little while,' I said.

'Of course!' She smiled warmly and held me close again. 'I'm making sweet and sour chicken. Come in!' I went in.

'How've you been? You never come and visit your old mum anymore,' she said as she set a dish in front of me and kissed me on the cheek. God knows what she'd done to it, but whatever she'd set down on the table definitely wasn't sweet and sour chicken. She must have noticed the way I was looking at it. 'I didn't have any chicken,' she said. 'It's tuna.'

I poked the food with my fork. It looked like she'd made the sauce and thrown in some frozen vegies and noodles, then just cracked a couple of cans of tuna on top. 'Thanks Mum,' I said, taking a cautious mouthful.

'What is it?' she asked, watching me like a jacked-up pigeon.

'Just needs a little salt,' I replied, battling to swallow both the literal and figurative lumps in my throat. It was pretty bad.

I finished the bowl somehow, and we chatted idly. I tried my best to allow the dinner and small talk to take my mind off the events of the morning. It wasn't working very well. I felt my phone buzz in my pocket and excused myself from the table. I went to the toilet and unlocked the screen. It was a message from Jenny.

Whatever you've done, you need to come back and sort this out.

I dropped the phone into the bowl and closed the lid. I didn't think about it, I just did it. I wanted nothing more than to turn myself off for a while, and switch back on once all of this had blown over. I flushed the toilet and left the small room. Mum was standing in the hallway. It was a little bit sad, but she still kept a spare toothbrush for me just in case I ever came to visit. She handed it to me in its dark-green plastic case, along with a fresh tube of toothpaste. Its bristles were as straight as the day it left the factory.

'You can sleep in your old room tonight, if you like,' she said to me once I'd finished in the bathroom. 'It's a bit of a mess. If I'd have known you were coming...' She frown-smiled at me.

It wasn't really messy at all. It was Mum-messy. Her definition of 'a bit of a mess' was clean things out of place, whereas my definition was more along the lines of filthy things all over the place. She'd half-converted my old bedroom into a sewing room. She had her Singer set up on a laminex sewing-machine table as you walked in the door, with half-finished creations in a tidy pile next to it. Along the back wall of the bedroom, under the room's only window, was my old single bed, dressed with blue and white covers I remembered well.

I gave her a hug and went to bed.

A week passed and I spent my time cleaning up Mum's backyard, doing work in the garden in an attempt to keep my mind focused on things other than Mel. I'm a little ashamed to admit it, but it sort of worked. I managed to spend the majority of the week not thinking about her at all, and when I did think about her, I would set my attention to another area of the garden and focus my mind on that. The night-time was when the thoughts managed to creep in. When the work was done for the day and I was lying in bed with nothing else to do, that's when the guilt would worm its way back into my brain. When that happened, I would usually just masturbate. It's strange how men can shut of their brains and their emotions, and just not think when it comes to sex, or in this case, masturbation. I don't think women can do that. I think it's more emotional for them. When I would start to feel bad, I would have a wank, and everything would be fine so long as I fell asleep right afterward. If I stayed awake, the guilt would creep back in and I'd lay awake for hours. I suppose I used it as a sedative more than a distraction.

At this point, I was pretty sure I was a bad person. The Karmic Exchange was way out of balance, and with everything I'd caused, I didn't think the scales would ever be level again.

I'd sort of made a deal with myself that I wouldn't smoke any pot while I was at Mum's house, mostly because she was terrified of drugs, and it was a sure way to get me booted out. She didn't understand the inherent differences between illegal substances; she just classed them under the one nasty umbrella of *Drugs*. In her mind, pot was just as bad as heroin or ice. It was all *Drugs*. She used to tell me a story, when I was a teenager, of her friend's cousin who smoked pot one time and jumped off the garage roof to his death. I'm pretty sure that never happened, but you'd have a hard time convincing her of that.

I was going to break my rule.

The masturbation had started to become ineffective. I'd manage to switch off for fifteen minutes, but afterwards I wouldn't fall asleep. I would just lie there feeling guilty. The lingering, background guilt that I'd grown accustomed to having around was being amplified by the guilt of having masturbated to alleviate that initial guilt. The *guilt-ception* was too much. I figured a joint before bed would make sleep come a lot more easily.

Next morning, I went and visited an old high school friend, Al. That's who Jake got his pot from, and he was pretty reliable. I'd woken up pretty early, around eight o'clock. I waited until eleven before I left the house, as a courtesy. Typically, pot dealers weren't that readily available in the early hours.

I got to the old weatherboard house and climbed the four concrete steps to the porch that stuck out of the front door like a swollen tongue. I knocked at a tempo that said, *I'd like you to hear me, but I'm not being impatient.* Or at least that's what I hoped it said. Four firm knocks on the fly-screen door: Loud enough to be heard, but not aggressive.

There was movement inside. I heard a guitar fall over, and saw a figure enter the hallway. It was one of those fly-screen doors where they can see you from inside, but you can only just make out the rough outline of the person on the other side of the door, so you just stand there smiling awkwardly until they open it, not really knowing how long they've seen you for. The door opened.

'Oh, hey man!' said Al. He was wearing red velour pants, and not much else.

Al had dreadlocks past his shoulders and a bright smile that contrasted well against his tanned skin. He was one of the most genuinely friendly people I had ever met. His eyes gleamed with a brightness that I'd always wondered if he was born with, or if it was just the glassy glaze of being baked most of the time.

'Bring it in, brother,' he said, wrapping his arms around me. He was a big-time hugger. I remembered that now. He smelled of a not-unpleasant mixture of deodorant and light perspiration. Holding out an arm, he welcomed me into his home. It was tiny, but warm. The kitchen flowed around the corner into a small loungeroom with a futon, T.V. and a fish tank of bright, tropical-looking fish.

'Can I get you a cup of tea?' he called from the kitchen as I stared, transfixed, into the fish tank.

'Sure,' I said absently, as I watched a clownfish follow my finger along the glass.

'What sort?' he asked.

Al was a big tea man, as well as a hugger. I knew at the moment he would be looking through a large wooden box filled with hundreds of varieties of herbal and fruity teas.

'Surprise me.' I didn't really care, to be honest. I was much more interested in the crab that had just sidestepped out from behind a fake rock at the bottom of the tank. He snapped at a tiny, bright blue fish that swam within his strike zone, missing it by just millimetres. After some clanging around, followed by the rhythmic clink of teaspoon on china, Al returned to the room with two cups of tea. He offered one to me and I took a sip.

'It's pomegranate and jasmine,' he said, smiling. It was delicious. He sat down gently on the futon and looked up at me.

'I suppose you didn't come here for the tea?'

Hitting his fist firmly and familiarly on one corner of the coffee table, there was a faint *click* from inside it. The top raised up slightly from the base, like a push-to-open cupboard, and he lifted it upward. Propped open on wooden struts, the tabletop-lid now revealed a large hidden cavity inside. The entire coffee table had opened up like an old school desk, and inside were ten or so big bags of vacuum-sealed marijuana. It was a real sight to behold.

Each bag had a different stickered description on it. *Purple Haze, Webstock Jade, Acapulco, Jack the ripper.* Al took out a bag that had already been opened, and closed the secret coffee-table lid. He put the bag down on top and selected a lovely big nugget.

He dropped it into a table-mounted grinder, which looked pretty much the same as an antique coffee grinder but had a marijuana leaf stamped into the metal face. Turning the crank, the nugget was ground and dispensed into a small metal dish underneath, which Al slid out and held up for me to smell.

I took a whiff. It was dense and sweet, and familiar.

'You'll like this one,' he said, as he pulled his bong out from beside the couch. I recognised it immediately. It was a large, ceramic wizard that looked just like Gandalf from *Lord of the Rings.* You smoked out of a hole in the top of the wizard's hat, and the cone-piece was on the end of his staff, which he was slamming into the ground. It was Al's favourite bong, and he'd had it as long as I'd known him. He took a pinch from the metal dish and loaded up the bowl. He lit it and took a hit, then passed it over to me. I was a bit hesitant, because I only really wanted it for getting to sleep, and it had only just gone midday, if that. That, and I still had to drive home.

I figured a little bit wouldn't hurt. He passed me the lighter and I lit it up, inhaling deeply from Gandalf's head. I didn't feel anything for a minute, and then it hit me. It was like I'd been punched in the eyes by a tiny fist. A baby was massaging my brain. It was incredible. I could hear what numbers looked like. My hair was hot. Like Keanu Reeves on an acid trip, all I could manage to say was 'Whoa.'

Then it was gone. Like a salty wave had washed over my head and down my back, I felt normal again. I was still lightly stoned, but all of the heavenly sensations, borne straight from God's vagina, had washed away.

'It's called Golden Euphoria,' Al said, smiling over at me. 'It's pretty great.'

He weighed the pot and I paid him for it after he rolled it up in some tinfoil and sealed it in a zip-lock bag. He threw in a second bag containing a heavier strain, in case the *Golden Euph* didn't send me off.

I took one last look in the fish-tank as I got up to leave. The crab had successfully clamped down on one of the little blue fish and was working out his next move. Although I would have liked to, I couldn't watch it all day. I had a retaining wall waiting to be finished in Mum's backyard, and it wasn't going to build itself. Al snuck in one last hug while I said goodbye, and I turned to leave, exiting out the beaten-up screen door. I was looking down at the bag of pot as I climbed down the four steps from the porch, and nearly knocked over someone coming up the other way.

'Jake?' I said, after I just about walked through him. 'How are ya, man?'

He was eating a sausage roll. 'Where've you been?' he asked between chews. 'I've been trying to get on to you all week.'

'Oh, my phone, it's ah,' I thought about the toilet, 'broken.'

He stared at me, then looked away, breathing deeply through his nose. His head snapped back to me. 'When were you gonna tell me about Ted's Melons?' he asked, heatedly. The question caught me off guard.

'I, uh, didn't think it was important,' I replied.

'Not important? You didn't think it was important to maybe tell your best friend, and business partner, about a deal with Ted? Instead, I have to find out when I'm at the supermarket, and your head is dotted through the fresh produce section!'

Wow. Ted moved fast.

'Do you want to know what I was doing in the fresh produce section, Dan?'

'What were you doing in the fresh produce section, Jake?' I responded weakly.

'I was looking for ideas for our sequel!' He was fuming. His grip tightened on the sausage roll.

'I didn't think it was such a big deal,' I said. 'If I had've known you'd get so cut up about it, I would have told you.'

'I reckon I've got pretty good reason to be cut up about it.' He said. A vein pulsed in his forehead. 'Ted's Melon's are the biggest melon distributor in Victoria. Second largest in all of Australia.' He waved his sausage roll around dramatically, flakes of pastry fluttering to the ground. 'How much did he pay you?'

There it was. It was about the money.

'Were you going to cut me in any?' he asked.

'I knew you were going to have a problem with it. I signed the contract, and I knew you would find out eventually, and I knew you would have a problem with it. I knew you would have a problem with it, and I still signed. You know why? *Fuck it!* I thought, you've already made tens of thousands of dollars from the video and the interviews, and they were asking for me. Specifically. They only wanted me this time. So, I didn't tell you about it. They only wanted me. My head. It's *my* head Jake. You don't get to cash in on my head!' I was shouting now.

'But it was *our* idea. If it wasn't for me, no-one would ever have seen your head. Without me, you would never have made the video!'

I was getting pissed off. I ticked items off on my fingers. 'The cantaloupe was *my* idea. *I* am the focus of the video. It is *my* face that has been circulating the Internet. *I* am the one everybody recognises. You could have just as easily been replaced by a tripod, or a fucking selfie stick!' Jake looked shocked. I wasn't done yet. 'You uploaded a video to YouTube, whoop-dee-doo! There are ten-year-old kids who run YouTube accounts! '

I felt it before I realised what was happening. A hard, wet, warm smack in the eye. Jake had thrown his half-eaten sausage roll squarely into my left eye, and it had exploded across my face. I reeled back, shaking my head like a wild beast. Jake stood in the driveway, staring at me remorselessly. Before I knew what I was doing, I'd charged at him, my shoulder making good contact with the bottom of his rib cage as I tackled him into the wheelie bins at the edge of the driveway. Recycling spewed out across the drive. There was a smash of glass uncomfortably close, followed by severe pain in the side of my head. Jake had smashed a beer bottle on my ear. The pain was immense. My vision blurred, and a constant, high-pitched whine took over my senses.

I grabbed for his shirtfront and we rolled across the front yard. I tried to punch him in the face, but my mind and body were out of sync, and I never completed the fist. I just sort of slapped him in the forehead with a malformed fist. He made a noise that I'd only ever heard cows make, on my Uncle's farm. He was on top now, and return-served with a solid headbutt. I was sent into a spin.

A hand reached down out of nowhere and grabbed a hold of Jakes shoulder, pulling him back. It was Al, Gandalf-bong in hand.

'Whoa, hey! Guys, guys! Let's all just chill out.'

He pulled Jake off of me with a weird, calm strength. 'Just relax, my man. Chill. Good vibes.'

He went to hand the bong to Jake at the same time as Jake tore his arm free of Al's grip. His wild movement sent ceramic-Gandalf into a spin, flying out of the dealer's hand and into the air. There was a moment when time stopped, and Gandalf stared down at me from his mid-air suspension; then everything literally came crashing down.

#howtofuckacantaloupe

No one breathed. All eyes were locked on the pool of brown water and broken pottery that Gandalf had degenerated into. It's not often that I'm reminded of nineteenth century Norwegian Expressionist Edvard Munch, or his paint and pastel composition of *The Scream,* but that was the expression that had taken up occupancy on Al's face. It was twisted into an emotion somewhere between violent grief and organic fear.

There was a sudden shift, and the temporarily-lodging emotions were evicted from his face, to be replaced by pure, white-hot anger. All traces of the chilled-out stoner were gone, and a deep, animal noise was released from within him as he threw himself into Jake in a flurry of fingernails and fists. Jake was knocked off his feet and onto the ground as Al laid into him with everything he had. My head was still ringing from the bottle that had been smashed on it, and all I could do was watch as the scene played out before me. It was pretty full-on. Sometimes Jake was up, but most of the time it was Al who seemed to be winning the fight. The punches kept on coming relentlessly before each of them began to get worn out. Their tired bodies weren't able to muster any more throws. One arm would be raised, coming down in a slow, lethargic blow, followed by the other, returning in sloth-like retaliation. I took the slow-motion fight scene as an opportunity to crawl back to the van and lick my wounds. I tucked the bags of pot under my arm and commando-crawled over to the old Bedford. I got inside and leant forward heavily against the steering wheel as I clumsily tried to find the ignition with the key. Eventually, I found it, and the van coughed itself into life. I shifted into reverse and pulled out of Al's drive, my tyres squealing on the concrete. In a state of dazed confusion, I backed over his mailbox. I made a mental note to come back and fix it for him another day.

Not today.

The street disappeared in my side-mirrors.

Chapter Twenty-One

I pulled into the driveway of my family home and went inside. Mum popped her head out from one of the spare rooms that lined the hallway. A welcoming smile was wiped quickly off her face by horror.

'Oh Daniel!' she cried, rushing over to me. 'What's happened to you?'

'It's not important,' I said, pushing past her.

I just wanted to get in a hot shower and rinse the dried blood off the side of my head. I wasn't sure it was all mine. I took myself to the bathroom, fending off Mum's consoling attacks on the way. I closed the door and locked it behind me, falling back against it. Today was not a good day.

I turned on the water and watched the steam fill up the room. The mirror fogged up until I became an out-of-focus blur. I felt the temperature of the water. It was hot. Stepping into the shower, I watched the dried blood break down as it mixed with the water, running over my chest and down my legs in rivulets of browny-red. The side of my head stung to touch. I probably should have gotten stitches. Instead, I just winced and let the hot water unclump my matted hair, as it worked away at eroding the blood caked into it. I stood under the water until it went cold.

I retreated to my bedroom after half-heartedly drying off. Mum had moved the sewing machine into the lounge room when she realised my stay was going to be more than just a few days. She pretended not to be bothered by it.

I smoked a bit of Al's pot out of the bedroom window. The window was on one of those old-style winders, so I was able to lean my head out a little way. The effects took hold fairly quickly, and I flopped onto the bed, falling asleep on top of the doona. I slept all the way through to midway into the next morning. I dreamt about nothing.

A lawn-mower next-door ultimately broke the surface-tension of my resting conscious. I'd left the bedroom window open, and it sounded like it was right outside my room. I stepped into the living room, bleary-eyed. Mum was in the kitchen. *Right.* It must have been Wednesday. Mum never worked Wednesdays. Something smelled amazing.

'Morning, Buggo,' she said brightly.

That was a blast from the past. *Buggo.* She hadn't called me that in years. When I was about nine years old, my uncle had given me one of those green and clear plastic bug catchers. I'd wanted to take it everywhere I went, hence, *Buggo*. Butcher-boys were my favourite.

'What? Too old for Buggo?' she asked, when I didn't respond. I told her it was fine. 'Well, good. Cause I've made Buggo some breakfast. One or two?' She'd made pancakes. Big pancakes. I could take the piss out of Mum as much I wanted for her cooking, but the woman made good pancakes, no argument.

'Two, please.'

She handed me a plate with two big pancakes on it. I added butter and sugar, the only way I enjoyed them.

'A letter came for you this morning,' she said kindly, handing me a bright gold envelope. 'Looks fancy.'

My fingers ran over the raised monogram at the bottom corner of the envelope. 'Thanks,' I said, slipping it into my pocket.

'Not going to open it?' She looked a little disappointed.

'After breakfast,' I said, taking a bite of the pancake.

I scoffed down the rest of my breakfast and quickly thanked Mum before going back into my room. I tore the top edge of the envelope off and dropped it to the floor, pulling the letter out. The monogrammed *O&O* of the envelope floated down to the ground as my eyes locked on the first line of text.

Mr Savage,

It has been brought to our attention that you have entered into a financial contract with Mr Theodore Schilling of Ted's

Melons *on behalf of the How to Fuck a Cantaloupe Enterprise. O&O Law Firm has been engaged by Mr Jake Saunders to represent him in the matter of monies owing.*

As a co-founding member, Jake is entitled to fifty per cent of all decision-making involving the enterprise, as well as fifty per cent of any monies accrued on behalf of the business or any of its subsidiaries.

In light of this, it has been deemed that the only fair and satisfactory conclusion to this discrepancy is the remuneration of funds to Mr Saunders, amounting to the sum of four-hundred-and-twenty-five-thousand dollars, what is deemed to be his share of the Ted's Melons *deal.*

We at O&O Lawyers *believe it would be prudent for all parties involved if this matter were to be kept from the courtrooms, and an agreement reached through private settlement; however, it is our understanding that Mr Saunders is prepared to take a more public route if necessary.*

At the bottom of the letter was their stamp, the swirling O&O emblem. My stomach dropped out of my arse. *Half of my money.* I'd only just gotten it, and Jake wanted to take it away from me. Fuck, he moved quickly. At a moment where I'd crawled back into the safety of my Mum's house to lick my wounds, he'd visited a law-firm and arranged to sue me. It was definitely the most proactive he'd been in a long time. I would have been almost proud of his hutzpah had he not been trying to take my money. I folded the letter up and tucked it into my pocket. I needed to get out of the house and clear my head.

'Everything okay?' Mum asked as I passed her in the hall.

'Fine,' I said, feigning a smile. 'Just going for a walk.'

'Okay...' She seemed unsure; I think she might have said something else, but I didn't break my stride. I was definitely not ready to try and explain the whole mess to her right there in the hallway.

I stepped out of the front door and walked to the end of the driveway, turning right to head down the street. I turned right at the first street I came to, which led down a slight hill. As a kid, in the springtime, I used to ride my bike down this street with a helmet on and a mask on my face. I would wave a stick above my head and shout out to the sky, trying to stir-up the protective magpies that I knew would be sitting up in the trees, looking after their eggs or newly hatched magpie chicks. I was the only person I knew that enjoyed the thrill of being swooped. When other people would be avoiding that street during spring for fear of aerial bombardment, I would tear down it with joyous abandon.

The reminiscent daydream was interrupted by a low, steady hum of a car engine slowly approaching. I looked over my shoulder in time to see the sun bouncing off gold lettering on a black door. The Chrysler pulled up alongside me. The window rolled down.

'Get in,' said a man with a thin moustache.

'Fuck off, would you?' I said to him as I began to walk away.

'I really think you should get in,' he said. There was something in his voice that I couldn't ignore. I stared at him for a while. Against my better judgement, I got in the car. It was incredibly comfortable.

'What?' I asked him, bluntly, as my arse sank into the amply-cushioned passenger seat. It was hard to sound assertive when your butt was being swallowed by a marshmallow.

He said nothing, but slid a tablet computer along the dash until it was in front of me. I picked it up. A video player loaded up with a clip entitled 'D. Savage.'.

I clicked on it.

The thumbnail expanded and a full-screen video began to play. There was no audio, but the image was startling. The footage was filmed from high up, somewhere in a corner of the small room; it was grainy, and the playback was in black-and-white, but it was undeniable what I was looking at. It was me, from behind, completely naked apart from a pair of socks. The footage started half a second before my back stiffened and arched, and I ejaculated onto the floor in front of a disabled boy and a man with a flaky scalp. The video showed me quickly look left, then right, then bolt out of the room, almost knocking the disabled boy from his chair, and crashing into his carer as I tore out of sight. The screen went black. The man with the thin moustache turned to me, looking me dead in the eye.

'Something to think about when you are weighing up our proposal.'

'Where did you get this?' I asked

'McCormack,' he replied.

'Why didn't you use this the first time? How come I'm only seeing this now?' I asked him.

'It was inadmissible,' he said, still staring into me. 'She wasn't meant to have cameras in the bedrooms, so the footage couldn't be used in court. Lucky you. However, that doesn't prevent us from anonymously leaking it online. I can't imagine that would do wonders for your public image. Now get out.'

I got out of the vehicle, and he pulled away from the kerb before I'd even closed the door. It thunked shut with the car's acceleration.

Fuck.

I felt sick. That footage would destroy me. I could imagine the headlines now, *'Guy who fucks fruit also gets off over vegetables.'* I'd be worse than Rolf Harris. I needed time to think. I walked down to the local park, about a block over. There was no-one there, so I sat on the swing. I opened up my banking app and checked the balance. In recent times, I'd found comfort in doing that when I was feeling low. The payment from Ted had appeared in my account last month, and I still got butterflies in my stomach whenever I logged in. *Current balance: $865,032.64*

I thought about it seriously: $425,000 was a lot of money to lose, but it would still leave me with a bit over that sitting in my account, and that was a hell of a lot more than I'd had in there a couple of months ago. It was still more than enough money to set me up well in the world if I was smart with it.

I thought about what Jake used to say when I would go around to his place empty-handed, and he would split his last six-pack with me. 'I'd rather have three beers with you, than six by myself.' He'd always shared with me, and never thought twice about it. I wasn't sure why I'd even tried to keep the Ted's Melons deal from him. It was important for me to have him as a friend. I knew it wasn't going to happen right away, not after we'd beaten the living fuck out of each other, but it wouldn't happen at all if I didn't take a step in the right direction.

I tried to transfer the money to Jake on my phone, but a message popped up saying I would exceed my daily limit if I transferred more than a grand. I'd have to go into the bank. As I got up to leave, I heard a noise nearby. Looking around the playground, I couldn't place it. I went to leave and heard it again.

The playground was made up of two swings, standing alone on a timber frame; one of those horses mounted on a big spring that kids could hop on and bounce back and forward; and a wooden jungle-gym structure with a green slide coming off it. The jungle-gym had a wobbly wooden bridge that led to a steering wheel, just before the entrance to the slide. Beneath the wobbly bridge was a round, red plastic tunnel that you could crawl through. With the way the light hit the plastic, I could see a dark silhouette of something inside the tunnel, moving around.

I heard the noise again: deep, guttural grunting. I bent down and peered into one end of the plastic tunnel.

'What the fuck, dude!' Was the first thing that came out of my mouth. I'd been met by the confronting sight of a man with scraggly hair and a very worn beanie, in a long brown Drizabone-style jacket and old boots, facing me, moving his body up and down as though he were fucking someone, but there was no-one else there. He stared up at me like a crackhead caught in the headlights.

'It's not my fault!' He said, before leaping to his feet and tearing out of the park. Only then did I realise what he'd actually been doing. In his haste, the man had left something behind, and it sat there in the eerie red light of the plastic tunnel, slowly spinning around: a cantaloupe, with a rough hole carved out of the top.

'Jesus Christ,' I called after him, 'not in the fucking playground!' I couldn't stand the thought of a kid coming across it, so I picked it up and carried it over to the bin. I passed a bloke in a skivvy walking a greyhound. He looked at me knowingly.

'It's not mine,' I said. He just winked at me and whistled on his way.

Chapter Twenty-Two

I went to the bank; it sucked. Banks suck. They smell musty and dusty and no one smiles. I spent forty-five minutes queuing up before being served by a frog-faced man. I hoped that in his spare time he was performing in pantomimes, because he was a dead-ringer for Toad out of *The Wind in the Willows*. 'Next,' he croaked into the void.

I stepped forward. His customer service skills were lacking, and his chin never left his chest whilst he processed my payment. Coated in a layer of slimy sweat, like someone had rolled him in Vaseline, the most personality I got from the man was a solitary raised eyebrow when I told him how much I wanted to transfer.

'Four-hundred-and-twenty-five thousand?'

'That's right' I said, and he processed the payment. I signed a stack of paperwork, and that was that. I walked from the Perspex window, past the long line of miserable-looking customers. I heard frog-head croak, 'Next', as I got to the door. I imagined him flicking a long tongue from that sweaty mouth and curling around a blowfly on the service window.

I smiled to myself. I was half-a-fortune lighter, but confident that I'd done the right thing; that, and no one would have to see a video of me dropping a load onto the carpet at McCormack's, now. *Tick.* That was a big one for the Karma Exchange.

Chapter Twenty-Three

Walking into the kitchen, I heard the repetitious chopping of vegetables, the *distinct chop-chop-chop* of carrots on the board. Mum said nothing.

'Hi,' I said, walking round to the other side of the bench.

'Hi,' she replied, without emotion.

'How was your day?' I tried.

'Fine.'

The house was filled with nothing but the metronomic rhythm of knife coming down on wooden board as it broke through the other side of carrot after carrot. I felt concerned with the amount of carrots she'd cut up. I couldn't think of a dish that would call for so many carrots.

The look on her face told me not to say anything, to walk away and keep clear of the area, at least for a little while. Her mouth was crinkled up, scrunched tightly against her teeth, and she hadn't made eye contact with me once. I ignored the warning signs.

'What's with all the carrots?' I asked. 'Are we housing rabbits?' It was supposed to be funny. The cutting quickened, then ceased abruptly.

'*He* left,' was the first thing she said. 'I didn't tell him to go. I didn't push him out the door. He left. He packed up his things while I was out doing the grocery shopping and never came back. It was *his* choice. Not mine.'

She was talking about Dad. She'd never really spoken about Dad, even when I'd pressed her. After my eighth birthday he'd stopped sending cards. By my tenth birthday, I'd stopped looking for them. I sometimes thought I could remember what he was like, though I'm pretty sure all of my memories of him were just cut and pasted together from stories I'd heard from other people.

'You were two.' She looked me in the eyes for the first time since I'd arrived. Hers were red and watery, like she'd been cutting onions. She hadn't been.

'He took the good car, he took all the money, and he left me to take care of you on my own. I didn't have a job then, you know.'

I didn't know what to say. I decided not to say anything. She was shaking, and her grip on the knife had turned her knuckles white. She dropped it. It clanged down onto the bench top. A long silence followed. Neither of us spoke, only looking at each other.

She looked away. Slowly, she opened a drawer on her side of the bench, removing something from inside it. She put it down on the bench in front of me. A Ziploc bag filled with rice.

'I found it in the toilet,' she said.

I really wasn't sure what she was getting at. I picked the bag up. Through the rice, some black glass peeked back at me.

Oh no.

I shook the bag and the rice fell to the bottom, uncovering my phone. *Fuck.*

'It wouldn't fit round the bend, you dickhead.' Mum didn't really swear that much, but when she did, *dickhead* was her preferred expletive.

I really should have known it wouldn't fit around the bend. Half the time my shits wouldn't fit round the bend and I'd have to break them up with a stick. I wasn't sure why she'd decided to store it in a bag of rice, though.

'The rice dries up the water,' she said, as if she'd read my mind. She held down the 'on' button through the bag by way of demonstration. The screen lit up.

'You received a lot of messages from one girl, and since you were obviously finished with this phone, I took it upon myself to read them.'

Mum was always snooping through my private things, generally under the pretence of something else. When I was a teenager, it was always, 'I'd like to talk to you about the magazines I found in your room when I was cleaning up.' Or, 'I was just putting your socks away when I came across a packet of cigarettes.'

This time she was much more direct.

'I thought I'd raised you better, Daniel.'

I said nothing. I couldn't think of a single thing to say.

'If you've gotten—' she began, then stopped. Took a breath. 'Do you know how hard it is to raise a child on your own? With all of the financial responsibilities left to you alone, and the sleepless nights, trying to scrape together enough energy just to give the little thing the love it deserves?

'If you've gotten some poor girl pregnant, and she's sitting in a room somewhere wondering whether she's going to be doing it all on her own, you need to man-up and go 'round there. Talk to her and make things right.'

She paused for breath. Tears had formed in her eyes.

'Just take some responsibility for yourself, for fuck's sake!'

She slapped the carrots aside with the back of her hand, and they were sent rolling around the kitchen. She stood in front of me, literally shaking with rage, then abruptly left the room. I stood in stunned silence.

I couldn't disagree with a single thing she'd said.

I pulled myself together and picked up the bag of rice, emptying its contents onto the benchtop. I picked up the phone.

Time to suck it up. I went out the back and lit a cigarette. Scrolling through my contacts, I found Mel's number.

Call.

The phone began to ring, and I waited patiently for her to pick up. It rang all the way out. She had no voicemail. The line just went silent.

Fuck it.

I stubbed the cigarette out and left the house.

I pulled up to the Clayton apartment block just as the sun began to set. I climbed the stairs to the third floor and walked nervously up to the apartment door. I took a breath and knocked. I could hear voices inside. The handle turned and the door opened just enough for me to see a face. To my great surprise, it was Jenny. The door was slammed on me almost immediately. *What's she still doing there?*

'Jen, I'm here to see Melinda,' I said through the door.

'Go away or I'm calling the police,' she called back.

I heard Mel's voice in the background; it was muffled by the door and I couldn't make out what she was saying. I heard my name.

'You sure?' I heard Jenny ask.

There was a pause, and the door opened slowly. Jenny stood in the way. She looked over her shoulder to Mel.

'It's okay. Let him in.'

Jenny moved to the side. I took one step in. Far enough, given the circumstances. Mel was sitting at the bench.

'Hi,' I said. I felt so awkward.

'Hi,' she said.

There was a pause. I realised I should be talking, but I had no idea what to say now that I had arrived.

'So?' Mel asked.

'We should talk,' I said.

'Go ahead,' she returned.

'Could we talk privately?' I asked, looking over to Jenny.

'Jen stayed when you left. I didn't hear from you for weeks, but she stayed with me while you went off and did whatever you were doing. Probably raping someone else, no doubt,' she added with fire.

'I didn't rape you,' I told her. It had almost become a catch-phrase for me. I put my hands together to stop them from shaking, and continued, 'but I'm pretty sure it was me who got you pregnant.'

She just stared on, eyeing me resentfully. I took a breath.

'It was the day you killed my bird,' I began, and I didn't stop until the entire story was out of me. Throughout the telling, Mel's emotions ranged from anger to disgust, to wide-eyed horror, then back to anger again.

'Who does that?' she said in disbelief.

'I was drunk.' 'It wasn't really my idea.' Were two of the many reasons I wanted to use to justify my actions, but when I went to verbalise them, I realised that they were simply weak excuses. I chose to not say anything.

'Who does that to a person?' she asked again.

'I don't know...' I replied dumbly.

She stood up. 'You don't know? *You* must know, because *you* did it. Did you think it would be funny? Did you do it for a laugh? Did you think it would be just hilarious to joke about with Jake?!' She was shaking now. 'Did you just think, fuck Melinda, the uptight cunt, I don't give a fuck about her, lets ruin her life!?'

'I don't know,' I mumbled. 'I was angry. I made a mistake.' I looked away from her. Looking her in the eyes hurt.

'You did,' she said, with finality.

'I'm sorry,' I said, looking up. She was glaring daggers at me. 'I want to help. I want to make up for it. I want to be a part of the baby's life.'

'Ha!' she laughed. 'You have got to be fucking joking. You will never get anywhere near this baby. You will never see this baby, and you will certainly never be part of this baby's life.' She spat the last words at me. 'Get out.'

I took a dazed step backwards, and the door was closed on me once again. I pulled an old receipt out of my pocket, folded it in half, and scribbled on the back of it.

'I know you're angry now,' I called through the door, 'but if you need anything, anything at all, here is where I'm staying. I've fixed my phone, too, so give me a call if you need anything.' I felt stupid saying it, but I didn't want to leave without letting her know I'd be there if she needed me. I needed her to know I was there for her.

I got some shit food from a drive-through on the way home to Mum's and finished it before I pulled up out the front. I rolled a little joint and sparked it up, inhaling deeply. I cracked the window a bit and exhaled into the night air. Jungle tunes were playing on PBS. My face started to crinkle around the edges as the marijuana took effect. Closing my eyes, I tilted the seat back a fraction and allowed it to wash through my body in thick, syrupy waves.

Chapter Twenty-Four

A loud thump on the side of the van jolted me awake. My eyes shot open violently, light burning into my retinas as they struggled to adjust. It was daytime, and a pain shot down the left side of my neck.

'Get a job and sort your life out,' said a voice from outside.

Mum. I saw her walking away in my side mirror, dressed for work. After her car had pulled out of the drive and disappeared down the road, I climbed out of the van, rubbing the side of my neck. It was killing. I stretched it to the side in an attempt to ease the pain, but it didn't help. I guess that's what you get for falling asleep in the driver's seat.

I caught a whiff of my armpit while I was stretching my neck. It smelled pretty mean. I went inside and hopped into the shower, turning the heat right up to let the hot water loosen up my stiff body. Steam quickly filled the room. The exhaust fan in

Mum's bathroom was about as active as Helen Keller's Spotify account, and the thick steam had begun to mould the ceiling above the shower again. Mum always said you had to open the window a bit to let the steam out, but I never did. I enjoyed the sauna effect.

Through the fog and the sound of running water I thought I heard something. I stuck my head out of the water and listened out. There was a faint knock coming from the front of the house. I wasn't entirely sure I'd actually heard it at first, but it came again, louder this time. They'd have to wait. I put my head back under the stream and sudded up my pits. They'd need a double-dose today. Relaxing into the hot, steady flow of water, my neck slowly began to feel better again.

Knock. Knock. Two solid thumps that I thought might shatter the faux stained-glass pane by the front door.

'Hang on!' I called out, shutting the water off. I hadn't had a chance to rinse off my underarms. The knocking came again, more urgently this time. As I threw a towel around my waist, the knocking increased with such intensity I was sure the pane of glass would give out, or the knocker would break their knuckles. I pulled open the bathroom door and called up the hallway, 'Just a minute!'

Fuck me, it wouldn't want to be Mormons.

The knocking only sped up as I climbed the four steps that divided our home into two split-levels. I could see the front door now, and the shadow of a knocking hand coming down viciously on the glass panel. I was surprised not to see blood dripping down the outside from the sheer ferocity. The knocking reached a stressful crescendo as I was about two metres from the front door, and then it stopped immediately. I'm not sure why, but I stopped too. I guess I was waiting for something to happen. Nothing did. I took two long strides to the entranceway and tore the door open. There was nobody there.

'Hello?' I called to the street.

Nothing.

As I went to close the door, light reflected off something shiny on the welcome mat. I looked down and there, staring back at me, were two letters, one word, and a symbol, in a familiar curling font: *O&O Lawyers.* I looked around, and quickly bent down to pick up the hyper-reflective gold envelope. I closed the door, retreating back into the house. Taking the envelope down to the kitchen, I tore it open, hands still wet from the shower.

To Mr Savage,

You are being contacted by O&O Lawyers on behalf of Miss Melinda Eckhardt. It is her firm belief that you are the father of her expected child. Miss Eckhardt has agreed to undergo blood analysis for the investigative purpose of the identification of the child's father. The blood sample and relevant analysis will take place at the Waverley Blood Clinic. Miss Eckhardt requests your attendance.

Non-compliance with this request will result in immediate legal action being taken against you.

We await your response before the week's conclusion.

O&O Lawyers.

I put the letter down and tried to call Mel. It went to voicemail. She'd gotten a voicemail account. 'Hi, you've reached Mel,' it said, 'I must have missed you, so leave a detailed message and I'll get back to you.' Then at the end she added, 'Unless you are Dan Savage, then you can piss off.' I heeded the message and left no voicemail.

Weighing up my options, I saw that there weren't any. I was too tired to fight. I had told Mel that I would be there for her, and I intended to keep that promise. I went to the blood clinic. *Time to swallow the frog*, I thought as I pulled up out front of the dull, white building. That was something Chris used to say. *Swallow the frog*. There was this quote, I think it was Mark Twain, which said, 'If you know you have to swallow a frog, swallow it first thing in the morning.' I'd never really put much thought into it until now. I think the whole idea was that if you knew you had something unpleasant to do, you should do it as soon as possible, so that it's out of the way.

'Dan Savage,' I said to the woman at the reception desk.

'Take a seat,' she said, handing me a small brown clipboard with a pen hanging from it. I did as instructed and cast my eyes over the form I was to fill out.

'Do you consent to this, do you agree to that, do you give permission for your analysis to be submitted to a third party, do you agree to waive liability, blah blah blah.' I scribbled my name in the box down the bottom and waited to be called through. The room was filled with middle-aged men. I wondered how many of them had wanked into bodywash dispensers. Probably none.

My name was called after about an hour of waiting. I was halfway through an article entitled *Jolie's Adoption Addiction* and was interested to see how it would pan out. Apparently, she was getting free postage if she ordered more than one at a time. I reluctantly put the magazine down and went into the room to get my blood taken.

I was met with a stern woman who looked remarkably like Lou Carpenter from *Neighbours*. 'You might feel a little prick,' said the woman as she tightened the colourful strap around my arm. I was going to make a dick joke, but decided it would probably be poorly received, so I bit my tongue. She filled up six whole vials.

'You got Count Dracula waiting in the back room?' I asked.

Her face didn't crack. 'We are very thorough,' she said blankly. 'You're done.'

She taped a cotton ball to my arm with robotic efficiency and sent me on my way. She said I might feel a little light-headed, and gave me a packet of jelly beans which were supposed to combat the nausea. I didn't think a woman who couldn't smile should be allowed to hand out jelly beans. I chose not to tell her that.

I got back to Mum's place and straight away stripped the doona and a pillow off the bed. In the garage I found an inflatable camp mattress in a faded cardboard box. I threw the lot into the back of the van. I'd already overstayed my welcome and didn't feel like being any more of a burden on my mother. I had no idea where I was going to stay, but I'd made up my mind that it wasn't going to be there. Even after giving away half of my money to Jake, I still had a good amount sitting in the bank. Maybe it was time I started looking to buy a place of my own. In the meantime, a few nights in the back of Van Go wouldn't hurt.

I wasted a couple of hours driving around looking for somewhere to park up and spend the night later on, eventually settling on a little park with a small lake in the middle of it. I ended up getting stoned and spending the entire afternoon sitting beside the water feeding bread to the ducks. It helped, not to think about anything.

The night was cold, and Van Go was poorly insulated. I kicked myself for not grabbing another doona from Mum's place. It was a bit upsetting that I didn't hear from her at all. I slept on the blow-up mattress with my phone beside me all night, but it never went off.

Next morning, I got up and stretched my back in the car park. There isn't much to be said about the chiropractic benefits of sleeping on inflatable mattresses. I was as stiff as a board. I went to the front of the van to get my cigarettes from the passenger seat. As I leant in through the door, I noticed something out of place from the corner of my eye. I had absolutely no idea how they'd found me, but under the driver's side wiper-blade was a golden envelope, with that same, familiar insignia on the front. I lit a smoke before opening it up, not sure I was ready for whatever news I was about to receive. I didn't rip it this time. I carefully peeled one edge of the envelope's seal open, then slid my thumb along the length of it. I withdrew the letter from inside. There were three pages.

To Mr Daniel Savage,

Enclosed in this envelope are the results of yours and Miss Melinda Eckhardt's paternity test. In light of the result, and the moral cloudiness surrounding the conception of the foetus, Miss Eckhardt has tasked O&O Lawyers to retrieve the finances she believes she is owed. Together with Miss Eckhardt, we at O&O have established an estimate that we believe fairly represents the funds Miss Eckhardt is entitled to. Based on the average settlement reached when a typical de facto relationship of twelve months or more breaks down, the reasonable settlement, in ideal circumstances, would result in a 50/50 split of finances and assets. As your relationship with Miss Melinda Eckhardt was not one of a regular, de facto relationship of twelve months or more, and taking into account the aforementioned cloudiness of morality surrounding the conception, we at O&O lawyers, in conjunction with Miss Eckhardt, have arrived at the judgement that a 60/40 split would better represent fairness in this particular settlement.

Attached is a breakdown of the division of finances as we deem fair and reasonable. We request that you read and sign the attached document, and send a copy back to us within ten business days.

If you have any queries or require any additional information, do not hesitate to contact us.

Regards,

O&O Lawyers.

I flicked through the attached pages. The blood test was positive; no surprise there. I set that page aside, tucking the corner of it under the windscreen wiper. The division of finances stated that sixty per cent of mine and Mel's total combined finances and assets were to go to Mel, and forty per cent were to go to me. Any assets or finances Mel had to her name were negated by the massive student loan she also had in her name; this resulted in her personal net worth coming in at negative twenty-thousand dollars. Based on O&O's recent acquisition of my financial information, their estimate deduced that my personal net worth was $445,032.64. She was to receive sixty percent of that—that is, of course, after we split her debt 60/40, too. All of these numbers came together to produce a grand total of $234,516.32. There were numbers for a bank account at the bottom of the financial summary.

I felt like I might be sick.

My hands trembled as I set the letter down on the windscreen. I didn't know what to do. I didn't have anyone I could talk to. I'd alienated everyone I was ever close to. Normally if I had a problem, I'd hash it out with Jake. He wasn't really a great one for advice, but he could be a pretty good sounding board sometimes. I hadn't heard a word from him since I put the money into his account. I guess that was to be expected.

I went back over to the lake with the little bit of bread I had left. I sat by the water and waited for the ducks to approach. There were only a few out this early in the morning; I suppose the rest were still in bed. I wondered where ducks went after the sun goes down. I know most birds go back to their nests, but I'd never seen a duck nest before. I imagined a big muddy cave, where all of the ducks would sleep together. I think they would like that. I tossed a crust out to the early risers. Breakfast had arrived.

Watching the ducks calmed my mind and helped me to think more clearly about everything. I wanted to be a part of Mel's life. I wanted be a part of the baby's life. Mel had made it clear that wasn't going to happen. Nevertheless, I wanted to help out. If I couldn't be there in person for the baby, I was at least in a position to set it up on the right foot financially.

I upended the bread bag into the shallows of the lake, crumbs spilling out across the surface and drifting apart. I stubbed my cigarette out in the grass and headed back to the van. It was still a bit too early for the banks, but I had nothing else to do and I'd run out of bread, so I pulled out of the car park and drove there anyway. I got a park right out the front, and as soon as the doors opened, I was the first one in the place.

I was served by the same toad-like teller that served me last time. His amphibious charm hadn't developed any further, I noticed, as he croaked, 'Next', without ever looking up from his monitor. I thought it was unusual for him to have called out 'Next', as I was clearly his first customer for the day. I also thought it was unusual that the unfortunate-looking banker was covered in the same, familiar layer of slimy sweat he had been glazed with last time. It wasn't even hot. The sun had barely surfaced from the night, and it was actually reasonably chilly for a summer's morning.

'I'd like to transfer some more money,' I said to him.

'Account?' he croaked in reply.

I gave him my details, then Mel's details. I filled out the required paperwork whilst his sausage-y fingers stabbed away at the keyboard, and it was done. No great fuss, just numbers falling out of my account and into someone else's. Life goes on, as they say in the classics.

And so it did.

Chapter Twenty-Five

I got a job, ladies and gentlemen: I got myself a real, honest-to-goodness, forty hour per week, cog-in-the-machine job. But first I got myself a house.

It all happened quite quickly, really. I got pretty sick of eating junk food and sleeping in the back of my van in seedy car parks, so I started looking around. Even after the financial ravaging I'd taken, I still had a good chunk of money left in the bank, a little over $210,000. It didn't get me the whole house, but it got me most of it, with a small mortgage.

I looked around the Scoresby area, thinking it would be nice to buy a house in the area I'd grown up in. It turned out to be supremely out of my price range. Apparently, people saw great appeal in living in an area with medium-sized backyards and nothing else. Seriously—there were absolutely no draw-cards to living in Scoresby. There was no swingin' nightlife, there were no beaches or forests or...fucking art galleries. There was no culture, and no real soul to the place. Just a neighbourhood in the suburbs, where everyone lives so close together but no-one knows your name. And it was fucking expensive, for some maddening reason. I had no idea why people wanted to live there. I wasn't even sure why I wanted to live there; and then I realised, I didn't.

I threw the idea of Scoresby in the bin and took Van Go on a tour of the surrounding suburbs. They were all much the same as Scoresby, just a bit closer to things. One was closer to a shopping centre, one was closer to a big lake (not like the lake I'd been sleeping at, which was more of a glorified duckpond, and didn't really deserve to be called a lake), and one had a train station. They were all an improvement; yet, still so far out of my price range. I found myself driving further out, eventually winding my way up into the mountain range which had hemmed the horizon for most of my life, but which I had only really visited once or twice when I was quite small: The Dandenong Ranges.

I'd been there once when I was six, for a friend's birthday party on Puffing Billy, an old steam train which took you on a slow journey through the mountain towns. You could sit up on the side of the carriage with your legs dangling out the window. We had ice cream that day.

As the old van wound its way up the mountain, the air became noticeably fresher. It was somehow cleaner and crisper than down in the suburbs, like a salad for your lungs. I breathed in deeply through the open driver's window. Something felt right about the area. I grabbed a coffee to go from one of the cafés in the main street of Belgrave, before wandering into the local real estate agents.

'I want to buy a house,' I said. No point beating around the bush.

The man that greeted me introduced himself as Michael.

'Would you like a cup of coffee?' he asked. I held up the cup I'd just purchased. 'Tea?' he suggested.

I wasn't sure what sort of person would drink a cup of coffee and a cup of tea at the same time, but I was about to find out, as I took a seat at Michael's desk, two hot drinks in hand. I sipped the tea first, just to be polite. I didn't even like tea, really, unless it was from Al's collection, and especially not green tea. It tasted like sucking water from a hot cloth. I went back to the coffee. Michael beamed at me magnanimously from his chair.

'How many bedrooms?' he enquired enthusiastically, and it went from there. We leafed through a few brochures for a while before Michael deduced that anything printed on glossy paper didn't fall within the scope of my finances. Lifting a substantial bunch of keys from a hook at the end of his desk, he said to me, 'Let's go for a drive.'

We took his car, a light-blue Ford Focus that smelled of cinnamon painted over the top of cigarettes. I noticed a few small ash-snowflakes around the front of his gearstick, just below the ashtray.

'Do you mind if I smoke?' I asked him.

'Life is for the living!' he declared. I wasn't sure that made sense, and couldn't confidently identify whether or not it had been a yes or no answer. I tentatively withdrew a cigarette from my packet. He nodded at me and flipped the centre console open, pulling out a twenty-pack. I lit up.

'I'm a menthol man,' he said as we pulled out of the car park. I couldn't stand menthol cigarettes. They were like smoking a peppermint crisp and made me feel nauseous. People only really smoke them because: A) They can't stand the taste of regular cigarettes, or B) They believe that the menthol leaves them with fresh-smelling breath, not the usual acridity of a smoker's mouth. It doesn't.

'Keeps your breath fresh,' he said, struggling with his lighter. It was a Zippo—gold, no less. He nearly burnt the end of his nose off when it eventually ignited.

'I think you are going to love this one,' he said excitedly. 'A real *hills cottage*. Two-bedroom, plenty of character.'

We arrived at the house and Michael showed me through. It was nothing flash, just a small weatherboard house on a flat block in Belgrave South. Michael told me flat blocks were very desirable in the hills. I told him if people wanted flat blocks, they shouldn't live on a hill. He laughed and smacked me on the back jovially.

'How much is it?' I asked. It was well outside of my price range. We moved along.

'There are a couple more I could show you,' Michael said to me. 'They're great places, with loads of potential. Just need a bit of love.'

'Great,' I said.

'You much of a handyman?' he asked.

'Sure,' I replied. I wasn't really, but I had a few tools and I'd watched a lot of *Home Improvement* growing up. He showed me two more houses. They were both in a lot worse shape than the *Hills Cottage,* and only mildly less expensive. In one of them, you could see the ground below the house where the floor had rotted out under the shower. I was beginning to lose hope.

'Look, I don't really have a whole lot to spend,' I said to Michael. 'I really just need a place to sleep, with a roof over my head.'

He thought for a moment. 'How flexible are you with the *roof over your head* part?'

I thought he was joking, until we hopped back in his car and he drove me to the final house for the day. The trip only took a few minutes. The term *renovator's delight* cropped up a handful of times. We pulled up out the front of a huge red-brick place.

'It blew off in the storm,' he said, indicating the street-facing side of the house, where the roof-sheets were completely missing. 'Pretty superficial, really,' he added, his mouth pulling back into a half-smile-half-frown, the Mona Lisa of realty.

We had to enter via the back door, as the front entrance had become overgrown with climbing vines and wisteria. From the back door, the house looked even more mammoth than the front. The block sloped downwards from the street, and what I'd initially assumed was a two-storey house actually had a whole other floor carved into the hill beneath it.

'Should we take a tour of the garden before we go inside?' Michael asked.

'Sure,' I said, looking around at the overgrown mess of weeds and blackberry bushes. There was an old woodshed by the house, made from corrugated iron and an old door. A chicken wandered out from inside.

'Does the chicken come with the house?' I asked.

'Yep,' he said, not sounding overly convincing.

We walked further down into the garden.

'The block goes all the way down to that back fence.' He pointed down the hill to a fence that I couldn't see.

'What's that?' I asked, pointing to a small structure down the hill where a section of the ground had been levelled. It looked like someone had slapped together a shed, maybe with their eyes closed.

'That? Oh, you'll love this. Let's go down there,' Michael said, leading me deeper into the yard. 'The previous owner had used it for bean-drying,' he explained as we came to a stop in front of the old shack. 'This is probably my favourite part of the whole house,' he said, slapping the side of the ramshackle building. It looked as though it might fall over. He breathed in deeply. 'Yep, you just don't get craftsmanship like this anymore.'

From the looks of it, that was probably a good thing.

'It's got a real seventies feel to it,' he added.

It was almost exclusively made out of asbestos.

'Want to take a look inside?' he asked.

I declined. If this was his favourite part of the property, it didn't exactly herald great things for the actual house. I asked if we could look inside the house.

'Sure,' he conceded flatly, visibly upset that I hadn't gone inside the bean-shack. We trudged back up the hill in silence. When we arrived back up at the house, Michael snapped back into realtor mode, becoming his usual, enthusiastic, sales-pitching self. The back door was heavy and wooden, and groaned loudly as it reluctantly swung open on rusted hinges.

'The house is an original build and boasts a whopping amount of rooms. I haven't had a chance to count them all yet, but I can assure you, there are plenty.'

We stepped inside. The place was cold, but Michael assured me that the concrete and brick were an excellent insulator. He was right about the rooms. Although the place looked huge from the outside, the inside of it was packed with so many rooms that you could easily get lost. It was like a maze, and they were all just that little bit too small to actually be used for anything. The largest room on the ground floor was set up to look like a chapel, and it was creepy as fuck. There were rows of pews, and a makeshift altar out of an old table with a sheet over the top of it. There was a portrait of a man I didn't recognise on the wall behind the altar. The floor was covered with green carpet-tiles; that seemed to be a theme throughout most of the house. One-foot by one-foot samples of carpet in varying colours were spewed across the floors in almost every room. They made me feel itchy.

We moved into the kitchen, which was crammed into place on either side of a narrow walkway which lead to a small room, or 'spacious pantry' at the end. I took a step into the pantry. Michael waited in the kitchen while I looked around. It smelled damp.

'It's at this point in the tour which I'm obligated to tell you that this is a deceased estate,' Michael said. It felt like he was holding his breath. The deceased estate thing didn't bother me. Everybody dies.

'Did they die in the house?' I asked.

'Yes, he did,' Michael replied.

'Where?'

'There,' he said, without pointing anywhere.

I looked down. There was a light brown stain on the floor beneath my feet.

'Are you superstitious?' Michael asked.

'Not really, no.'

'Good,' he said firmly. 'I'm the only agent who will come here. Everyone else thinks the place is haunted, but I haven't seen anything.'

He really knew how to sell the place.

We looked around a while longer. It was much of the same throughout: big house with too many awkward-sized rooms, defeating the purpose of having a big house. I wasn't much of an engineer, but I figured a few walls could be knocked down here and there to open the place up a bit. The brick walls were screaming out for more windows to let some more natural light through, too. I was hesitant to ask about the price, considering how far out of my range the smaller ones were. I asked anyway. Michael seemed startled by the question.

'Sorry?' he asked.

'How much do they want for it?' I said again.

The guy who'd carked it in the pantry had seven children, apparently. They didn't live in the state and had no plans to do anything with the place, so were keen for a quick sale.

'They are asking two-ninety,' he said to me, 'but between you and me, they'd probably take two-seventy.' I didn't think they were supposed to do that, real-estate agents, down-sell a property. Michael obviously saw the question on my face. 'This place has been on the market for ages. People get freaked out by it. I don't know, I guess we'd just be happy to get rid of the listing and be done with it. Two-seventy and it's yours.'

I shook hands with him after a moment of thought. It was better than sleeping in the back of the van, and it's not as if I were drowning in options. Even with its pokey rooms, its creepy chapel, and the death pantry, it would be a place to call my own. Its only major downfall was all of the fresh air where the roof should have been, but that would only be a problem when it rained.

Chapter Twenty-Six

It rained all the time. I learned this shortly after I moved in to the house. The geriatric neighbour next door, who used the waistband of his trousers to keep his armpits warm, said to me when I moved in, 'It rains for nine months of the year in the Dandenong Ranges, and for the other three, it drips from the trees.' It had been raining when he told me that.

The open-air roof situation wasn't too much of a problem if you just treated the floor of the third storey as a makeshift roof. The water built up on the top floor until it reached the edge of the stairs, which it would then cascade down like a waterfall. I learned that if I just left the back door open, the water would run straight out once it reached the ground floor, and wouldn't come anywhere near the kitchen, which was where I slept.

In my haste to sign the paperwork for the house, I'd neglected to ask important questions like, 'Is there gas or water or electricity on the property?' Luckily I didn't ask those questions, because I would have been sorely disappointed by the answer. When I eventually rang Michael to ask about the utilities, he told me that they, too, along with half the roof, had 'blown off in the storm.'

I slept in the kitchen, in front of an old wood combustion stove, to keep me warm. I was a little creeped out by the death-pantry after the first night of sleeping on the kitchen floor. The next day I dragged an empty bookcase from one of the many spare rooms and moved it into position in front of the opening to the pantry. If I couldn't see it, it wasn't there.

There were so many rooms in the house that I realised I'd missed during the initial inspection with Michael. Most of them were empty, save the odd piece of rundown furniture. Occasionally I'd come across an old newspaper or a blanket, a photo frame, a walking stick; lonely remnants of a solitary life.

I was torn between two areas of the house as contenders for the one that creeped me out the most. It would have to have been either the third floor, which was really just a big attic, I realised; or the bathroom on the second floor. The attic was definitely a strong contender. We hadn't been up there when Michael was taking me through the place. To get access to the area, you had to climb a flight of home-made stairs which had been breakfast, lunch and dinner for white-ants for quite some time. Every third or fourth step was either broken, or about to break. I ascended with caution.

It was early in the morning when I first went up there, and the eerie light of a crimson sunrise spilled through the hole in the roof where the sheets had blown off. The only things in the roof-space were a small wooden chair facing out to the street, and a little black radio-cassette player with a silver carry-handle. It was coated in a thick layer of dust. I hit the *play* button, and to my surprise, it actually fired up. The sounds of swing music filled the attic.

The old-timey music only lasted for about twenty seconds before the batteries gave out and the tunes melted down into silence, leaving me to question whether it had ever actually started up in the first place. I watched the sun come up in silence, then climbed back down the dilapidated steps. There was an overwhelming sense of loneliness up there, and I didn't want to spend too much time with it.

Contender number two for the creepiest area of the house: the second-floor bathroom. The second-floor bathroom just plum didn't make any sense. There was no shower or toilet, just a pedestal basin below a dirty, cracked mirror-cabinet jutting out from the wall. Beside the pedestal basin was a bathtub, which was where the room began to get interesting. The rim of the bathtub came in at about chest-height, which I'd never seen before. The hob had been constructed from the same red bricks the rest of the house had been built from, at such a height that you had to climb four home-made steps to get in to it, and even then, you would have had to swing your hips to get in there, as though you were getting on a horse. I had no idea how an old man could have managed getting into a tub with such a challenging point of access. By the looks of the grime that lined the inside of the bath, and the cobwebs that had formed around the spout, it hadn't been used in some time.

A tall bath on its own isn't inherently creepy, and would certainly be no competition when pitted against a solitary chair in an attic, but when you took a look at what was going on below the bath, the playing field began to even out.

On the left-hand side of the bath-steps, built into the side of the brick-hob, was a small metal door, the kind you would sometimes see used as an access point for getting underneath a house. It was rusted around the edges, and secured shut by an equally rusty bolt and hasp. I slid the bolt out and jiggled the door open. Inside the bath-hob was a scrap of pink clothing next to a single-serve box of cereal. It was like the beginning to a horror story I didn't want to know about. I closed the door and decided it was best not to open it again.

The rain had let up at some point during the early hours of the morning, while I'd tried to sleep on the kitchen floor. As it turned out, there was a rainwater tank down the side of the house. I'd heard water thundering into it overnight. The ground was mud at the base of the tank where it had been overflowing. A single tap ran up the side of it, which I could get water from. There was a neglected pump connected to the tank, covered in a tangle of weeds, that I supposed was meant to service the house, but without electricity it was as useful as Stevie Wonder's reading glasses. I filled up a kettle from the kitchen and made a cup of instant coffee on the combustion stove. I'd found a jar of coffee powder underneath the small, greasy kitchen bench. I'd been feeding small pieces of scavenged wood into the combustion stove every few hours to keep it going overnight; the water didn't take long to boil.

I took the cracked mug of hot coffee out into the yard and, taking a seat on an upturned wheelbarrow, surveyed the land that was now mine. The yard was a jungle. Aside from the two metres along the back of the house that was sort of clear, the entire back yard hadn't had any attention in years. I finished my coffee and cleaned the redbacks out of a pair of work boots in the woodshed. They were about one size too big, but they'd do fine. There was a heavy rake and bow-saw leaning against the side of the woodshed, and a chainsaw sat atop the pile of split gum inside. I eyeballed the piece of machinery; it would be a huge asset if it worked, but something in its dirty, rusted appearance had me doubting it would ever fire up. A pair of gloves hung on a nail just inside the shed; I put them on and had a go at starting the chainsaw. No love. I spent the next twenty minutes tinkering with it trying to get it to start. I wasn't a very mechanically minded person, so tinkering mostly involved banging it on the floor of the shed, spinning the chain back and forth, and nearly pulling my shoulder out reefing on the pull-cord. I was covered in sweat already and hadn't even managed to start the bloody thing.

I took a breath and stepped back, before picking the piece of machinery up and looking over it. Just below the handle was a small switch, sitting in the *off* position. I let out a small, inward laugh, and flicked it into the right position. I pulled the cord, and to my great joy, it roared into life—which was fleeting; it soon spluttered itself into silence once more.

Fuel.

I opened the cap to the fuel reservoir, and I could see all the way to the bottom. After a bit of fucking around, I found an old jerry can outside, around the back of the shed in the undergrowth. It had the words *Two-Stroke* written on the top of it. I filled up the tank and it started up beautifully on the second pull. Wasting no time, I took it straight into the garden, and went the hack on pretty much anything I could see. I spent the entire day hacking at the undergrowth, the overgrowth, and the growth that grew between them. I pulled weeds, and dragged branches, and didn't stop for more than a glass of water. I piled everything I pulled out or cut down in a heap on the side of the property. I worked hard, and went all the way through, missing lunch, working right the way up until the sun hung low in the sky, ready to set. Sweat rolled off me in fat beads, and my shirt was saturated, as I took up my seat on the upturned barrow at the top of the yard. I looked out over my day's efforts and thought to myself, *I've hardly made a fucking scratch.*

I'd spent an entire day, non-stop, on vegetation demolition, and I hadn't even made a dint. And I was starving. The house was

351

walking distance from the main street, which was home to a small, unassuming bar that I'd been keen to check out. I wandered down and went in. It was warm and quiet. There were a handful of people in there and a woman was playing acoustic guitar in the corner on a low stage. I ordered a beer and took up a seat at the bar. The guy working the taps told me they didn't have a kitchen there, but you could order a pizza from the shop a few doors up and bring it in, so I did just that.

I sat quietly, enjoying the atmosphere, sipping on my beer. The guy behind the bar asked me where I was from, and I told him I'd just bought a place down the road. He was friendly and welcoming, and told me which cafés were good and which ones to stay clear of. There were two bakeries in the main street, one where you could get a good meat pie and a shithouse dessert, and one where you could get a shithouse meat pie and a good dessert. If you got a membership at the local cinema, you could see movies for twelve bucks, but don't go there if it's a windy night, because the power goes out. He was a wealth of knowledge. He introduced himself as Carey.

I finished my pint and went up to collect my dinner from the pizza shop. They were flat out, and mine wasn't ready yet, so I took a seat by the window. There was a small noticeboard behind my seat, and I casually looked over it while I waited. There was a billy cart race coming up soon in the next town over. Someone was running a spiritual healing workshop on the first Sunday of next month, and a guy called Graham was looking for a room to rent with his pet ferret. Pinned at the bottom of Graham's notice was an A4 poster with little tabs and phone numbers at the bottom that you could tear off and take with you. It was an ad for a *Fitter Machinist* apprentice on the Puffing Billy Railway. I looked around to make sure no-one else was watching me, then tore the entire thing off the wall and stuffed it into my pocket. The money that still trickled in from the video was helpful, but I knew pretty soon, I was going to need a more steady income flow. I'd applied for a stack of jobs online when I'd first decided that Belgrave was the town I was going to plant myself in, but I hadn't heard back from a single one. I couldn't work it out. Maybe I shouldn't have put Mrs McCormack down as a reference, I don't know.

'Twenty-three,' called out the guy making the pizzas.

That was my number. I thanked him and left, heading back to the bar for a couple more beers. The place had gotten busier since I left, and there wasn't any room at the bar to sit, so I moved out the back to a small decking area, taking up a seat at an outdoor table. The seats were empty kegs, with rounds of timber sitting on top of them so you didn't get a taphole up the arse. I unfolded the ad I'd taken from the noticeboard as I bit into a slice of pizza.

Are you good with your hands, have a strong work ethic, and want to be part of a dynamic team that keep our heritage locomotives on the tracks?

No, not really; and not overly, were my answers, however I did want a regular source of income, so I could pay for things.

353

'What's that?'

The voice startled me. I instinctively folded the piece of paper up quickly. I'm not sure why. It was the guy from the bar. Carey. He'd come out the back for a smoke. I slowly unfolded the paper. He looked at it over my shoulder.

'Oh, yeah. We've got one of those inside, on the wall.' He exhaled a white cloud. 'Rare as hen's teeth, those jobs. Everybody wants to work on the Puffing Billy around here. Not sure why. Shovelling coal's not really my jam,' he said, with a slight laugh.

'Smoke?' he offered, holding out a pack.

'Thanks,' I said, sliding one from the box.

'I'll take it down,' he said. I looked at him quizzically. 'The ad. For the train. I'll take ours down inside. Increase your odds.'

He was a nice guy, with a kind face under a mess of dark facial hair that was too patchy to be considered a beard. I thanked him. Carey sucked down the second half of his cigarette the way hospitality workers do—not wasting any time—and went back to tend to the bar. I stayed outside a little longer, finishing off half of my pizza before heading home; the other half in the box under my arm would make for a nice breakfast in the morning.

I looked up the Puffing Billy hours of operation on my phone when I got back to the house. Google Maps said they opened at 9 a.m., so I set my alarm for a little before then. As I built a fire in the combustion stove, I decided I'd call the electricity people tomorrow to see about getting the power back on. It would be nice to get a little electric heater and set myself up in a room other than the kitchen. I still had a bit of money coming in from the video. The hype had died down, and I wasn't being recognised in the street anymore, but people were still watching it, and money was still trickling in. The stream had slowed, but it hadn't yet come to a stop.

The fire caught on, and I waited up for ten minutes or so to make sure it wouldn't go out, before finally curling up under the blanket on my camp mattress and drifting off to sleep.

I needn't have worried about setting my alarm, as I was awoken at the ungodly hour of 5.30 a.m. by the furry face of Satan, staring at me from atop my box of leftover pizza. A persistent scratching noise beside my head was what initially tore me from my slumber, and as my eyes blinked open blearily, I realised I was near-on nose-to-nose with a possum the size of a wombat, trying to get into my pizza box.

'Oi!' I shouted, a little less bravely than I'd hoped. He stared back at me, unblinking, like a junkie who'd just been caught going through a bin. I threw a bit of wood at him and he scrabbled off out of the kitchen. I could hear his little paws clambering up the stairs. I guess he was wondering what I was doing in his house. He'd no-doubt lived here longer than me.

I couldn't be arsed with the fuck-around involved with making a cup of coffee, and decided to try my luck with the main street. I wondered if there were any early-openers ready to serve coffee at this hour. As it turned out, I was in luck. The first place I came across, after turning the corner into the main drag of Belgrave, had its lights on. A young girl was lugging a stack of chairs to the front door to set up the outside dining. I held the door for her as I stepped inside. I always felt uncomfortable when holding a door open for a woman. I wasn't sure if I was being chivalrous or condescending. I was just trying to be nice.

The temperature was the first thing I noticed as I walked in, followed closely by the aroma; both were warm and welcoming. A stack of freshly baked pull-apart loaves was piled on a trestle table at the end of the front counter. You could still see the steam coming off them.

'Hi! How's it going?' asked a very peppy young lady with a high ponytail who was cleaning the coffee machine.

'Better now,' I replied, picking up one of the pull-aparts. I hadn't intended my reply to come across as creepy, so I lifted up the loaf to show her what I'd been referring to. She didn't seem to notice.

I ordered a coffee. Large, strong, one sugar. I chose to eat in, and took up a stool at the long, rustic-style wooden bench by the window. There was something pleasant about sitting there, taking my time drinking my coffee, watching the rest of the town wake up and slowly come to life.

The bakery over the road opened up first, at around 6.30, and by 7 a.m. the street was busy with cars taking their drivers to work and shop owners getting in early to set up for the day's trading. I finished off the rest of my coffee, and rolled up the final third of the pull-apart in the brown paper bag it had come in. It had proven to be just as delicious as it looked. I took to the street, finding a quiet corner in which to unfold the piece of paper I'd pulled off the pizza-shop's wall the night before. I tried the number.

'Puffing Billy Railway,' said a deep voice, answering the phone. They'd gotten in early. I told him I was calling about an apprentice job I'd seen advertised in town. 'Oh yeah, when can you come in?' he asked.

'Right now, if you like,' I said with a laugh, 'I'm just in the main street.'

'Great. See you in five.'

He saw me in three. It was a two-minute walk from where I was, and I spent a minute tidying up my hair in the back of a teaspoon before I left for the station.

'You the bloke who called?' said a big man whose voice matched the one on the phone. He had a big face, and a curly beard of grey and black.

'Yeah.'

'Great. Put this on.' He threw a heavy blue jacket at me. I caught it awkwardly and followed his instructions. 'I'm not gonna bother with any sort of interview,' he explained, 'I won't know what you're like as a worker until I've seen you work.'

I couldn't believe my luck. He didn't ask for a single reference, and certainly didn't look as though he were going to do any background checks. The bearded railworker put me to work right away. I spent the day lugging heavy train parts around the yard. The boys in the workshop were rebuilding a steam engine – an old *Garratt*, they'd called it. I wasn't of much technical assistance, but I could drag and lift heavy things, and hold them in place while the other workers took care of the engineering and assembly.

It was the hardest day's work I'd done in a long time, maybe ever; but I was determined to make a good impression, so with each heavy locomotive part they got me to drag into position in the hot shed, I blinked through the sweat that stung my eyes and obliged. When I got home, I collapsed onto the floor-mattress with a big smile plastered across my face—absolutely knackered, but content. My working day had finished with the big-faced man, Tony, saying to me, 'Good work. I'll see you at six tomorrow.' *Good work.* I fell asleep smiling, and didn't even bother to light the combustion stove.

Chapter Twenty-Seven

The days rolled into weeks, which melted into months, and before I knew it, an entire year had passed living in the hills. Out of my first pay-check, I bought a heavy tarp from a seconds yard. It came from an old circus tent which had been torn to pieces during *the storm*; apparently, my roof and utilities hadn't been its only victim. I used the half circus-tent to cover the open-air viewing deck that the house's attic had evolved into. It was definitely a disappointment saying goodbye to the relaxing sounds of the house's indoor waterfall of an evening, but the wooden staircase and sodden carpet-tiles certainly thanked me.

Two weeks into the railway job I had the utilities reconnected and a plumber out to replace the hot water service. He charged me exactly one arm and one leg for the privilege, but thankfully my remaining limbs were appreciative of the transition from icy-trickle to cascading heat in the creepy high-rise bathtub-shower upstairs.

Mel would have had the baby by now, I realised one night, as I was taking the bins up to the street. The thought staggered me, knocking all of the air from my lungs. I must have stood there for twenty minutes, staring into the darkness of the street, the thought slowly unwrapping itself inside my mind. *Mel would have had the baby by now.*

I'd suppressed the notion of her shamefully well up until that point, but the thought moved in and wouldn't leave. Mel had blocked all forms of contact from me with a firm letter from O&O, and I had almost completely followed the note to a tee; save one time, feeling brave after a skinful of beers, I caught an Uber to the apartment in Clayton. I was met at the door by an elderly Sri Lankan woman and her rather wary-looking son. The program had ended, and she had moved on: to where, they couldn't tell me.

Mel would have had the baby by now.

It's a strange feeling, knowing that you have contributed to making a human that you will more-than-likely never see. It sits, heavy, inside the stomach.

I have a child that will never know a father.

I didn't even know what sex it was.

I hoped it was a boy. The world didn't feel like a good place for a girl.

I'd tried to contact Mel a few times in those initial weeks of living and working in the hills, before the letter from O&O arrived. Each time, my call had been met with her message bank. I sent her multiple text messages, seeing how she was doing, and checking in to see if she needed any help with anything. I received no reply. When my third pay-check came in, I forwarded the entire sum into Mel's bank account. Call it guilt, maybe; perhaps it was a sense of loyalty, or duty, to her and the life that she had inside her. Each week from then on, I transferred exactly half of my pay into her bank account. I used the other half to cover my mortgage repayments and other expenses, but I really didn't need it all. The weekly wages of a mature-aged apprentice on a steam train were meagre, but my expenses were few. The house needed a lot of work, but I planned to simply chip away at it over the coming years. I felt grounded in Belgrave. I'd never really felt connected to an area I'd lived in before, but there was certainly a strong sense of community, and when you told people that you worked for the Puffing Billy, it was always met with a smile. I began to feel as though I belonged. I'd made a good friend out of Carey, and would often stay on past close, when he'd come around to the other side of the bar and we'd have a beer together. It was a good way to debrief at the end of a long week. An opportunity to get things off your chest, or talk about plans for the future, or debate as to whether the Doritos *Nacho Cheese* flavoured corn chips were superior to their *Cheese Supreme* counterpart. We still hadn't reached an agreeable consensus on this.

Sometimes our conversations would only last one beer, but on more than one occasion we'd found ourselves talking smack at the bar as the early rays of daylight punctured the enveloping dark outside. It was on one such occasion, as he leant over from the wrong side of the bar to pull a beer from the tap, that he asked, 'Why don't you give Jake a call?'

It caught me off-guard. As much as we'd spend late nights talking about the world after hours, I'd only ever mentioned Jake once, maybe twice. I tried to leave the old life in the past, where I could bury it beneath the new experiences and memories I was creating in the hills.

'I've tried,' I said. I had. It went straight to voicemail. I surmised he'd blocked me.

'Recently?' he pressed.

'No,' was my answer. I'd tried to get onto him a few times over the space of a week, but each time I'd gotten sent straight through to voicemail. I'd eventually given up.

'You should.' Carey looked at me seriously.

I took a mouthful of my beer and said nothing. The sun peeked through the trees on the hill, bouncing purple-crimson light off the furniture against the front window of the bar. We called it quits and walked home.

Whether he had realised it or not, Carey had planted a seed that morning, and it wormed away inside my brain to the point where I wasn't sure whether or not he'd planted a seed or a worm. Maybe the worm was planting the seed, I'm not sure; but I wanted to see Jake. He went from being a person that I had pushed to the furthest corner in the back of my mind, the place where you would store Christmas decorations or camping gear, and only ever looked in once a year, if that, to being situated squarely in the forefront of my consciousness. I'd packed him away emotionally, probably behind the Christmas decorations if I'm being honest, and Carey had dragged him back out.

The thought niggled away at me over the coming days, and I eventually succumbed to it one Saturday morning. I'd been lying in bed, enjoying the sunlight streaming in through the window and the fact that I didn't have to work. The railway had someone else for the weekends.

I'd been thinking about how far I'd come since I first moved in to the house. I'd relocated my sleeping quarters to one of the upstairs rooms, and no longer went to bed on an inflatable camp mattress in the kitchen. I'd picked up a nice double bed on Gumtree, from a middle-aged couple who were just giving it away. An electric heater buzzing away beside the bed added to the new luxury I found myself living in. My head sank back into the pillow and I smiled to myself. That's when the thought crept in. I was tired of the idea of Jake quietly taking over my subconscious, so I picked up the phone and selected his name from the contacts list.

I got voicemail. I didn't leave one. Instead, I got out of bed, put some clothes on, went outside, and got into my van before I could talk myself out of it. I wound my way back down the mountain, rattling away through familiar streets until, eventually, I pulled up at the end of a street. My van was too conspicuous to park out the front of McCormack's, and if you looked closely at the side of it, you could still faintly make out the word 'PEDO', so I decided it would probably be for the best if I didn't pull up right out the front of his house.

I killed the engine under the shade of a small tree on the nature strip, on the wrong side of the road. Not completely out of sight, but better. I flipped the hood of my jumper over my head and walked up the street to his place, what used to be *our* place. As I got closer, I stole a cautious glance over the road. The words 'The McCormack Home for Disabled Youths' leered out at me, sending a cold shiver swimming down my spine. I quickened my pace to the front door and knocked firmly. The door swung open within a few seconds of knocking and my heart jumped. I was met with a sight of confusion. Unless Jake had had some serious work done, the person who had opened the door was almost certainly not him, in fact, they appeared to be a young oriental woman. She smiled and said hello.

'I'm looking for Jake,' I said awkwardly. 'Is he home?'

He was not. He had not been home for some months. The young woman explained to me that he had moved out almost a year ago, and they had been renting there ever since. My heart dropped.

'Hold on,' she said, turning back inside. The screen door closed behind her. I heard a drawer open just around the corner. I tried to see what she was doing through the wire-mesh, but I couldn't make out much. There was a jingling of keys and rustling of paper and a rubber bouncy ball escaping to another section of the house. *The junk drawer*, that's what I could hear. Every house had one. That one drawer where all rules and any sense of organisation went out the window. A place where paperclips and rubber bands were at home with bills from four years ago, old receipts, and a surplus of forgotten keys which you couldn't find a lock for, but would certainly need the moment they were thrown away. Oh, and a golf ball for some reason; that was another one of the usual suspects of the junk drawer, rolling around with an assortment of dead batteries and batteries with full charge, all free from their packaging.

The drawer closed and the young woman returned to the front door. She handed me a piece of paper, with some words written on it in black marker.

'What's this?' I asked; I couldn't make sense of it.

'A forwarding address, for his mail.' I looked at the piece of paper. It still didn't make any sense. 'I had to get the landlord to chase it up for me after his magazines kept getting delivered here,' she frowned, adding, 'we have children in the house.'

I could only imagine what magazines Jake had been having delivered. The woman went to close the door.

'Wait,' I said, 'are you sure this is the whole address?'

She shrugged her shoulders, frowning again, and told me that that was all she had been given. I was about to thank her, when a booming voice fired across the street like a cannon.

'YOU!' it declared.

I turned quickly on the spot, confirming what I already knew: I'd been spotted by Judy McCormack. 'Shit,' I hissed, but McCormack was already advancing across the road. 'I gotta go,' I said to the woman in the doorway. 'Thanks.' Grasping the paper tightly in one hand, I began to shuffle quickly across the front lawn.

McCormack's steps quickened.

Mine did too. I dared not look her in the eye.

I'd almost reached the edge of the lawn, and she was half way across the road when, out of nowhere, she charged at me like a wounded bull. She had some serious pace about her as she heaved her bulk across the road, like an Olympic sprinter. She reached me before I knew what was happening, and out of sheer luck only, I ducked and spun my body at the right moment, avoiding her outstretched arms with just millimetres to spare. The rapid evasion took her a moment to recover from. Her size made it difficult to reverse her trajectory right away, and she had to hook back in a wide arc to avoid toppling over. I didn't waste any time in getting out of there and hit the pavement as fast as my feet would take me.

I was about half way to my van when I chanced a look over my shoulder. McCormack was back on the footpath and rocketing along with impressive propulsion. The gap was closing. I couldn't believe a woman of her carriage could move faster than me, but there you go. It was going to be too close to call as to whether I would make it to the van before she made it to me. My heart pounded in my head as I pushed myself onwards. I reached the van and stabbed my key into the door's lock, turning it with shaking hands. McCormack was just rounding the tree, about three metres away from the van, when I tore the door open and threw myself in. She was moving too quickly to slow herself down in time, and slammed hard into the open driver's side door. I was sure there would be a McCormack-shaped impression left in the panelling. She fell heavily onto the grassy strip dividing the footpath and the road. A loud groan was released from inside her.

'You okay?' I asked, leaning out the van's window. I wasn't a complete arsehole. There was no response. Her chest expanded and contracted slowly.

'McCormack?'

She stirred, shaking her head from side to side before sitting up. Her eyes flicked open, locking on me.

'You!' she said emphatically, seeing red once again.

I turned the key in the ignition and spun the tyres on the asphalt, speeding away down the street. When I was a safe distance from the area, I pulled over and unfolded the piece of paper again, looking it over. I scratched my head.

Skinners Flat

Gibson

Platform 9.

It didn't seem a whole lot to go off.

I typed the words into Google, hoping it might make sense of it and spit out an address. It didn't. It just came up with camping suggestions for Skinners Flat Reservoir. I tried just typing, *Gibson. Platform 9.* There were no relevant results. Lastly, I typed in *Skinners Flat. Gibson.* It was a little more promising. The first result, at the top of the page, was a screenshot from Google Maps: Gibson road, running through a town called Skinners Flat. The place was in the middle of nowhere, out near towns with stupid sounding names and not much else around. The *Platform 9* part was still confusing me. I opened the Maps page and scrolled right the way along the length of Gibson road, and there didn't look to be any train stations anywhere along it. I reasoned that the only way to make sense of it was to go out there. And so I did. Right away.

Skinners Flat. It definitely sounded made up -something from a comic strip or a B-grade slasher – but if Jake's magazines had been getting there, then so could I. Maps said it was close to a four-hour drive away. I filled the tank and grabbed some snacks for the road, settling in for the long drive.

I passed through Sunbury, Gisborne, Woodend, Kyneton, Malmsbury, Inglewood and Kurting on the way, all towns that gave a driver absolutely no reason to stop. A bakery near Wedderburn was the only place the van came to a halt. I got out and stretched my legs, ordered myself a pie, and used the toilet. I was served by an older, sunburnt woman with deep lines carved into her chest by time and the country sun. Skinners Flat was the next town over, so I asked the woman if she'd heard of any train stations, or Platform 9, in the area. She shook her head and told me she hadn't. It was only a ten-minute drive from the bakery, so I took the time to eat in, pulling up a chair at a small table by the window. I took a bite of the pie and watched as a big green tractor drove past the bakery.

I wasn't sure how I felt about seeing Jake after so long. I wondered how he might react to me turning up on his doorstep unannounced. It wasn't the way I would have liked to have gone about it, but I wanted to make things right between the two of us, and in my defence, I would have announced myself if I had the means to; I'd certainly tried.

The pie downed, I jumped back into Van Go and took on the last leg of the journey. A little while later, I came across the road marked out as his, and found myself turning into the dusty mouth of Gibson road. Deep corrugations almost rattling the inside panels of the van off, so I slowed right down. I slowed down partly for the sake of my spine, and partly because I had no idea what I was looking for. Bouncing my way along the road, leaning out the window, looking closely at the frontage of each of wide-spread country block, I searched for anything that might be considered *Platform 9*. Gibson was a long road, stretching out for a couple of kilometres at least. I crawled along, a little over walking pace, scanning each block as I rumbled past, finally coming to a stop where Gibson intersected with another road. I attempted a three-point turn, which inevitably turned into a five-point turn, and trawled back along the other side of the road, my sights refocused. This side, like the other one, was lined with tall gum trees and thick undergrowth made up of native grasses and bracken ferns, making it difficult to see through to the properties behind. Perforating the bushland every now and again, dusty long driveways wound their way off through a break in the tree-line, stretching off into the distance to faraway houses. Again, I came to the end of the street without spying any *Platform 9*. I spun the van around quickly and completed another circuit. Nothing.

The gearstick clunked into reverse as I backed up from the intersection, pulling over in a cloud of dust on the side of the road. I opened up the map, checking to make sure I was in the right place. I even unfolded the piece of paper the address was written on and checked it again. It was definitely the right street. I was beginning to think I would end up having to doorknock every house along the stretch of road. There would have to be a hundred of them at least. I lit a cigarette and tipped my head back against the seat, exhaling. I didn't know what I was doing there. I didn't have a plan. I suddenly wasn't sure what I'd been thinking, driving all of the way out there with no proper address.

Maybe I'd hoped to just drive past a house and see Jake conveniently retrieving some mail from the letterbox. Perhaps his special magazines, I don't know. I felt pretty stupid sitting there, watching as a big green tractor bounced its way around the corner into the entrance of the street. I think it was the same one from town, except now it was towing a long, rusted trailer filled with hay bales. The driver lifted two fingers off the steering wheel in an obligatorily polite wave. I responded in kind and he rolled on by, turning into a driveway a little further down the road. I got out and had a piss by the side of the van, nearly blowing-out my urethra when a tremendous bang went off on the other side of the tree-line. I stemmed the flow and pushed through the bush until I was staring out over an open, sloping paddock. I could see the green tractor idling not too far down the hill, a little way up from a long metal shed, which stretched across a levelled-off section of the paddock. The driver was walking down the hill toward the shed, one arm raised.

BANG!

He fired a shot from the pistol in his outstretched arm, up into the air. I watched as he dropped his hand back down by his side and slogged the other object he'd been dragging along up onto his shoulder. I squinted my eyes hard, straining to work out what it was. Only when the lumbersome man shifted its weight and I could see the sun glinting off its blade, did I realise it was an axe.

The guy was carrying a gun *and* an axe.

It seemed excessive.

A scream tore my attention away from the tractor driver as a woman in a floral sundress came into view. The driver lifted the heavy axe up above his head as he approached her. I couldn't believe what I was seeing. The guy was going to butcher her. My legs moved before my brain, and I was carried toward the scene as fast as they would take me.

'Hey!' I roared, pelting towards the woman's assailant. He didn't flinch.

'Hey!' I yelled again, still running at full pace. The woman stole a nervous glance toward me, then flicked her attention back to the man. Before I knew it, I was launching myself headlong into the man, spear-tackling him to the ground. The axe flew from his hands and he landed heavily with an 'Oof!' I scrambled quickly to my feet, standing over the man. He had rolled onto his side and was clutching his lower back where the pistol had dug in. I kicked it to the side.

'Cut!' came a voice from nearby. I turned towards it.

'Jake?' My brain was having trouble processing the visual.

He was wearing a beret.

'Dan?' he responded.

'Ugh,' groaned the man on the ground.

'What's going on?' I asked, confused.

'We are in the middle of a shoot,' Jake said. 'We *were* in the middle of a shoot before you ran across my property like a madman and attacked Serge, my leading man.'

'Oh,' I said, taking in the situation with fresh eyes. There was a lighting tree set up and a guy in black holding a boom microphone, who I swear hadn't been there before. I looked around, bewildered, seeing the place clearly for the first time. I looked over at the female actor, who was leaning against the building, a little shaken up.

'That's Caroline,' Jake said. She gave me a meek wave, before heading into what I had initially thought was a long, narrow shed, but now realised was actually a repurposed train carriage. Something fell into place.

'Platform Nine,' I said, dumbly.

'Yep,' said Jake.

'You live here?'

'Yep,' he said again. 'Gets a bit cold at night, but apart from that, it's great. How'd you find me?'

'I went by our old place this morning.' I had a haunting flashback of being chased down the street by Mrs McCormack. 'I can't believe you live in a train.'

'It's great,' he said, 'I've got a bed and a kitchen set up in the front carriage, and there is enough room for my students to stay in the back one if they want. The middle is a greenhouse.' He tapped the side of his nose.

'Students?'

'Yeah, well I didn't learn *nothing* from the cantaloupe video. I've taken my skills in film-making and experience in the industry and I'm imparting them onto the younger generation.'

'Unh,' groaned Serge from the ground.

'It's getting a really great response so far,' he beamed.

I stepped over the injured man on the ground and held out my hand to Jake.

'Well, it's great to see you,' I said.

He took my hand firmly and pulled me into a hug.

'We were just about to have a cook-up. Did you wanna stick around for dinner?'

I told him that sounded great.

We had roast beef and vegetables cooked in a pot-belly stove. It was surprisingly good. Country living seemed to be doing good things for Jake. I'd never seen him cook more than an egg. After the sun went down, we had a beer and smoked a spliff together from the comfort of a couple of deck chairs, sitting alone in the middle of a paddock beneath a sprawling tapestry of stars.

'I love it here,' Jake said, 'I really do.'

I'd never seen so many stars before. It was breathtaking. And the place was dead quiet. The only thing to be heard was the distant voices of Serge and Caroline, rehearsing a scene for the next day in the back carriage.

'It's pretty beautiful,' I said to him.

It was.

A long quiet set in. After a while I made an attempt to breach it, bringing up the elephant in the room—or paddock, as it were—that was the Ted's Melons fiasco.

'Water under the bridge,' Jake said, waving it off casually.

'It's not really, though, is it?' I said.

'It is to me,' he said, taking a happy toke on the joint.

'It was pretty horrible, really,' I said to him. 'We've never had a disagreement before; next thing we are in the middle of a legal battle.'

'If you are gonna do it, you may as well do it right,' he said, smiling, handing me the smoke. I inhaled lightly.

'How can you be so chill about it?' I asked. 'I've felt terrible about it for the last year, and I don't know if I can ever get over the way I went behind your back.'

He swung his arm out in a sweeping arc. 'Look around, mate. We are in paradise. I'm doing something that I really love. Things are going well.' He smiled kindly at me. 'And I got half of your money.'

I thought about it for a moment.

'I'd rather have three beers with you than a six-pack by myself,' I said, knocking my drink gently against his. 'Sorry for being a dick.'

'Apology accepted,' he said, taking a sip of his beer.

There was a bloodcurdling scream from the train carriage. My heart jumped before I realised it was just part of the rehearsal.

'I better go see how they are doing,' Jake said, 'We've got a pretty big day tomorrow.' He got up and headed back toward the train, assuring me he'd be back in a moment. I leant back in the chair, taking a long drag of the joint Jake had left me, trying to soak in the entire solar system. The country night's sky was too vast to take in.

My phone buzzed in my pocket.

Fighting hard against the all-encompassing calm produced by the marijuana, my heart-rate increased significantly when I saw the little banner that had popped up on the phone's lock-screen. *Mel: 1 new message.* My hands trembled as I slowly slid my thumb across the glass to unlock it.

Do you want to meet your daughter?

My breath caught in my throat, and I was floating above myself, looking down on the scene, reading the message over my own shoulder. I was drawn back into reality as a second message appeared below the first. A thumbnail of a photograph. I tapped it, expanding to full screen. Decorated with a pink bow headband and chewing on the head of one of those *Sophie* giraffes, there was no mistaking that I was looking into the face of my daughter. She had eyes like mine. The nose, the ears, everything else was quite obviously from Mel, but she had my eyes. It was quite staggering to look at an image of a person who is quite clearly a part of you. I read over the text slowly.

Do you want to meet your daughter?

I wanted to respond with 'Yes! Yes I do! I can't think of a single tiny thing in this world that I would rather do more than meet my daughter! I want to hold her tightly and support her tiny head with my hand and cover her tiny face with kisses! Yes, I want to meet my daughter!' I wanted to respond like this, but the stone from the pot had set in and I was worried I would mess it up.

'Yes,' I replied simply.

The phone made a sound which let me know that the message had been sent. A long moment passed where I wondered whether I'd said enough. I didn't want to come across as ambivalent in my single-worded response. The longer I stared at the screen, the more concerned I became with the inadequacy of my reply. She hadn't asked me if I liked chicken salt, for fuck's sake. She'd asked me if I wanted to meet my only daughter whom I had, up until this point, believed I would never see. I began to type out a fresh text, but was interrupted by another message popping up on the screen.

Meet me at my place at 3pm tomorrow?

There was an address at the bottom. I backspaced the message I had begun to write and sent back the words 'Can't wait.' I opened up the image of the baby girl on my phone and stared at her, mesmerised by her tiny features. She was so fragile and soft and I could have stared at her for hours, but the battery life on my phone finally submitted, and it was time to turn in for the night.

Chapter Twenty-Eight

Next morning, I awoke having slept only perhaps two or three hours, at best. Nervous excitement had been a strong opposition for my need to sleep, but my body had finally given in at some stage during the early hours of the morning.

I hadn't mentioned any of it to Jake. It didn't feel real yet, and I was worried that if I told him, that would make it real, and if it were real then there was a chance it wouldn't work out, because in reality, things often don't work out. It was much safer, for now, to keep it as a gentle fantasy until she was in my arms.

I thanked Jake for having me and took leave from the carriage at around eight o'clock. If he was at all curious about me leaving so abruptly, he didn't let on. I didn't stop the entire way home. I'm not sure I breathed either; the excitement had placed itself squarely in my chest, and it buzzed around inside my ribcage, making it very difficult to relax. I pulled up in my driveway and had to consciously remind myself how to breathe. I inhaled deeply, held for five seconds, then released, before climbing out of the van.

I ignored the grime built up on the edge of the bathtub as I climbed in to have a shower. Since moving in, I'd retrofitted the bath spout with a rubber hose that slipped over it and had a handheld shower head at the other end. It was a little awkward, washing yourself like this, but it was certainly more pleasant than sitting down in a bath that someone had probably been murdered in at some point in time. And besides, the hot water didn't last very long so I only ever spent a few minutes in there anyway.

Today I washed thoroughly, and was in there well past the point where the hot water turned to ice. I remembered hearing somewhere that babies formed their strongest memories and attachments through smell, and didn't want my daughter to confuse her first association of her father with a dumpster. When I was satisfied with the way I smelt, I got dressed again, brushed my teeth, and even combed my hair. I'd never combed my hair in my life, but today I was combing it.

I didn't even own a comb.

I used a fork.

I wasn't happy with the t-shirts I owned for my first meeting with my baby girl. Although I thought the 'bugger' t-shirt was comic excellence, I didn't want her associating me with a dog that's been run over by a car, either. I left the house and went to the fanciest place I could think of to by a nice button-up shirt. It was a place called *Linton's*, which I'd only ever walked past. Today I ventured to the other side of the glass door. *Linton's* was one of those places where the people working there introduce themselves to you when you walk in, and they learn your name. A man called Dominic greeted me and asked how he could be of service. I told him I needed a nice shirt. He called me *Mr Daniel*, and with confident familiarity, began to measure my chest.

'You have a big chest, *Mr Daniel*,' Dominic commented, his South American accent putting a hint of 'J' into the letter 'Y'.

I wasn't sure if a big chest was something to be proud of or not. I thanked him anyway. He disappeared into a clothing rack on the side-wall of the shop and came back with a navy-blue shirt. It was excellent. He held it up against me and beamed.

'What is the occasion *Mr Daniel*?' he asked, 'No! Let me guess. A job interview?' He was very emphatic in the way he spoke. I thought about it for a second. I guess it sort of was. 'Blue is very good for job interviews,' he carried on, 'it makes you appear confident and promotes trust.'

I told him I'd take it. The problem, I learnt, with buying a very nice shirt, is that it makes the rest of what you are wearing look rubbish.

Dominic told me, 'You don't wear a bad hat in a Bugatti.'

I'm not too sure what he meant, but I ended up buying a pair of pants, new shoes and a set of cufflinks as well. I walked out of the store having spent two week's pay, but feeling excellent. I knew if Mel saw me now, she would be looking at a different man to the one she had shared an apartment with in Clayton. I checked my phone. *Two o'clock.* I'd spent almost an hour at *Linton's.*

'Shit,' I said, picking up the pace as I headed back to the van. The address Mel had given me was in Pakenham, and I was worried I wouldn't get there in time. As I pulled away from the kerb, an orange light glowed dimly on the dash. Low fuel. I'd just about run the tank dry on the way back from Skinners Flat. I'd have to stop and top up on the way. *Fuck.*

I stopped at the first servo I saw and chucked twenty bucks in. While I was at the counter paying for the fuel, I noticed a small display above the newspapers, left over from Easter: a pile of stuffed toy bunnies holding packets of chocolate eggs. I grabbed one. It was blue. I would have really preferred it to be pink, but they were all blue. I paid for the lot and got back into the van. I ate the chocolate eggs on the way.

A wave of nervous apprehension pulsed through my body as I pulled up at the address Mel had sent me. I was out the front of a small brick house with a simple garden of rosebushes in no particular order. Something dry had caught in my throat, which I couldn't quite clear, and the palms of my hands were clammy. I checked the text message from Mel again, to make sure I was in the right place. I was. I tilted the rear-view mirror to look at myself and ran a shaky hand through my hair. I looked okay. I tried on a friendly, approachable smile. It scared me a bit. I got out of the van.

I made it halfway to the front door before turning around and jogging back to the road. I pulled the passenger door open. The rabbit looked up at me from the seat. I picked it up, tearing off the *Happy Easter* badge it had sewn on its chest and stuffing it in my pocket. I flared out my fingers and stared at the back of my hand. I tried to steady it. The veins on the back of my hand stood up and I couldn't stop shaking. A million different thoughts were smashing into each other inside my head. *What if she's scared? What if she cries? What if Mel cries? What should I say? Do I smell okay? What if she doesn't like me?* I think the last one scared me the most.

I took a moment, breathed in, and straightened up before taking up the stuffed rabbit in my hands, and turned around. I began to walk slowly toward the doorway, each uncertain footfall making me want to run away from the house, and toward it, all at the same time. Reaching the front door, I held my breath, standing as lightly as I possibly could on the doorstep.

I raised an unsteady hand to ring the bell.

I coughed into my hand.

Thirty seconds or a week passed.

I swept my hair to the side, then pushed it back again.

The rabbit clutched in my left hand, I rang the doorbell once more.

Another thirty seconds.

I knocked.

Maybe the doorbell wasn't working.

'Dan?'

The voice came from behind me.

I turned around to see a police officer closing the gate at the side of the house from which they had silently approached. She moved to join her partner by the doorstep.

'She's not home, mate,' said the one who had just closed the gate.

'Dan Savage?' the first voice asked again, belonging to the taller of the two officers, a strong-looking man with a solid torso and dark hair. I looked up at the officer.

'Yes?' I responded.

'You are going to have to come with us,' he said.

I turned away and knocked at the door again. I was here to see my daughter.

'No-ones home, Dan,' he said, putting a hand on my shoulder.

He didn't understand.

I kept knocking.

'I'm just here to see my daughter,' I said, still knocking. 'I just want to see my daughter.' I felt my left hand being pulled behind my back whilst my right kept knocking. 'You don't understand. She sent me a message.' I felt my right arm being pulled down to meet my left. I yanked it free and slammed it onto the door, pounding.

I called out for Melinda.

The second officer, who had been so far waiting on the sidelines, joined in. There was a sharp pain in the back of my knee and I fell to the ground on the concrete landing. Handcuffs were slammed onto my wrists.

'Dan Savage, you are under arrest for the sexual assault and unlawful impregnation of Miss Melinda Eckhardt,' the officer said. 'You are not obliged to say or do anything unless you wish to do so, but whatever you say or do may be used in evidence. Do you understand?'

I blinked up at him.

'You don't understand,' I began, slowly. 'I am here to meet my daughter.'

'Mr Savage, do you understand?' he asked again.

'I am here to meet my daughter,' I repeated blankly.

They heaved me to my feet. As they marched me to the kerb, I twisted my neck around as far as it would go to look back at the house. I could have sworn I saw the curtain move.

'You don't understand,' I said, getting more agitated. I twisted my wrists in the cuffs. 'I am here to meet my daughter!'

I tried to break free.

'She sent me a message!' I said, yanking my shoulders around. 'If you just let me show you! ... I'm here to meet my daughter!'

They marched me around the corner to where a police car sat by itself under a tree. The first officer held the door open while the second guided me toward the back seat. I thrashed wildly.

'I'm here to meet my daughter!' I howled, kicking off the back end of the car, my body jolting violently. My head launched backwards from the force, slamming into officer-number-two's face with a sickening crunch. She released her grip on my wrists and I spun around like a wounded animal, tearing back up the street toward the house. I got maybe fifteen paces before I felt the powerful mass of the first officer, driving his entire body into my lower back. I hit the deck like a sack of shit. The policeman threw me in the back of the car. The door shut heavily after me. I could see blood pouring between the second officer's fingers as she cupped her face in her hands. We pulled out from the kerb and turned the corner, an air of hostility in the car. No one said anything.

Passing back in front of the house, I pressed my face to the glass, straining to keep the building in my vision for as long as I could, until finally it disappeared, existing, now, only in my memories. We rounded a corner at the end of the street.

Chapter Twenty-Nine

I've read children's books that lasted longer than the court trial, and ones with more difficult decisions to make than the Australian judicial system had to make for me.

They had video footage from University Housing Experiment that showed me admitting what I had done to Mel.

'It's okay. Let him in.'

A deep sense of shame engulfed me as the video played to the court. I sunk back in my seat, trying to make myself as small as possible. There was a heavy, cold stone in the pit of my stomach, which only grew heavier and colder as Mel took the stand and delivered her Victim Impact Statement to the courtroom. Hot tears sprung into my eyes as I saw how nervous she was, the pieces of paper clutched between shaky hands barely staying still long enough for her to read the words.

'Dan Savage,' she began, choking on the words. She raised a trembling hand to her face and wiped away a stray tear with the back of it. Looking over the top of her paper across the courtroom, she took a jagged breath in, an attempt to steady herself, and tried again.

'Dan Savage, I thought, was a nice guy,' she said quietly. 'I thought Dan was a nice guy, because he never gave me cause to think otherwise.' She straightened up a little. 'Not to my face. I thought Dan was a nice guy, because that is the way he comes across. Certainly, we had grown up in different worlds, and I knew from the start that our moral compasses pointed in slightly different directions. I attributed this difference to my growing up with the guidance of religion, and the love of both of my parents. What I didn't realise was that when reading Dan's moral compass, I had been looking at the wrong end of the needle.'

The cold stone in my stomach turned over.

'A person who can smile to your face after committing a despicable act as he did, is surely worse than a person who instead spits in it.' She looked over the top of her page, directly at me. Her eyes were bloodshot. She looked as though she hadn't slept.

'He cooked me breakfast and we went for a walk that same weekend. We talked candidly, for the first time, as friends. How can it be that the only time he felt close enough to me to open up about his life and to listen to mine, was after doing something so revolting? What does that say about his character?'

She turned the page over.

'It has taken me over a year to bring myself to the point where I understand that all of this is real, and needs to be dealt with. I have lived through the past eighteen months, and the birth of my daughter, without ever properly addressing the issue. If I didn't give it attention, it wasn't real, and if it wasn't real, then the world would never have to know about it. Well, now I think the world needs to know about it.

'For a long time, I blamed myself. I believed that I was at fault in all of this, at least partially. I thought, if only I hadn't killed that fucking bird –' her voice was strained. 'If I hadn't accidentally killed that bird, then none of this would have happened to me.

'It's taken me eighteen months to drum up the courage to make this real. At the time of the video, when Dan confessed to me what he had done, I contacted lawyers shortly afterwards. It was more of a knee-jerk than anything. I panicked. They encouraged me to report the incident to the police, but I couldn't. I couldn't deal with the publicity around it. I couldn't make it real. Dan had become something of a celebrity at that stage, with the cantaloupe thing at its peak, and I knew there would be a media circus. I didn't want my face, or that of my baby, flung across the tabloids. I couldn't bear it.' She paused, looking out across the sea of faces in the courtroom.

'Dan Savage and my lawyers reached an agreement on a sum that Dan would pay, as a means to support the child financially, and, credit to him, Dan put forward the money - one of the first decent acts I'd seen from him. Dan's financial contribution, however, didn't excuse the fact that he had done something abhorrent. It didn't excuse the fact that he had invaded my body. It didn't excuse the fact that he had committed a crime. For a long time, I thought that it did.

'For a long time, I thought that because I had taken his money, that meant that we were even; but that money was provided to support my daughter, not as recompense for the vulgar way in which she was created.' She folded the paper twice, then held it tightly at her side, her eyes welling up with tears once more.

'I haven't been able to leave the house in more than a year,' she said shakily. 'I had a good life before I met Dan. One of my favourite things to do was go for a walk through the park—a pleasure I can no longer enjoy. I am scared. I am frightened of the world outside my door. I'm frightened not just for myself, but for my daughter, too. I am afraid to bring her up in the world she was born into. Something has shifted in my life, and I'm not sure it will ever shift back. I've even, in the quietest, darkest hours, begun to question my faith, something that has been a constant in my life. The foundation of who I am as a person.

'I love my daughter. I love her dearly, despite where she came from. I love her dearly, but every time I look into her face, I see Dan Savage in her eyes, and if that's not the cruellest joke of our Creator, then I don't know what is.'

Chapter Thirty

The jury delivered their verdict the same afternoon, and the judge passed his sentencing the following day.

The jury's decision was unanimous and met no opposition from me. I was convicted of three charges. The first, one count of sexual assault, carried a sentence of three years imprisonment. The second, one count of recklessly causing injury, for the broken nose of my arresting officer, came with two-and-a-half years. Thirdly, resisting arrest. A further six months.

The papers said it was a light sentence, and I tended to agree with them. Mel was left with a physical reminder every day of what had happened, in the shape of a child, and I was only getting six years. Mel's mother spat at my feet as I was escorted from the courtroom.

I never saw my daughter.

The End.
Sort of.

The End, dear reader, is a curious thing, and is often a matter of perspective. *The End* holds the implication that the story has, in fact, concluded. *The End* brings about a sense of finality, a sense that it is all over. But how can a story have found its end when the characters that helped shape it are still alive? Don't they carry on, once the final page has been written?

Perhaps my death would have been a more satisfying ending, and you would have found your finality there, but my death has not yet arrived, and how can I be certain that anyone would pen a fitting conclusion after my demise? As the many years between my birth and the beginning of this story were omitted, so too will the years between its ending and my own. I haven't paper enough, nor inclination to write any further. And so, we find ourselves arriving at the point in the story that is deemed fitting enough to be called *The End.*

The final page. This is the point where we will conclude our story.

But not right away.

First, and paradoxically, last, we must address the Karma Exchange. Does it work? Did it work? Will it work for you? The answer is, and always will be, a resounding *no*. No, it doesn't. No, it didn't. No, it won't.

The Karma Exchange is a flawed philosophy. On the surface, it seems to work: Do something bad, do something good, balance it out. Try to be a good person. However, not all wrongs can be righted by just trying to be a good person. Trying to be a good person doesn't undo all of the shitty things that you did before you were *trying to be a good person.* That, dear reader, was my mistake. Life can't be reduced to such a basic system of give-and-take. It is far more complex than that, and the individuals affected by your negative actions are no better off from you having done some good elsewhere to make yourself feel better.

If there is one piece of advice I can offer the dedicated reader, before signing off indefinitely, it is this: don't live like me. Don't try to be a good person—just BE a good person. Don't do what I did, don't live the way I did, and for God's sake, don't wank into anyone's bodywash.

That's it. That's *The End.* It's all over. Finished.
You can shut the book now.
My name is Dan Savage, and this is my story.
(At least, the parts worth reading.)

#howtofuckacantaloupe

About the Author

Pete Young spent his formative years growing up on an illegal mushroom mine in country Victoria. His youth was mostly spent toiling away as a subterranean rock-blaster in the family mines, where he would be responsible for blowing apart layers of bedrock, then sifting through its rubble for the treasured green-top mushrooms, which were distinguishable by their bioluminescent glow. When he wasn't bottling bootlegged mushroom oil, which his family peddled as the only cure for walking into a room but forgetting why you went in there, Pete would sometimes look out the window. At the age of twelve, after finally growing tired of combing mushroom spores out of his beard at the end of each day, Pete abandoned the family business to pursue his dream of becoming a plumber. Many years later, he realised that was a terrible decision and wrote a book. This is it. I hope you enjoyed it.

You can connect with Pete via his social channels on Facebook and Instagram to stay up to date with his latest releases (pete.young.author) or via email at
pete.young.author@gmail.com
Be sure to follow the hashtag #howtofuckacantaloupe to see what everybody is saying about it.

#howtofuckacantaloupe

Pete Young